COA

STAR TREK®

THE ORIGINAL SERIES

FOUL DEEDS WILL RISE

Greg Cox

Based upon *Star Trek*
created by Gene Roddenberry

POCKET BOOKS
New York • London • Toronto • Sydney • New Delhi

Pocket Books
A Division of Simon & Schuster, Inc.
1230 Avenue of the Americas
New York, NY 10020

First Pocket Books paperback edition December 2014

POCKET and colophon are registered trademarks of Simon & Schuster, Inc.

For information about special discounts for bulk purchases, please contact Simon & Schuster Special Sales at 1-866-506-1949 or business@simonandschuster.com.

The Simon & Schuster Speakers Bureau can bring authors to your live event. For more information or to book an event, contact the Simon & Schuster Speakers Bureau at 1-866-248-3049 or visit our website at www.simonspeakers.com.

Cover design by Alan Dingman
Cover art by Joe Corroney and Brian Miller

Manufactured in the United States of America

10 9 8 7 6 5 4 3 2 1

ISBN 978-1-4767-8324-6
ISBN 978-1-4767-8326-0 (ebook)

*In memory of Richard Matheson,
whom I had the pleasure of working with
for more than twenty years.*

"Foul deeds will rise, though all the earth over-whelm them."

—*Hamlet,* Act I

One

Captain's log. Stardate 8514.6

  The Enterprise *has embarked on a peacekeeping mission to the Savinia system, where two warring planets, Pavak and Oyolo, are attempting to end years of bitter hostility. Although neither planet is a member of the Federation, we have been invited by both parties to act as an impartial mediator. The* Enterprise *will serve as neutral territory for the upcoming peace negotiations, while also patrolling the space between the two worlds in order to deter any attacks. Given the atrocities and bloodshed on both sides of the conflict, there are bound to be hard feelings among the delegates. I don't envy the Federation ambassador assigned to this mission.*

  Who just happens to have a familiar face . . .

"Well, they're not shooting at each other yet," Ambassador Kevin Riley said. "That's a positive sign, I suppose."

The *Enterprise* approached the rendezvous point. On the bridge's main viewer, two small diplomatic courier crafts from Pavak and Oyolo faced off against each other in the demilitarized zone between the planets. The couriers were essentially streamlined shuttlecrafts, designed for interplanetary travel within the solar system. Kirk recalled that both races possessed rudimentary warp technology, but had scarcely ventured beyond their own system. He briefly considered raising the *Enterprise*'s shields, but he decided against it. The shuttles posed little threat to the starship, and arriving with shields up, as though expecting trouble, hardly sent the right message.

"I admire your optimism, Ambassador," Kirk said from the captain's chair. He was wearing his dress uniform in anticipation of the delegates' imminent arrival. Medals adorned the front of his double-breasted maroon jacket. "From what I gather, you have your work cut out for you."

"You can say that again." Riley stood beside Kirk's chair in the sunken command circle at the center of the bridge. His conservative gray suit was a good deal less colorful than the then-regulation gold tunic he'd worn when he'd first served aboard the original *Enterprise,* some two decades ago. Years in the diplomatic corps had added some seasoning to his face and a neatly trimmed brown beard made him look more mature as well. "I have to say I've enjoyed the trip here, though. It's good to be back on the *Enterprise* again . . . well, *an Enterprise* at least."

"I know what you mean," Kirk said. This new vessel wasn't quite the same as his old ship, which had gone down in flames above the Genesis Planet a few years back, but he was getting used to it. And certainly it had proven itself during some tight situations, beginning with that business on Nimbus III. "And it's been a pleasure to have you back aboard, if only for this mission."

"We're being hailed by both delegations," Uhura reported from the communications station. "They're ready to be beamed aboard."

"Thank you, Commander." Kirk rose from his seat and marched briskly toward the starboard turbolift. He nodded at Spock and Chekov. "Let's not keep our distinguished guests waiting."

The first officer and security chief fell in behind Kirk and Riley, leaving the bridge in the capable hands of Commander Sulu. Heela, a young Saurian lieutenant, took the helm as Sulu occupied the captain's chair. Like Kirk, Spock and Chekov had donned their dress uniforms for the occasion. A short turbolift ride brought the reception party to the main transporter room on G Deck, where they found Doctor McCoy and Commander Scott waiting for them, along with a pair of discreetly positioned security guards. Kirk wasn't necessarily expecting any trouble, but he was pleased Chekov wasn't taking any chances with the safety of the delegates or the crew. In the captain's experience, peacekeeping could sometimes be anything but peaceful.

"The Federation's only interest is promoting peace in this sector," Riley stressed. "It's vital that we remain impartial and avoid even the appearance of taking sides."

"You don't need to remind us, Mister Ambassador," Kirk said lightly. "This is hardly our first rodeo."

"Of course, Captain," Riley said, sounding slightly abashed. "I didn't mean to imply otherwise."

"At ease," Kirk teased him. "You can count on us to be thoroughly even-handed where our guests are concerned."

He had to admit that Riley's respectful manner was a pleasant change from the sometimes overbearing attitude of many high-ranking Federation officials. Still, Kirk made a mental note to remember that Riley was indeed an experienced ambassador now, not the enthusiastic young lieutenant who had once served under Kirk's command—and who had later been his chief of staff at Starfleet HQ, back when Kirk was an admiral flying a desk. All joking aside, the captain had no desire to undercut Riley's authority by continuing to treat him as a subordinate. Ambassador Riley had come a long way.

"Who gets beamed aboard first?" Scott asked, occupying the transporter control booth. Transparent partitions divided the control console from the transporter platform. "If ye don't mind me asking?"

"The order was determined randomly," Riley explained. "The Pavakians go first."

"You heard the man, Mister Scott," Kirk said. "Proceed."

"Aye, Captain."

As Scott operated the controls, Kirk looked forward

to meeting his first Pavakians. He had never encountered either species before and, despite the weighty
nature of his mission, felt the same thrill he always experienced when visiting a new planet or civilization.
The joy of discovery was a big part of why he had joined
Starfleet. He hoped he never got so jaded that he lost his
natural curiosity about alien races and cultures.

Twin pillars of coruscating energy shimmered above
the transporter platform before coalescing into two humanoid figures, who were clearly Pavakian. Their most
distinguishing characteristic, which had been noted in
Kirk's briefings on the species, was a velvety layer of
fine fur that lay flat against the elegant contours of their
otherwise very human-looking faces. The rest of their
bodies were covered by crisp white military uniforms
with black piping. Matching white gloves protected their
hands, while polished black boots rested squarely on the
transporter pads. The Pavakian delegation consisted of
an older male and younger female of basic mammalian
design. It had been arranged in advance that each senior
delegate would be accompanied by a single aide.

"Welcome aboard the *Enterprise*," Kirk said, and
greeted the new arrivals. "I'm Captain James Kirk, one
of your hosts for this summit." He gestured toward
Riley. "And this is Ambassador Riley."

Riley stepped forward. "It's a pleasure to meet you.
On behalf of the United Federation of Planets, let me
extend my own welcome . . . and our sincere hopes for
a productive conference."

"Thank you, gentlemen." The senior Pavakian, accompanied by his aide, stepped down from the platform. He was lean and grizzled, with a stiff military bearing. His fine brown fur had been infiltrated by streaks of silver at his temples and chin, but his pale green eyes were sharp and alert beneath bushy black brows. Medals and ribbons festooned his double-breasted white tunic. His voice was slow and sonorous, as though weighing each word carefully. "General Vapar Tem of the Pavakian Civil Defense Force," he introduced himself. "And this is my aide-de-camp, the indispensable Colonel Gast."

"Captain, Ambassador." Gast's tawny golden fur was sleeker and more lustrous than Tem's, no doubt because of the difference in their ages. She appeared young and fit and self-assured. Tiger stripes streaked the top of her scalp, meeting in a widow's peak atop her brow. Cool brown eyes, darting briefly to note the presence of the security guards, regarded Kirk and his crew. Kirk got the impression that she missed very little.

"A pleasure." He took a moment to introduce the other officers present. "Captain Spock, my first officer and science officer. Doctor Leonard McCoy, ship's surgeon. Commander Montgomery Scott, head of engineering, and Commander Pavel Chekov, navigator and chief of security."

"Officers." Tem nodded at the reception committee before calling their attention to his aide. "Colonel Gast is an accomplished engineer and space traveler in her own right. She was originally assigned to our fledgling star exploration program before the war intervened."

"The general is too kind," she protested. "I merely saw my duty, like any other loyal Pavakian. Defending our world and interests took precedence over a purely scientific expedition."

Kirk suspected that the war's gain had been their space program's loss. "Perhaps peace will open up new possibilities for all Pavakians—and for the Oyolu as well."

She shrugged. "We shall see."

Kirk found her remark worryingly noncommittal, but let it pass. As he understood it, the cease-fire had been in place for just a few months. It was only natural that soldiers on both sides might be skeptical of the chances for a lasting peace.

"The Oyolu delegation is ready to board," Riley remarked. "We should not abuse their patience."

"Heaven forbid," Gast said drily.

Tem shot her a warning look. "Colonel." He turned apologetically toward the *Enterprise* officers. "You must understand, gentlemen, that there remains little love lost between my people and the Oyolu. Much blood has been spilled, many friends and family maimed or buried, cities and homes reduced to rubble. Such wounds are not easily healed, and old grievances die hard."

Kirk recalled his briefings on the painful history of the system. Oyolo, the inner world, was a lush green planet whose abundant resources and biodiversity had inevitably attracted the interest of rapacious traders and merchants from the neighboring world of Pavak. Although Pavak had never officially conquered or colonized Oyolo, its military government had vigorously defended the traders' interests against those of the native Oyolu, eventually provoking a violent insurgency devoted to driving the Pavakians from the planet. The result had been an escalating cycle of violence, of vicious attacks and brutal retaliation, which had spilled oceans of blood over the past several generations.

"I understand," Riley said. "My own homeland, back on Earth, was torn apart by bitter, often bloody Troubles only a few centuries ago, but in time peace and forgiveness came. You know what they say: Shaking hands with your friends is easy, but with your enemies? That's a challenge that calls on the best we can be."

Tem nodded solemnly. "Let us hope we are up to the task, then, for the sake of both our worlds."

"Mister Chekov will escort you and Colonel Gast to your quarters," Kirk said. It occurred to him that it might be better to postpone any meeting between the delegations until both were comfortably settled aboard the *Enterprise.* "We've prepared guest accommodations for both of you."

Tem shook his head. He appeared to see through Kirk's tactics. "I appreciate your prudence, Captain, but there is no point in delaying this encounter. Let us greet the Oyolu."

Very well, Kirk thought. He nodded at Scotty. "Energize."

Within minutes, two new figures materialized upon the transporter platform. The Oyolu were larger and stockier than the Pavakians, with broad chests and faces. Curling horns jutting from their brows indicated that both of the Oyolu delegates were male. Flowing manes of hair framed leathery yellow complexions the color of fresh lemons. In contrast to the stark white uniforms of their enemies, the Oyolu sported much more colorful and elaborate attire. A fur-lined burgundy cape hung from the wide shoulders of the senior delegate. A belted silk tunic, intricately embroidered, bared his muscular arms and legs. Beaded wristbands and greaves adorned their limbs. Cloven hooves rendered footwear superfluous.

The younger delegate, who had a shorter cape and less ornate tunic, as well as a rich, slightly accented voice, stepped forward to introduce his superior.

"May I present to you our revered leader, A'Barra the Defender!"

"More like A'Barra the bloody-handed rabble-rouser," Gast murmured under her breath, earning her another cautionary look from General Tem. Kirk hoped her remark had gone unheard by the Oyolu.

"Welcome aboard the *Enterprise*," Kirk said, before introducing himself and his crew. "And this is Ambassador Riley."

"Greetings, Minister A'Barra," Riley added. "I hope we did not keep you waiting."

"Not at all," A'Barra said in a deep baritone. "Peace

has been a long time coming. A few stray moments here or there will make little difference." His right horn had been broken off or severed so that only a truncated stub remained, while a pronounced limp was noticeable as he stepped down from the platform to address Kirk and the others. Flowing white hair fell past his shoulders. "Is that not so, Ifusi?" he asked his aide.

The other Oyolu had long black hair and a youthful intensity that reminded Kirk of Chekov back during their first five-year mission. Kirk noted an empty holster upon Ifusi's belt. Both delegations had been instructed to leave any weapons behind.

"As you say, sir," the aide replied.

So far, so good, Kirk thought as the two delegations regarded each other warily. *Now for the tricky part, introducing the recent enemies to each other.*

Riley came forward to do the honors. He gestured toward the Pavakians. "You know General Tem, of course."

"Only by reputation," A'Barra said in a tone that made it unclear if this was a compliment. His eyes narrowed as he contemplated the enemy commander. His hand absently fingered his broken horn. Beside him, Ifusi openly glared at Tem, not even trying to conceal his hostility. Kirk found himself grateful for that empty holster.

"Likewise," Tem said drily.

A tense, awkward silence ensued. "Well, I'm sure we'll have plenty of time to get to know each other better in the days to come," Riley said. "That you're both here in the same place, ready to talk, is a historic first step that can only lead to—"

Chekov sneezed loudly, interrupting the ambassador.

"Commander?" Kirk asked.

"Excuse me, Captain." Chekov sniffled. "My apologies."

McCoy gave Chekov a look of professional concern, but Kirk took advantage of the distraction to try to move things along. A crowded transporter room was not the ideal place to bring the wary adversaries together; if nothing else, it was far too easy for one delegation to beam away in a huff.

"Now that we've completed the introductions," he said, "why don't we get you settled into your respective quarters. No doubt you'll want to relax and freshen up before we get down to business."

"Thank you, Captain," A'Barra said. "Your hospitality is most welcome. I confess, the hedonist in me is looking forward to enjoying the creature comforts of your fine starship." He patted a prominent belly. "Particularly some of your exotic Federation cuisine."

"We're honored to have both delegations aboard." Kirk turned to the security officers at hand. "Mister Hernandez, please escort the Oyolu to their quarters. Mister Yost, please do the same for our Pavakian guests."

The ship's VIP staterooms were all located on

D Deck, one level above the senior officers' quarters. Kirk wondered if he should have arranged matters so that the rival delegations were on different decks, but he saw no way to do so without possibly slighting one faction. Better that they receive equal accommodations, even if that meant putting them in uncomfortably close proximity to each other. At least they were at opposite ends of a curving corridor, he reflected, with a few empty staterooms in between. One more buffer zone couldn't hurt.

Colonel Gast paused on her way to the exit. "What of our personal effects and baggage?"

"They're being beamed aboard via the cargo transporters as we speak," Scotty assured her. "Ye can count on them to be delivered to your quarters in no time at all."

"Understood." She let Yost lead her toward the exit, giving the Oyolu a wide berth on her way out. A look of mutual contempt passed between her and Ifusi. Her nose wrinkled in distaste. "Until later, gentlemen."

Ifusi snorted in disdain.

Yes, Kirk decided. Kevin Riley definitely had his hands full. You could practically smell the bad blood between the old enemies. They could be sitting on top of a powder keg.

Here's hoping nobody lights a match.

Two

"Approaching Oyolo, Captain," the shuttlecraft pilot reported.

"Thank you, Lieutenant Hua," Kirk said. "Bring us in at the designated coordinates."

"Aye, sir."

While the peace negotiations got under way aboard the *Enterprise,* the *Copernicus* was delivering medical supplies and other humanitarian aid to the war-torn planet. Kirk and McCoy, along with a small contingent of nurses, orderlies, and security personnel, occupied the shuttle's passenger compartment. Kirk admired the lush, blue world before them. Years of bloodshed had yet to mar the M-class planet's intrinsic beauty.

Not too surprising, he thought, given that it was Oyolo's natural resources and abundant biodiversity that had attracted the avaricious Pavakian traders in the first place. Small wonder that the Pavakians would not want to annihilate the golden goose even while asserting their "right" to exploit those resources to their own advantage. Meanwhile the Oyolu, lacking the vast military-industrial complex of their foes, had pursued a campaign of insurgency to drive the foreign merchants from their planet. Both sides had chosen to wage a war of attrition instead, with the goal of wearing the enemy down until they sued for peace, with the Oyolu wanting the Pavakians gone and the Pavakians wanting unrestricted access to Oyolu markets and territory. That strategy had cost each planet dearly, resulting in a generation of carnage and destruction.

"Looks like a pretty world," Kirk observed. "It's a shame that we're not visiting it under happier circumstances."

"Tell me about it," McCoy said, seated beside his friend. "I'm not looking forward to checking out the conditions planet-side. Beyond the direct casualties of the fighting, reports indicate that there's also widespread malnutrition, disease outbreaks, problems with contaminated food and water, and lack of decent medical facilities. Their whole infrastructure has been bombed to bits."

"So I hear," Kirk confirmed. As he understood it, the bulk of the violence had taken place on Oyolo, but he fully intended to visit Pavak as well. Reports and briefings could only tell you so much. "I want to get a firsthand look at the situation, see for myself just where we might be able to render assistance."

"Glad to have you along," McCoy said, "but you sure you're not needed back on the ship to play referee between our feuding guests?"

"That's Riley's bailiwick, and it's likely to be a slow,

tedious process. Even with the cease-fire in place, there are still plenty of thorny issues to be ironed out: territorial boundaries off-world and throughout the rest of the solar system, prisoner exchanges, more equal trading practices, reparations, prosecution for war crimes, and so on, none of which are likely to be settled in one afternoon." He shrugged. "I think the negotiations can spare me for a few hours."

"And you don't want to step on Riley's toes," McCoy guessed correctly.

Perceptive as always, Bones, Kirk thought. "Let's just say I'm erring toward restraint in that respect. If Riley needs my assistance, he only has to ask. In the meantime, I'm perfectly happy to let him haggle over tariffs and immigration quotas while I set boots on the ground."

"Can't blame you there," McCoy said. "Heck, I'm a doctor, not a diplomat. I figure I can do more good on that poor planet than babysitting some fractious dignitaries." He glanced over his shoulder at the rear of the shuttle, which was loaded with packed medicine, nutritional supplements, and medical equipment. "I just hope that this stuff makes a difference, and the same with the supplies Spock and Scotty are delivering to Pavak."

The *Galileo,* bearing the two senior officers, had departed the *Enterprise* shortly before the *Copernicus* on its own vital mission. Besides enforcing a no-fly zone between the two planets, Starfleet had also agreed to provide qualified weapons inspectors to oversee the disarmament efforts on both worlds. Kirk had dispatched Spock and Scotty to personally verify that Pavak's threatening stockpile of interplanetary missiles was being dismantled. In the interests of both efficiency and parity, the *Galileo* also had been loaded with a quantity of humanitarian supplies for Pavak.

In theory, Starfleet inspectors also would oversee the dismantlement of the Oyolu's weapons stores, but that was more of a symbolic gesture than anything else, simply to provide a token attempt at even-handedness. Of much greater and more immediate concern was Pavak's ability to decimate Oyolo with interplanetary weapons, which was why Kirk had put his best people in charge of that end of the operation. If anybody could ensure that the Pavakians were holding up their end of the bargain—and truly disposing of their overwhelming offensive capacity—it was the *Enterprise*'s top science officer and engineer.

"Entering the planet's atmosphere," Hua announced from the cockpit. "Brace yourself for some turbulence."

She wasn't kidding. Heavy winds buffeted the *Copernicus* as they descended toward a continent in the planet's northern hemisphere, which was conveniently still facing the sun at this hour. Kirk calculated that it was roughly late afternoon in that time zone, several hours ahead of the *Enterprise*'s shipboard clock. *Not too bad of a time lag,* he thought. On strictly exploratory missions, he often attempted to coordinate the landing party's location with the ship's own chronology, but in this case there was less flexibility regarding the landing coordinates. Their destination was the main hub for the relief efforts on the planet, which just happened to be located in this particular corner of the world.

At least it's not four o'clock in the morning our time.

A bumpy ride deposited the shuttle on what appeared to be a large muddy field on the planet's surface. A shattered city skyline could be glimpsed in the near distance.

"Thank goodness," McCoy muttered, visibly relieved to be on solid ground at last. "I was starting to feel like we were going through the Galactic Barrier again."

"What's the matter, Bones?" Kirk asked. "Forget your air-sickness pills?"

"I have a rock-solid stomach and you know it," McCoy said. "But let's just say I take back some of the complaints I've made about the transporter over the years." He unbuckled his seat belt. "*Some,*" he repeated. "Not all."

Beaming down to Oyolo had not been an option. With the *Enterprise* patrolling the buffer zone between the two worlds, the ship had been well beyond transporter range of the planet, which was why the courier shuttles had been required to ferry the delegates to the rendezvous point. Those shuttles, Kirk recalled, had since returned to their respective home worlds.

"Remind me to get that in writing," the captain joked as he rose from his seat, eager to get his first real look at Oyolo. He nodded approvingly at the pilot. "An excellent landing, Lieutenant. Considering."

"Thank you, sir." She killed the shuttle's engines and opened the starboard hatch. Muted sunlight and a gust of hot, humid air invaded the passenger compartment. "Local temperature is approximately thirty-two degrees Celsius," she reported, consulting a display panel in the cockpit. "It's pretty muggy out there."

"Duly noted," Kirk said, appreciating the warning. He shed his field jacket, but kept on the red vest underneath. He contemplated equipping himself with a phaser from the weapons drawer, but he decided against it. The security team's discreet type-1 phasers were probably more than enough to guarantee their safety in the unlikely event of an altercation. This was an errand of mercy after all. "Let's get to it."

As usual, he was the first one out of the shuttle. Earth-level gravity sank his boots into the mud as he took a moment to get his bearings and look around. The shuttle had landed on the outskirts of a sprawling refugee camp that had taken over what had once been a large urban park, approximately three square kilometers in size. A battle-scarred metropolis, strewn with rubble and damaged buildings, encircled the grounds on all sides. An overcast orange sky threatened rain, making Kirk rethink leaving his jacket behind, but the oppressive heat and humidity already had him sweating through the white turtleneck shirt beneath his vest. He felt bad for the hundreds of homeless refugees inhabiting the camp, as well as the Federation relief workers assisting them. He was already missing the *Enterprise*'s controlled environment.

"Captain Kirk?"

A middle-aged Andorian woman, wearing a muddy green coverall, approached the landing party members, who were piling out of the shuttle after Kirk. The woman was short and stocky, with weathered blue features, and she radiated a certain indefatigable energy. Her twin antennae tilted in Kirk's direction.

"Guilty as charged," he said.

She held out her hand. "Doctor Sala Tamris. For my sins, the director of the emergency efforts here. I can't tell you how grateful we are for the fresh supplies you've brought us. The Galactic Relief Corps is supported by a variety of civilian and government agencies, but it sometimes seems like there's never enough aid to go around, especially in severe circumstances like this."

Kirk knew the GRC was a largely civilian organization, comprised of dedicated volunteers from dozens of different worlds, that provided humanitarian aid throughout the Federation and beyond. They had arrived on Oyolo before the cease-fire took effect, risking their own safety to care for victims on both sides of the conflict.

"We're glad to be of assistance," Kirk said.

McCoy joined them and introduced himself. Like Kirk, he'd left his jacket back on the shuttle. A medkit was slung over his shoulder.

"A pleasure," he drawled. "You and your people do good work."

"We do what we can." She glanced at the rear of the shuttle, where the rest of the landing party was already unloading the supplies via the aft hatchway. Eager volunteers, dressed similarly to Tamris, helped transfer the containers to a waiting ground vehicle, which looked as though it had seen better days. Cracked and abraded treads would have been discarded by Starfleet due to their distressed condition. "Any little bit helps."

Kirk contemplated the sizable camp ahead of them. "How bad is it? I've read reports, of course, but . . ."

"Let me show you around," she said.

Confident that Hua and the others had the unloading in hand, Kirk let Tamris lead McCoy and him through the camp on foot. Temporary structures, fabricated from thermoconcrete and transparent aluminum, were supplemented by weather-beaten survival tents that had been patched over so many times that it was hard to make out the original color. Kirk estimated that there had to be at least a dozen shelters, but even that seemed insufficient to house all the ragged-looking Oyolu crowded into the camp. Displaced men, women, and children lined up for emergency rations of food, clothing, and clean water, while clinging to their meager possessions in the sweltering heat. Families huddled around portable stoves and even old-fashioned cooking fires, or sought shade beneath makeshift awnings and umbrellas. The air smelled of unwashed bodies, rotting garbage, smoke, and open latrines. Torched and bombed-out buildings rose in the distance, where a once-vital city had been.

"Good Lord," McCoy murmured.

"Believe it or not," Tamris said, shaking her head, "this used to be the city's biggest and most beautiful park, complete with spacious lawns and gardens, riding paths, playgrounds, and so on. I've seen recordings of happy Oyolu families enjoying carefree afternoons here, before the planet turned into a war zone and large sectors of the city were rendered uninhabitable."

Kirk peered past the camp to the shattered buildings looming on the horizon. Pavakian missiles had clearly reduced much of the city to rubble. He was reminded of the charred and crumbling cityscapes left behind by Earth's World Wars. Thankfully, Pavak had so far refrained from launching their most apocalyptic weapons against Oyolo, but that was probably small comfort to the wretched masses struggling to survive in the aftermath of even non-cataclysmic bombings. The lawns and gardens mentioned by Tamris had long since been trampled into an ugly, muddy expanse. It was hard to imagine that this place had ever been as idyllic as she claimed.

"What a waste," he said.

"Indeed," Tamris said. "And there are camps like this all over Oyolo. The cycle of attacks and reprisals has left the planet with much rebuilding to do, if and when the cease-fire holds. And we still have security concerns, what with occasional riots, looting, and violence against alleged collaborators. Sadly, it's not just a matter of Oyolu versus Pavakians. There are rival factions and violence among the Oyolu. Minister A'Barra deserves credit for holding the new coalition government together. At times I fear he's the only thing uniting his people."

Kirk had second thoughts about forgoing a phaser. "Sounds like a difficult situation."

"That's what I call an understatement," McCoy said. "This is a damn tragedy."

Tamris nodded gravely. "You'll get no disagreement from me, Doctor."

On the other hand, Kirk was pleased to see volunteers from across the Federation lending a hand. Glancing around, he spied humans, Deltans, Rhaandarites, Arcturians, Tellarites, and even a Horta assisting around the camp. The latter was excavating a large heap of stony debris that appeared to be the remains of a collapsed tower or monument. Vapor rose as the lumpy, silicon-based being literally consumed the rubble, dissolving it with a highly corrosive acid secreted from its own body. Hortas were the finest natural miners in the Quadrant; Kirk could see where they would be well suited to cleaning up after disasters as well. Shattered stone, steel, and concrete were like a buffet to Horta.

Too bad the Oyolu couldn't feed on the wreckage as well.

"Looks like your people are keeping busy," he commented.

"And then some," she agreed. "It's hard work, but satisfying." She led them toward one of the larger structures. Armed guards, both Oyolu and otherwise, were posted by the entrance. "This is our main medical facility. I imagine this will be of interest to you, Doctor, but I warn you in advance: This is a far cry from a Starfleet sickbay."

"I've delivered babies in caves," McCoy replied. "Trust me, I'm no stranger to frontier medicine."

"Good to know." She approached the entrance. "After you, gentlemen."

Kirk paused to indicate the guards. "Part of the security issues you mentioned before?"

"Exactly. We need to protect our supply of drugs and medicines, as well as some of our less popular patients. Those believed to have collaborated with the Pavakians, and profited by their dealings with them, although the line between 'collaborating' and cooperating can be a blurry one that is too often lost when it comes to reprisals. People have been attacked and run out of their homes simply for not opposing Pavak as fiercely as others might like . . . and even for supporting the peace process too vocally."

"Understood," Kirk said. Guaranteeing the safety of alleged "collaborators" was one of the many prickly issues to be hashed out in the negotiations taking place aboard the *Enterprise*. As Kirk recalled, many of the Pavakians' Oyolu allies and trading partners were already seeking asylum on Pavak and the preservation of their personal fortunes and property, while Oyolo had its

own claims on various assets "stolen" by Oyolu expatri-
ates currently living on Pavak. It was a messy situation
that had apparently already resulted in hard feelings
and bloodshed, even among the Oyolu themselves. "I
can see where you'd need to take precautions."

"I wish they weren't necessary," Tamris said, "but
I'm in the business of dealing with harsh realities." She
stepped aside to let the men pass. "As I suspect you are
as well."

"On occasion," Kirk admitted.

A riveted steel door sealed the entrance to the facility. Kirk expected it to slide aside at his approach and
was momentarily thrown off his stride when it didn't.
Automatic doors were apparently a luxury the camp
could not afford to indulge in.

"The knob," McCoy suggested.

"Thank you, Bones. I think I can manage."

Kirk tugged on the handle and held the door open
for McCoy and Tamris. The first thing he noticed as
they entered was that it was possibly even hotter and
stuffier inside the structure than outdoors, despite the
best efforts of various fans and open windows. The next
thing he observed was just how many sick and injured
people appeared to be crammed into the warehouse-
sized building. Spock would have been able to estimate
an exact head count at a glance, but Kirk registered that
there were several dozen at least. He also could tell at
once that there were too many patients and not enough
doctors, medics, and nurses.

"Dear Lord," McCoy murmured. "This makes that so-called 'hospital' back in the twentieth century look positively civilized."

Tamris gave him a quizzical look. "Come again?"

"It's a long story," Kirk said, recalling their tumultuous voyage through time a few years ago before turning his attention back to the situation at hand. Movable partitions divided the facility into separate sections: triage, recovery, intensive care, and quarantine. Tamris pointed them out as she guided the men through the overtaxed medical center, which nonetheless struck Kirk as impressively clean and organized under the circumstances. The majority of the patients occupied cots instead of proper beds, with sophisticated monitor systems reserved for only the most severe cases. Bags of plasma and saline hung on old-fashioned IVs, while hyposprays were deployed conservatively, the better to extend the center's limited supplies. Kirk spotted another guard posted outside the quarantine area and wondered how many "collaborators" had been stowed there, away from the other patients, for their own safety.

There's healing to be done here all right, he thought. *In more ways than one.*

Grief and suffering were everywhere to be seen, as were compassion and dedication. Exhausted-looking volunteers tended to patients suffering from burns, infections, hacking coughs, missing limbs, and other conditions. Kirk had hardly lived a sheltered life, having witnessed his fair share of plagues, massacres, and battlefields in his time, but he was still deeply moved and disturbed by the heartrending sights and sounds around him. Labored breaths and pain-racked groans tugged at his heart. He watched in sorrow as an orderly somberly pulled a sheet over the face of a patient who hadn't made it. A friend or family member stood by, sobbing.

"And this planet looked so peaceful from above," he mused.

"There's still beauty to be found here," Tamris assured him. "You just have to look a lot harder to find it. And make no mistake, gentlemen. Those supplies you delivered are going to make a tremendous difference. We were running dangerously low on anti-virals, anesthetics, cardiostimulators, and working surgical lasers, among other things."

McCoy nodded. "We also brought you a cartload of hemozinate, to accelerate red-cell production in suitable patients. That should cut down on the need for transfusions and help stretch out your blood supply."

Kirk recalled McCoy using the same drug decades ago when Spock had to donate a large quantity of T-negative blood to his father. Hemozinate had been dangerous and experimental then, but had since become a standard part of the Federation's medical arsenal.

"Tailored for Oyolu physiology?" Tamris asked.

"Absolutely," McCoy promised. "I double-checked the specifications myself."

"Perfect. That's just what we need."

It hardly seemed enough. Kirk glanced around the overcrowded facility. He wished he could beam all these patients up to the *Enterprise*'s sickbay, but that was hardly practical, especially if there were indeed camps like this all over Oyolo—and injured on Pavak as well. The best he could do was to make sure that the peace process went forward, so that both planets would have a chance to heal.

After touring the medical complex, Tamris showed them around the rest of the camp. Kirk considered it time well spent, but eventually began to think about returning to the *Enterprise*. There was a diplomatic reception being held in the ship's observation lounge this evening, shipboard time, and he was curious to hear how the first round of negotiations had gone.

"This has been very illuminating, Doctor Tamris," he said. "I appreciate your hospitality and the truly heroic efforts of you and your people. The galaxy is a better place because of selfless and hardworking organizations like yours. But we should probably start making our way back to our shuttlecraft. I'm sure all of those supplies have gotten where they belong by now."

"But you can't leave just yet," she protested. "It's almost time for tonight's performance."

Kirk didn't understand. "Performance?"

"The GRC does more than simply see to a distressed population's basic physical needs, although that naturally takes priority. The arts serve a vital role as well, if only to provide some relief and distraction from the emotional toll of the disaster. Many of our volunteers put on entertainments for the refugees, on top of their ordinary duties. Indeed, we have some very talented performers in our ranks—musicians, storytellers, actors, and so on—who generously share their gifts with the struggling people here, whose spirits are so much in need of lifting. 'Make art, not war,' as it were."

"A laudable sentiment," Kirk said. "And would those talented performers include yourself?"

"Hardly." She chortled at the very idea. "Believe me, the last thing any Oyolu needs is for me to sing or dance. That would be a whole new category of atrocity. But several of my fellow volunteers are staging an abbreviated production of *The Tempest* tonight, adapted from a play by one of your fellow Terrans, I believe. They've been rehearsing it for weeks, during their rest periods, and I know they'd be honored if you and Doctor McCoy could attend. I'm quite looking forward to it myself."

Kirk thought about it. He did have that reception on the *Enterprise* coming up, but the time difference between the ship and this part of the planet worked in his favor. The reception was still a few hours away, which, in theory, gave him more than enough time to catch at least part of the play and still make it back to the *Enterprise* in time to join Riley and the delegates at the reception.

And he did like Shakespeare.

"*The Tempest*, you say?" Kirk was tempted. "A play

all about reconciliation, forgiveness, and leaving old wrongs and grudges in the past. I can't think of a more suitable choice at this particular juncture."

"You won't regret it," Tamris insisted. "Our leading lady, Lyla Kassidy, is a most remarkable actress. I'd say she was wasting her talent here, if not for the crucial importance of our work. You really owe it to yourselves to experience her performance. It will give you chills."

Kirk admired her powers of persuasion. No doubt a useful skill when it came to mustering donations and volunteers, not to mention wrangling with local authorities and bureaucracies. He doubted that she ever willingly took no for an answer.

"Well, when you put it that way . . ." He turned to McCoy. "What do you say, Bones. You up for a little Shakespeare?"

"I don't know." McCoy glanced back at the medical facility. He was obviously still thinking about all the stricken patients they'd observed there. "Maybe I can lend a hand at the medical center while you take in the show. . . ."

"Absolutely not," Tamris said firmly. "You've already done enough. Please allow us to repay your kindness in some small fashion. It's the least we can do."

McCoy hesitated. "But—"

"No buts," she declared. "If there's one thing I've learned from this business, it's that martyrs burn out fast and even the most motivated humanitarians need to take a break once in a while. Besides, what's the point in saving lives if we can't stop to appreciate the things that make life worth living?"

"All right," McCoy said, giving in. "Far be it from me to refuse such a gracious invitation."

Spoken like a true Southern gentleman, Kirk thought. "That goes double for me."

"I'm so glad." Tamris took them both by the arms. "Step this way."

Twilight was falling as they arrived at an open-air amphitheater that had somehow miraculously survived the bombings. Hordes of bedraggled refugees were already filling the tiered rows that circled the central stage. Tamris pulled rank to get Kirk and McCoy front-row seats only a few meters away from the stage. A light rain was held at bay above the theater by a weak force-field dome, which crackled and sparked as the drizzle bounced off it. Kirk had just settled into his seat when an artificial thunderclap announced that *The Tempest* had commenced, in more ways than one.

The staging was minimalist but effective. Flashing lights and lasers, along with the amplified sounds of howling winds and booming thunder, created the illusion of a raging storm at sea. Actors portraying the imperiled crew and passengers of a foundering vessel tossed themselves about the stage, like modern-day spacefarers caught in an ion storm, while shouting to be heard above the simulated tempest.

"Now would I give a thousand furlongs of sea for an acre of dry land!"

Kirk noted that the bleachers circled the entire theater so that there was no backstage area. Scenery and
characters entered and exited the stage by means of
trapdoors and hidden stairways beneath the stage floor.
Lost at sea, the hapless mariners vanished from sight
as though disappearing beneath the waves. Applause
greeted the conclusion of the first scene.

Nicely done, Kirk thought, especially for an amateur
production put on by aid workers in a refugee camp.
I've seldom seen it staged better.

A change in lighting and a few prop trees switched
the location to Prospero's enchanted island. The wizard and his daughter emerged from an underground
"cave" beneath the stage. Miranda was played by a hairless young Deltan actress in a simple linen frock while
Prospero wore a hooded cloak adorned with arcane
Klingon hieroglyphics. A graceful hand clutched a
gnarled staff topped by what Kirk assumed was just
a replica of a dilithium crystal. He gathered from her
gait and carriage that Prospero was being played by a
woman in this production.

*Probably that talented volunteer Tamris mentioned
earlier,* he guessed. *Lyla Somebody?*

As ever, the gentle Miranda feared for the safety of
the men at sea, but her magisterial parent was quick
to reassure her:

"Be collected. No more amazement. Tell your pite-
ous heart there's no harm done. . . ."

Kirk frowned. There was something familiar—and

oddly unsettling—about the feminine voice escaping the wizard's concealing hood. He leaned forward in his seat, squinting at the stage, but he could not make out the face beneath the hood. Nor could he place the voice right away.

On stage, Prospero attempted to dispel Miranda's confusion. "'Tis time I should inform thee farther. Lend thy hand and pluck my magic garment from me—so."

Prospero threw back her hood, revealing the elegant features of an attractive human woman who looked to be in her late thirties. Flaxen hair complemented her fair complexion. With Miranda's help, she shed her wizardly garb and stood before the audience in a belted brown robe that flattered her trim figure. Sandals shod her feet.

Kirk's eyes widened in shock. The woman's face was two decades older than he remembered and her hair was styled differently. But there was no mistaking those striking features and captivating hazel eyes. Twenty-year-old memories surfaced from the past, confirming the startling truth.

The woman on stage, performing before the crowd, was Lenore Karidian.

Murderess, madwoman, and daughter of Kodos the Executioner.

Three

"My God!" McCoy whispered, obviously recognizing "Prospero" as well. "Is that . . . ?"

"Yes," Kirk said tersely. "Lenore Karidian."

The memories came flooding back. Kirk had first met Lenore in 2266, while investigating charges that her father, a distinguished Shakespearean actor going by the name "Anton Karidian," was actually Kodos the Executioner, the infamous mass murderer responsible for the deaths of some four thousand colonists on Tarsus IV decades earlier. Despite his suspicions regarding her father, Kirk had grown close to Lenore—until he'd discovered that the troubled young actress had and would murder to protect Kodos's guilty secrets. In the end, after accidentally killing her father during a confrontation with Kirk, she had suffered a complete mental breakdown. At the time, McCoy had assured Kirk that Lenore would get the best help available, but he hadn't laid eyes on her since.

Until now.

McCoy eyed him with concern. "Are you all right, Jim?"

"I'm fine," he lied none too convincingly. In truth, his mind was reeling, struggling to process this unexpected specter from the past. What was Lenore Karidian, of all people, doing here on Oyolo after all this time? Granted, it had been twenty years since her crimes and breakdown, which was presumably long enough for her to regain her sanity and be rehabilitated, but even still . . .

Clad in her humble robes, she gazed out at the audience as Prospero probed Miranda's childhood memories of their shared exile.

"But how is it that this lives in thy mind? What seest thou else"—her eyes met Kirk's and she briefly stumbled over the line—"in the dark backward and abysm of time?"

Kirk was impressed by her quick recovery. She had been a fine actress, he recalled. She had been playing Ophelia in *Hamlet* the last time he saw her perform, right before a phaser blast intended for him had killed Kodos instead. The realization that she had inadvertently slain her own beloved father had shattered her already questionable sanity, although the woman on the stage before him now certainly seemed lucid enough—and had clearly recognized him as well.

I wonder if she's as shocked to see me as I am to see her.

The rest of the performance passed in a blur, with Kirk barely aware of the classic story playing out on the stage. He vaguely registered a Troyian Ariel, with blond hair and blue skin, springing up from a hidden trapdoor like an airy spirit, and he was surprised to see that Caliban was being played by the Horta he had observed earlier; a universal translator affixed to his rocky carapace gave him an appropriately gravelly voice. But Kirk fidgeted restlessly in his seat whenever Lenore was offstage, unable to concentrate on the other actors. All thought of discreetly slipping away between acts had been disintegrated as surely as though it had been blasted by a disruptor set on maximum. She had already seen and recognized him. He wasn't about to leave without dealing with her return.

For her part, Lenore appeared to be doing her professional best to ignore his presence in the audience, but he caught her stealing furtive glances in his direction. Her reaction, however, remained unreadable, veiled as it was behind the assumed guise of Prospero. Shakespeare's venerable mage eventually forgave his ancient enemies, but had Lenore?

He whispered to McCoy, "Were you aware she'd been released?"

"I remember seeing some encouraging reports way back when, but, honestly, Jim, I lost track of her case decades ago."

"Me, too," Kirk admitted. He couldn't blame McCoy for not being up to speed on Lenore's psychological condition after all these years. That had indeed been a long time ago. Truth to tell, he hadn't thought of her in ages, except maybe once in a while.

"It's not like she was ever really my patient," McCoy pointed out. "At least not after she was carted off to a hospital for the criminally insane. . . ."

"Sssh!" protested an elderly Oyolu seated behind them. "Some of us are trying to watch the show."

Kirk gave the man an apologetic nod and piped down for the time being. He waited impatiently through the rest of the performance, grateful when it did indeed turn out to be a condensed adaptation of the original play, lasting only ninety minutes or so. He watched intently as Lenore was finally left alone on the stage to deliver the closing soliloquy, which now seemed to carry a hidden meaning.

"As you from crimes would pardoned be, let your indulgence set me free."

A standing ovation greeted the cast as they assembled on the stage to take their bows. Kirk and McCoy rose to their feet and joined in the applause, although Kirk felt uncomfortable doing so. Twenty years or not, Lenore had murdered seven innocent people and had tried to kill him.

But that was long ago, he reminded himself, *and she hadn't been in her right mind. Perhaps she is better now?*

"You see!" Tamris enthused, oblivious to Kirk's unexpected rendezvous with the past. She beamed at Kirk and McCoy, who had been seated to her left, while clapping enthusiastically. "Wasn't that completely worth sticking around for?"

"Absolutely." Kirk feigned a blithe and appreciative attitude. "I don't suppose . . . it would be possible to meet with the cast? I'd love an opportunity to extend my personal congratulations on a job well done."

McCoy shot him a glance, which flew completely over Tamris's antennae.

"By all means," she said. "I'm sure they'd be delighted to meet you."

Kirk was somewhat less confident about that, at least as far as the production's leading lady was concerned, but he saw no reason to convey those doubts to Tamris. He couldn't help wondering, however, if the dedicated GRC leader was aware that they had a former murderer in their midst. Was he morally obliged to inform Tamris of her colleague's checkered past or was Lenore entitled to a second chance?

I can't know that until I've had a chance to talk to Lenore again, he thought, *and see for myself if she's a new woman. If even then . . .*

Tamris waited for the bleachers to clear out a little before escorting them down toward the stage. While she led the way, McCoy sidled up next to Kirk and whispered to him too softly to be overheard.

"You sure this is a good idea, Jim?"

Kirk appreciated his concern, but he did not turn back. He lowered his voice. "And you're not curious to find out what she's been up to? And what she's doing here?"

"Of course," McCoy admitted, "but as a doctor I know the danger of re-opening old wounds."

Kirk smirked. "Didn't I say that to you once?"

"Yes. And you weren't wrong."

Kirk shrugged, dismissing the doctor's worries. "She's just an ordinary human who had to be institutionalized many years ago. It's not like we're running into Khan again."

"Maybe," McCoy groused. "But look how well that turned out."

A raised trapdoor exposed a lighted stairway leading down into the staging area below. High spirits, music, and laughter wafted up from the lower levels.

"Come with me," Tamris said. "Let me introduce you."

The stairs led down into a warren of musty underground compartments. Props, scenery, and costumes were strewn haphazardly about, looking a bit more cheap and tawdry without the magic of the theater investing them with glamour. The cast and crew were squeezed into one of the larger spaces, only one level below the stage. Flickering overhead lights illuminated the basement, banishing the shadows to secluded nooks and crannies packed with random bits of theatrical paraphernalia. A catchy Denevan pop song played over a sound system. Kirk spied a touchscreen control panel mounted to one wall. He assumed it was used to manage the audio and lighting effects, not that he really cared about that at the moment.

Where was Lenore?

Celebrating actors, basking in the success of tonight's performance, congratulated one another over mugs of foaming Oyolu beer. The Horta's universal translator was set loud enough to be heard over the hubbub. Kirk imagined the Horta felt quite at home in this cramped subterranean setting, given that its species tunneled deep beneath the surface of their native Janus VI. Boisterous laughter, like boulders rolling downhill, echoed off the exposed stone walls of the chamber.

"But what I really want to play is Falstaff," the Horta declared. "I like to think I have sufficient girth!"

The festive atmosphere was at odds with Kirk's own mood. Despite his bravado with McCoy, he anticipated their upcoming reunion with Lenore with some apprehension. Things had not ended well between them, to say the least. He scanned the crowded compartment, but did not immediately lay eyes on her. Had she already fled to avoid encountering him again?

"Friends, colleagues!" Tamris called out. "We have two very important guests with us tonight. Captain James T. Kirk and Doctor Leonard McCoy of the *Starship Enterprise*. They're here to tell you how much they enjoyed the show."

Actors, many still in costume and makeup, swarmed the visiting Starfleet officers, forcing Kirk to make polite conversation while keeping his eyes peeled for Lenore. Time was running short, and he had other places to be, but he wasn't about to return to the ship before finding her. Her presence here raised too many questions that he wanted answered—for his own peace of mind.

"Well, I'm no drama critic," McCoy drawled, keeping up his end of the chitchat, "but I'd say you did the Bard proud. I'm sure the folks in the audience appreciated a break from their troubles. . . ."

Kirk was only half-listening. Milling bodies jostled him and blocked his line of sight, making it hard to scan the party for Lenore. Someone opened a bottle of cheap champagne, provoking shrieks and squeals of laughter as the bubbly sprayed over the heads of the crowd. Nobody seemed too concerned that the star of the production had yet to make an appearance. Kirk began to fear that she was going to be a no-show.

Is she hiding from me?

Then, just as he was starting to wonder how far he was willing to search for her, Lenore emerged from a dressing room to a round of copious applause. Her pale face was scrubbed of makeup and she had exchanged Propero's monastic garb for a simple white sundress. She accepted the applause with a graceful bow, but her wary eyes immediately sought out Kirk. He could see, even if her jubilant costars couldn't, the tension behind her poise. Her jaw was tight, her smile forced.

"And there's our star," Tamris announced. Grabbing Kirk and McCoy by their arms, she dragged them over to Lenore, clearing a path through the party. "Captain Kirk, Doctor McCoy, may I present the lovely and talented Lyla Kassidy."

Kirk chose to overlook the alias for now. McCoy discreetly did the same. He hesitated, uncertain if he should acknowledge their history in front of Tamris and the others, but Lenore took the question out of his hands.

"There's no need for introductions," she said lightly. "I've met Captain Kirk before and the good doctor as well."

"Really?" Tamris reacted with surprise. She turned toward the two men, confusion on her face. "You didn't say."

"I wasn't sure it was the same person at first," Kirk fibbed. "It's been quite some time since I last saw you perform, Miss Kassidy."

For the time being, he saw no reason to blow her cover. Being the daughter of Kodos, and a convicted murderer in her own right, was a lot to live down. He could hardly blame her for assuming a new identity and trying to put the past behind her, if that was indeed what she was doing here.

"Yes," she agreed. "Quite some time."

Despite a certain understandable guardedness, her expression and body language remained unreadable. It was impossible to tell what she was thinking and feeling. Did she blame him for her capture so many years ago? Did she still want to kill him for exposing her father?

"Your acting is as impressive as ever," he said. "I've never forgotten your Lady Macbeth."

In more ways than one, he thought.

"Thank you, Captain. Prospero is a fascinating part, with so many layers." She turned her gaze on McCoy. "And you, Doctor, I see you're still looking after our indomitable captain."

"When he lets me." McCoy eyed her carefully. "You seem . . . well."

"I am, Doctor. Much more so, I think, than when we last met."

The oblique exchanges frustrated Kirk, who would have preferred a franker discussion away from so many other eyes and ears. He felt like they were fencing in the dark, stiffly and clumsily. Even Tamris began to pick up on the underlying tension. Her brow furrowed and her antennae twitched as she glanced quizzically between the three humans, clearly attempting to decipher the situation.

Probably figures there's some awkward romantic history here, Kirk guessed. And she wouldn't be entirely wrong, although that was hardly the whole story or even the most important part. Kirk had run into plenty of old flames before, but few came with as much bloody and tragic baggage as Lenore Karidian. Death, madness, and betrayal had long ago eclipsed whatever tender moments they had shared. *But if Tamris wants to suspect that this is just an uneasy reunion of exes, I can live with that. It's probably simpler that way.*

"I'm glad to hear it," McCoy said before casually inserting himself between Tamris and Kirk and Lenore. "You know, Doctor, I'd really like to drop in on your medical center one last time before we have to head back to the *Enterprise*. Just to make certain that those new supplies got where they were going without any complications. I hate to tear you away from the party, but if you wouldn't mind showing me the way . . . ?"

"Of course, Doctor," Tamris replied, perhaps a tad reluctantly, and she made her apologies to Lenore. "If you'll excuse us." She glanced curiously at Kirk. "Are you coming with us, Captain?"

"I'll be along shortly," he promised, grateful for McCoy's subtle intervention. "Miss Kassidy and I still have some catching up to do."

"I figured as much," McCoy said dourly as he steered Tamris away, giving Kirk and Lenore a little more privacy. Medical shoptalk was a ploy to distract Tamris from the cryptic conversation she'd just borne witness to. "As you know, it's crucial that hemozinate be kept refrigerated at precisely the right temperature. The last thing you want is for it to freeze up. Let me tell you about the time that . . ."

His voice trailed off as they left, although McCoy looked back in concern before heading up the stairs to the stage above. No doubt he was already having second thoughts about leaving Kirk alone with a woman who had tried to kill him a couple of times, albeit two decades ago. Kirk wondered himself if he should be glad that there was still a crowd of partying cast members around them. A humanoid stagehand thrust a glass of champagne into Lenore's hand, and Kirk recalled that he had first met her at a cocktail party on Planet Q. Little had he known at the time that she had just murdered an old friend of his, Thomas Leighton, less than an hour before. Leighton, along with Kirk, had been one of the last surviving eyewitnesses of the genocidal massacre on Tarsus IV—and one of the few people who might be able to identify "Anton Karidian" as Kodos the Executioner. That had made him a threat in Lenore's eyes and a target for assassination.

"That was deftly done," she remarked, watching McCoy depart with Tamris. "A neat bit of maneuvering. I suppose you have to be able to manage touchy situations if you want to be a physician. Develop a good bedside manner and all that."

"Actually, that was surprisingly smooth for Bones. He's not exactly known for his subtlety, although he has his moments, I suppose." Kirk changed the subject back to her. "So, do you consider this a 'touchy' situation?"

She smiled wryly. "How could I not? Don't get me wrong, Captain. I bear you no ill will, and I'm pleased to see you and Doctor McCoy looking so well, but you'll surely concede that . . . well, we have a complicated history."

"That's one word for it." He noticed that she hadn't taken a sip of champagne yet. "You're not drinking?"

She shook her head. "I avoid spirits these days. They disagree with me . . . and I prefer to keep a level head." She offered him the glass. "Here. Have mine." She chuckled darkly. "It's not poisoned, I promise."

"I'll take your word for it, but perhaps I should keep a clear head as well."

Declining the glass, he was about to say more when the charming Deltan actress who had portrayed Miranda came rushing up and threw her arms around Lenore. Her smooth cranium gleamed beneath the bright overhead lights. "Oh my stars," she burbled, "did you hear that applause? They loved us . . . and you especially!"

"I heard them, Jyllia," Lenore assured her younger costar. "And I'm certain that applause was for the entire company, including a certain incandescent Miranda." She gently disengaged from the other woman's embrace, always a somewhat tantalizing experience where Deltans were concerned, and nodded at Kirk. "I'm visiting with an old friend at the moment. Why don't you run along and join the others? I'll be by presently."

"Promise?" Jyllia grinned at Kirk. "What did you think, Captain? Wasn't Lyla the best Prospero ever?"

"I've never seen it done better," he said sincerely. About that at least there was no need to dissemble or couch his words. Lenore had brought depth and complexity to her performance, blending subtle shades of anger, bitterness, compassion, and wisdom into a seamless portrait of a world-weary mage tying up the loose ends of his life. "You had the audience under your spell."

"You're both shameless flatterers," Lenore stated. "Not that I'm complaining, mind you." She foisted her untouched drink off on Jyllia. "Now, shoo, you capricious 'daughter.' Attend to your revels while I converse on deeper matters with our esteemed starship captain."

"All right . . . but don't be long!"

Jyllia scampered off to join a bunch of tipsy actors who were trying to get a conga line going. Argelian belly-dance music blared from the loudspeakers. Kirk frowned at the increasingly raucous celebration. This was hardly the ideal environment for a serious conversation.

"Is there somewhere we can talk privately?"

Lenore arched an eyebrow. "You're not afraid to be alone with me, considering?"

Kirk thought about it, but he judged the risk to be minimal. She didn't appear to be hiding any weapons under her dress, at least as far as he could tell. And while he wasn't as young as he used to be, he liked to think he could still defend himself against an unarmed woman. As long as he kept his guard up, that was.

"Just keep your hands where I can see them," he quipped.

"All right," she said after a moment's consideration. "Follow me."

A back stairway led to another entrance onto the stage, which was now dark and empty, lit only by a pair of crescent moons overhead. The summer shower had passed, leaving the evening sky clear and the force field deactivated. Night had brought some relief from the heat, although it was still warm and muggy. Kirk followed Lenore up into the deserted amphitheater surrounding the stage until they reached the upmost tier, about as far as possible from the underground cast party. Although neither of them mentioned it, it wasn't by accident that Kirk walked behind Lenore. He wasn't quite ready to turn his back on her just yet.

"This should do," she said, taking a seat. "I doubt we'll be interrupted up here."

"Or overheard." Kirk glanced around, confirming that they pretty much had the "nosebleed seats" to themselves. He sat down beside her. "A much better venue, Miss Kassidy."

"No need to be so formal, Jim. 'Lyla' will be fine."

"Very well . . . Lyla."

An awkward silence descended as Kirk tried to come up with a diplomatic way to frame the questions nagging at him. Was she truly cured of her madness? Had she ever repented of her crimes? And what exactly had brought her to Oyolo?

"So," she prompted. "Here we are."

"I admit I was startled to find you here," he said. "Gave me a bit of a jolt."

"Likewise," she confessed. "I had heard, of course, that the *Enterprise* was in the vicinity and that you were involved in the peace negotiations, but it's a big planet and a bigger solar system. It seemed unlikely that we would run into each other, so imagine my surprise when you showed up unexpectedly in the audience . . .

and in the front row, no less. I fear I fell out of character briefly."

"You recovered admirably. Your father would be proud."

She flinched and Kirk felt a stab of guilt.

"I'm sorry," he said. "That was tactless of me."

"No need to apologize. After everything I did back then, you're entitled to a little revenge. I can't blame you for hating me."

"I don't hate you," he said, realizing it was true. "You were sick, damaged . . . unhinged by the knowledge of your father's crimes. I pitied you and was horrified by what you'd done, but I never hated you. If anything, I was angry at myself for not seeing the truth soon enough." A thought occurred to him. "So you *do* remember everything that happened? At the time, McCoy said that you wouldn't recall any of it, that you were convinced that your father was still alive, performing throughout the galaxy."

"I didn't remember, not at first." She shuddered and hugged herself despite the sultry night air. "It took years of therapy and treatment before I could cope with the memories, but I had to face them eventually . . . if I was ever going to move past them."

"And have you?" he asked. "Moved on?"

"I'm not plotting to kill anyone, if that's what you're asking." She looked him squarely in the eyes, as though he was another painful memory she needed to confront head-on. "I'll always have to live with what I've done, but for the last several years, I've been trying to atone for my father's crimes—and my own—by making a positive contribution to the universe."

"As in volunteering for the Galactic Relief Corps?"

"Exactly," she said. "I know it won't bring any of my victims back to life, or erase what happened on Tarsus Four, but it helps me sleep at night."

He wanted to believe her. Wasn't this entire mission about forgiving past crimes and conflicts to forge a better, more peaceful future? If the Oyolu and the Pavakians could attempt to move beyond their bloody history, why couldn't Lenore Karidian?

"I had no idea, about any of this," he confessed. "To be honest, I'm feeling somewhat guilty myself at the moment."

She gave him a puzzled look. "What for?"

"For losing track of you over the years and never bothering to see what had become of you." He shook his head ruefully. "Truth to tell, I've never been good at looking backwards."

Like with Khan, he thought. *And David . . .*

"Perhaps that's just as well," she said.

"Not always."

The last few years had taught him some hard lessons about the dangers of ignoring the past. He'd always been so busy boldly going forward that he'd seldom stopped to consider the consequences of his actions, and that negligence had eventually cost him dearly. Letting sleeping dogs lie was all very well and good, at least in the short term, but those dogs sometimes came back to bite you when you least expected.

As with Lenore?

"There's a difference, I think, between leaving the past behind and sweeping it under the rug. I've learned from experience that—" His communicator beeped, interrupting him. "Excuse me for a moment." He flipped open the communicator. "Kirk here."

"Lieutenant Hua from the Copernicus," a voice identified itself. *"Doctor McCoy asked me to remind you that we're expected back on the* Enterprise."

Kirk assumed that McCoy also wanted to make sure that he was still alive and not lying dead with a dagger in his back. Bones had a point, though. They did need to get back to the ship. This fact-finding expedition to Oyolo had already lasted longer than intended.

"Acknowledged," Kirk replied. "Tell Doctor McCoy I'll be with you shortly."

"Aye, sir. The shuttle is ready when you are."

"Save me a seat. Kirk out."

Lenore watched him put away the communicator. "Duty calls?"

"I'm afraid so." He knew he should get going, but he found himself reluctant to depart. It felt as though he and Lenore had only just begun to sort out the unfinished business between them. He wanted to hear more about her new life, if only to convince himself that the lies and losses of yesterday were not the end of the story and that second chances were still possible. "Damn."

"I know," she said. "Strange to say, but I'm glad we had this chance to talk. A pity there isn't more time."

A sudden inspiration struck him.

"We're having a diplomatic reception aboard the *Enterprise* later this evening. Why don't you come aboard as my guest? It will give us a better opportunity to catch up . . . and perhaps lay some old ghosts to rest."

"I'm not sure," she said hesitantly. "Perhaps we should just be grateful for this brief encounter and let it go at that."

He thought he understood her reluctance. The last time he'd invited her aboard the *Enterprise,* he'd been laying a trap for her father, she'd been conspiring to kill him, and the whole ugly affair had ended in tears. Granted, that had been an earlier *Enterprise,* but he could see where returning to the scene of her crime might be daunting. Her father had died on the *Enterprise* at her own hands.

"No, you were right the first time," he insisted. "We have twenty years to catch up on, and two decades of regrets to work through. One brief conversation isn't enough."

She regarded him thoughtfully. "Are you looking for closure, Jim?"

"Perhaps. And isn't that what *The Tempest* is all about? Prospero needs to confront those who wronged him, and forgive them, before he can sail off into the sunset."

"'Gentle breath of yours my sails must fill,'" she recited, nodding, "'or else my project fails, which was to please.'" She took a deep breath. "Perhaps I should board your mighty vessel again, if only for old time's sake. But it sounds as though the good doctor is eager to depart and I'm hardly dressed for a formal reception." She glanced down at her unassuming attire. "Plus, I really should join my cast mates in their celebration. I promised Jyllia."

"No problem. The reception isn't until twenty-one hundred, shipboard time. I'll send the shuttle back to pick you up in time for the party." She started to protest, but he held up a hand to fend off any objections. "It's no bother. It will give us a chance to deliver another load of supplies to the relief effort here."

"Well, if you're not making a special trip on my account . . ."

"I suspect we'll be making regular runs to Oyolo while the negotiations are under way. One more trip this evening is no hardship." He shrugged. "Besides, as you'll recall, I once diverted the *Enterprise* from its course to accommodate you."

"With ulterior motives," she pointed out.

"Yet another issue we'll discuss later and at leisure." He rose to his feet, making ready to leave. "I'll have the *Enterprise* contact the camp to arrange matters. Please don't get cold feet once I'm gone. I really want to continue this conversation. I think it will be good . . . for all concerned."

"Don't worry," she promised. "Stage fright is not among my many failings, and I have never been late for a performance."

"It's settled, then. I look forward to seeing you later, aboard the *Enterprise*."

He started down the aisle toward the nearest exit, already wondering how he was going to explain this to McCoy . . . and Riley.

"Jim?" she called out before he got too far.

He turned around to look back at her. "Yes?"

"You *are* being very forgiving and accommodating. Should I be suspicious?"

"I don't know," he answered. "Should *I*?"

Four

"You are cleared to land, Galileo. *You are requested to lower your shields. Do not deviate from the prescribed flight path or we will be forced to open fire."*

The stern instructions came over the shuttlecraft's comm unit as the *Galileo* descended toward the remote Pavakian military base, located near the planet's border. Piloting the shuttle, Spock confirmed that the fort had lowered its own defensive force field so that the shuttle could approach unobstructed. He made visual contact with the base.

"Not exactly what you'd call a warm welcome," observed Mister Scott, who was seated beside Spock in the shuttle's cockpit. At this stage of the disarmament process, the Pavakians were allowing only two Starfleet inspectors to visit the restricted site, so Spock and Scott were alone in the shuttle. Scott scowled beneath his mustache. "You'd think they weren't happy to see us."

"Pavakians are not known for the warmth of either their temperament or climate," Spock stated. "And it is unlikely that our mission is regarded with enthusiasm by every element of their military."

The Vulcan observed their destination as they descended through a cold, gray sky. The Pavakian base was located in a stark, inhospitable wasteland surrounded by barren, rocky hills sparsely dotted with scrub. Gazing down at the harsh terrain of this equatorial region, Spock could well understand why the Pavakians had found Oyolo's lush environment and biodiversity so tempting. By comparison, life on Pavak was a constant struggle to survive. That the Pavakians had managed to build an advanced space-faring civilization despite such obstacles did them credit.

The base itself appeared highly secure. Along with its force field, the complex was also guarded by high mesh walls that were surely capable of being energized or electrified. Guards and heavy artillery were stationed at every gate and watchtower while batteries of phaser cannons further defended the base's perimeter and airspace. A single paved highway connected the base with a large urban metropolis in the distance, although the base seemed to be quite self-sufficient. Inside its barricades were a variety of structures, including barracks, garages, hangars, and armories. A massive concrete silo, which appeared of newer construction than the rest of the base, dominated the site. The sun was just rising on the horizon, confirming that it was early morning on this part of the planet.

Galileo touched down on a landing pad, where a large contingent of armed Pavakian soldiers were on hand to greet them. Spock chose to view this as a demonstration of respect, but he acknowledged that the potentially intimidating show of force could be interpreted differently.

What message was truly intended?

He shut down the engines and opened the starboard hatchway. Under ideal circumstances, Spock would have preferred to leave a crew member to watch over *Galileo* in their absence, but that was not an option in this instance, so they would have to leave the shuttle-craft unattended. He rose from his seat and joined Scott at the open hatch. Befitting their role as peacekeepers, they left their phasers aboard.

"Let us meet our hosts, Mister Scott."

"Aye, sir."

The hatchway closed behind them as they emerged from the shuttle. A bracing cold immediately imposed itself upon their senses. Despite the base's location near the equator and the fact that it was technically summer in this region of the planet, the temperature was uncomfortably frigid, particularly by Vulcan standards. Even Scott, who'd been raised in the rigorous climate of his native Scotland, displayed evidence of discomfort. The men's breaths frosted before their lips, and Spock was grateful for their heavy-duty field jackets. He also found himself envying the Pavakians' layers of fur.

"Welcome to Fort Dakkur," a Pavakian officer addressed them in a frosty tone that rather belied the content of his greeting. He stepped forward to meet them.

"I am Brigadier-General Pogg. I will be responsible for you during your stay here."

Fine black fur covered a blunt, square face, except around his mouth and chin where snow-white fur created the illusion of a beard and mustache. His uniform and military bearing left no doubt as to his profession. The sable down upon his face made it difficult to gauge his age, but he conveyed an impression of vigorous middle age. A disruptor pistol was holstered at his hip.

"We look forward to your hospitality and cooperation, sir," Spock said. He introduced himself and Mister Scott. "Our mission here can only benefit all concerned."

"I have my orders," Pogg said stiffly. "You may rely on me to carry them out."

Unlike his father, Spock was not a diplomat, but he thought it best to bring any potential conflicts out into the open in a timely fashion. In his experience, reliable data was essential to achieving one's objective.

"May I ask, sir, if you personally approve of your orders?"

"My personal views are irrelevant," Pogg replied. "I subscribe to the chain of command."

"Nonetheless," Spock said, "I would be interested in knowing where you stand with regards to our mission."

Pogg's eyes narrowed and he contemplated the visitors carefully before responding.

"Let me make myself clear. As a soldier, I am all in favor of peace. I've lost too many good men and women to this ugly conflict and have offered my condolences to far too many families and orphans. But, as a patriot, I can't say I'm happy about the Federation sticking their nose in our business. Pavak is perfectly capable of keeping up its end of any agreements with Oyolo without outsiders looking over our shoulders."

"I appreciate your candor, sir," Spock said. "But let me point out that Starfleet's involvement and, specifically, our own arrival at this base, was a compromise agreed to by both parties. Because Pavak would not allow any Oyolu inspectors to visit your military installations, a third party was required. Were the situation reversed, would you be content to simply take the Oyolu's word that all weapons of mass destruction had been destroyed?"

"Not for a moment," Pogg admitted. "But this is a Pavakian base—and Pavakian weapons—that we are discussing. Allowing any outsiders to this fort rubs me the wrong way. I take Pavakian autonomy and sovereignty very seriously, gentlemen."

"As well you should," Spock said. "However—"

"This is a fascinating debate," Scotty interrupted, shivering, "but perhaps we could continue it somewhere a wee bit warmer?"

"Of course," Pogg said. "My apologies for forgetting that you are unaccustomed to our climate. We have prepared quarters for you in the officers' barracks. Follow me."

He escorted them across the grounds to a utilitarian, block-shaped building within walking distance of the landing field. A detachment of armed soldiers accompanied them, but they kept a reasonable enough distance that Spock felt more like a guest than a prisoner. As they passed through various levels of security, Spock wondered whether such measures had been upped in anticipation of their visit. He was aware from his briefings that both the peace talks and the disarmament agreement remained controversial on Pavak, with a significant percentage of the populace bitterly opposed to making any concessions to Oyolo. It was probable that the fort's defenses, both within and without, were at least partially intended to protect the base from disgruntled elements on their own planet.

Spock found this more troubling than reassuring.

Thankfully, the guards stayed outside as Pogg admitted them to a suite on the top floor of the barracks. The accommodations were Spartan, but adequate. Picture windows offered a view of the fort and outlying terrain. The temperature was still fairly chilly, but perhaps it could be adjusted; if not, years of living among humans had accustomed Spock to environments considerably cooler than Vulcan. He was pleased to note a computer terminal and work station in one corner, as well as what appeared to be a personal communications unit. He fully intended to keep the *Enterprise* apprised of their activities here.

"Aye, that's more like it," Scott said, although he appeared to be in no hurry to remove his field jacket. "It was a tad nippy outdoors, if ye don't mind me saying."

"By Pavakian standards, the weather is quite pleasant," Pogg assured them. Crossing the suite, he extracted a bottle from a cupboard. A viscous amber liquid sloshed inside the bottle. "This is an excellent local vintage. Perhaps it will warm your blood."

Scotty beamed. "Now that's what I call hospitality."

Pogg poured a drink for Scotty and himself. "And you, Captain Spock?"

"No thank you, Brigadier-General. I will abstain, as is my custom."

"Ye don't know what you're missing," Scott said and raised his glass to Pogg. "Your very good health, sir."

He downed the drink, then patted his abdomen in satisfaction. "Aye, that's a potent brew, just the thing to thaw out my bones."

"You approve?" Pogg asked, sounding vaguely impressed.

"I do indeed, sir. My respect for your people has just been elevated considerably." Scott fished a flask from the interior pockets of his field jacket. "Now then, in the interests of cultural exchange, might I interest you in a nip of good Scotch whiskey?"

Intrigued, Pogg accepted the flask and took a swig.

"Interesting," he declared afterward, wiping his lips with the back of his hand. His frosty demeanor also began to thaw. "A fit drink for a soldier."

Spock observed the exchange with interest. *An unconventional approach to diplomacy,* he noted, *but apparently an effective one.* He was not entirely sure his father would approve, but Spock could not fault Scott's results. If nothing else, the canny engineer had already found common ground with their host, which might well make their mission proceed more smoothly.

"Are ye quite sure you don't care to join us in a drink, Mister Spock?" Scott asked. "I realize it's hardly the Vulcan way, but it seems to me that, over the years, you've become a bit more flexible about such things than once you were, no offense."

Spock took no offense from what was in fact an accurate observation. Since his encounter with V'Ger several years ago, he had indeed come to realize that logic was merely the beginning of wisdom and not an end to itself. Nevertheless, he remained a child of Vulcan in many respects.

"Simply because I have become more comfortable with my human heritage does not mean that I intend to embrace its vices." He located a food processor unit and keyed in a request. "I will stick to tea if you don't mind."

"Suit yourself." Scott poured himself another glass and made another toast. "To peace . . . and beating swords into plowshares."

"A curious expression," Pogg said, "but I take your meaning." He raised the flask. "To peace."

"To peace," Spock echoed. He retrieved a cup of hot tea from the food processor and relocated to a dining table surrounded by simple but functional chairs. "In that spirit, perhaps we can begin to discuss the task at hand."

Reducing Pavak's ability to attack Oyolo was a complicated process that was likely to take weeks. The first order of business was to confirm the destruction of Pavak's stockpile of protomatter missiles, whose warheads were far more destructive, by several orders of magnitude, than the relatively low-grade photonic missiles Pavak had employed against Oyolo to date. Their very existence had only been rumored until the truth had been exposed by Oyolu intelligence agencies working in conjunction with Pavakian peace activists and the interplanetary press. Because the missiles were manifestly offensive weapons, serving no defensive purpose, and because the Oyolu lacked the ability to retaliate in kind, it had been agreed that the apocalyptic threat to Oyolo had to be eliminated if there was to be any hope of a lasting peace. That protomatter, a dangerously unstable substance, was banned by most responsible civilizations had also convinced the Pavakians to relinquish the weapons.

"Our entire supply of protomatter missiles are being transported to this site to be disposed of," Pogg said. "We can begin the process shortly."

"We anticipated nothing less," Spock said. "Your people are to be commended for their willingness to destroy this arsenal, and for your restraint in never employing it, no matter the provocation."

Pogg chuckled mordantly. "I'm not sure all my fellow Pavakians would agree with that," he said, the whiskey appearing to loosen his tongue to a degree. "There are many among my people who still think that we should have employed the missiles to bomb the Oyolu into submission once and for all. They blame weak-willed Pavakian 'traitors' and alarmists and sympathizers for tying the military's hands. They would prefer total victory to compromise, no matter the cost."

"Armageddon, once unleashed, has a tendency to spread unchecked," Spock said, "and even total victory often comes at a cost, if only to the victor's sanity and nobler aspirations. My own people nearly destroyed themselves in brutal, internecine warfare before we finally realized that reason yielded greater rewards than revenge, and that wanton destruction benefits no one in the end."

"Easier said than done," Pogg said. "Outsiders cannot truly appreciate how deep the enmity between Pavak and Oyolo goes. Generations of hatred and bloodshed cannot be put aside overnight."

"Perhaps not," Spock said, "but our work here could be an important first step to allowing you to at least peacefully coexist in the same solar system."

In truth, destroying the protomatter warheads was only the beginning of the disarmament process. In the weeks and months to come, teams of qualified Starfleet engineers, chemists, and other scientists would need to make regular inspections of various silos, bases, factories, and other sites to ensure compliance with the cease-fire agreement. Investigators would also need to conduct private interviews with Pavak's top weapon designers, who would have to be guaranteed freedom from government interference or repercussions. It would serve little purpose to destroy one stockpile of missiles if Pavak retained the capacity to manufacture more without delay. Spock recalled that Pavak was currently in opposition to Oyolo so that the two planets were closer together than at any other time. Now, he reflected, would be an ideal time for Pavak to launch a devastating attack at its neighbor, when the distance between them was a mere eighty million kilometers.

All the more reason to ensure that the most lethal missiles were destroyed in a timely fashion.

"We will, of course, require access to all relevant files and databases," Spock said, "to verify that all warheads are fully accounted for."

Pogg bristled. "Are you implying dishonesty on our part?"

"Not at all," Spock insisted. "I was merely stipulating the conditions required to produce the desired result."

"You needn't remind me." Pogg lifted the flask to his lips, then reconsidered and handed it back to Scott. His posture stiffened. "I have my orders. I understand what is expected of me."

Spock hoped that would be sufficient. Weapons-inspections operations could be unpredictable and even hazardous. It was not unknown in the annals of such missions that prior arrangements could come apart without warning. Only six months ago, Federation weapons inspectors visiting a suspected biogenic weapons plant on Samotta III had been barred from the premises at the last moment and even detained on the planet for a time. Spock was only too aware that, orders or no orders, full cooperation on the part of Pogg and his fellow Pavakians was by no means guaranteed. Indeed, some resistance was to be anticipated.

"I did not mean to imply otherwise," the Vulcan stated calmly. "I wished only to avoid any misunderstandings later on."

"You'll get what you were promised," Pogg said gruffly. "No more, no less."

Five

An antique ship's wheel, from the golden age of sail, was the centerpiece of the *Enterprise*'s forward observation lounge, which was located on C Deck at the stern of the saucer. The relic evoked a proud maritime tradition, as did the inlaid compass design at the center of the polished hardwood floor. Ceiling-high viewports overlooking the ship's twin warp nacelles also offered a panoramic view of the vast starry vista beyond. An inscription beneath the wooden wheel spelled out the ship's ongoing mission: "To Boldly Go Where No Man Has Gone Before."

At the moment, the lounge provided an ideal setting for tonight's reception. A lavish buffet offered gourmet food prepared the old-fashioned way in the ship's galley, as opposed to synthesized fare from the food processors. An open bar dispensed drinks both intoxicating and otherwise. Tinkling glasses imparted a festive note that was at odds with the somewhat less than convivial mood of the guests of honor. Kirk couldn't help comparing the tense, uneasy atmosphere to the more jubilant celebration he'd attended down on

Oyolo. He gathered that the first full day of negotiations had not gone well.

"Thank you for your hospitality, Captain," A'Barra stated, enjoying a second helping of sushi. He patted his rotund stomach. "You are to be commended on your ship's cuisine."

"On that at least we can agree," General Tem said, picking at his own small plate of hors d'oeuvres. He appeared to have less of an appetite than his Oyolu counterpart. "Although I confess that years of soldiers' rations have left me unaccustomed to such rich fare."

The delegates maintained a polite distance from one another as they mingled with Kirk, McCoy, and Riley in front of the panoramic ports. Kirk felt as though he and his colleagues had become a living DMZ, dividing the two delegations. He envied Sulu and Chekov and Uhura, who were enjoying one another's company over by the buffet. Conspicuously missing were Spock and Scotty, who were still carrying out their vital duties on Pavak. Scotty would be sorry to have missed the reception, Kirk assumed. Spock perhaps not so much.

"Nothing but the best for our honored guests," Kirk said, while keeping one eye out for Lenore. The reception had been under way for several minutes, but she had yet to make an appearance. He wondered if, despite her assurances, she had indeed gotten cold feet at the last minute, unable to face Sulu and Uhura and the others again. "And a fitting reward for all your hard work today."

"Such as it was," Colonel Gast observed drily.

"I believe we had some very frank and valuable discussions today," Riley said, putting a positive spin on matters, "which will aid us in making significant progress in the days to come."

"Perhaps," A'Barra said, "but we still have a long way to go, with many sizable obstacles to be overcome."

Tem did not dispute the other man's assessment. "Then let us hope that the destination proves worth the journey."

"A destination we may never reach," A'Barra persisted, "unless you are prepared to bend on certain crucial issues, such as surrendering complete administrative control of your spaceports on Oyolo."

"We built those spaceports at our own expense," Gast argued, "to accommodate our merchant fleet. Surely we are entitled to full compensation for those facilities." A sneer lifted one corner of her lips. "Including those senselessly damaged by sabotage, vandalism, and brutal terrorist attacks."

"Those ports were built against the will of our people," Ifusi said with heat, his voice rising. "Razing Oyolu lands and communities, displacing populations that had lived there for generations. All so you could send more ships to steal our resources and infest our world!"

"Your memory deceives you," Gast replied coolly. "Those facilities were constructed with the full permission and cooperation of the proper civic authorities. Everything was done in accordance with your own laws and government."

"You mean you bribed and intimidated corrupt officials to get your way. Those traitors did not speak for our people!" He stomped toward Gast, invading her personal space. "But you are not dealing with craven puppets and collaborators now. And those infernal ports sit upon the sacred soil of Oyolo. How dare you make claim to them!"

Riley stepped between Ifusi and Gast. "Hold on," he said. "Now is not the time to wrangle over such matters. There will be opportunity enough to air our respective views, on this and other vital issues, in the meetings ahead. For now, let's put the negotiations on hold and try to simply relax and set our differences aside for the evening."

"An excellent suggestion, Mister Ambassador," Kirk said. A yeoman came by bearing a tray of liquid refreshments. Claiming a glass of Saurian brandy, the captain lifted it and proposed a toast. "To journey's end . . . and new beginnings."

"To new beginnings," Tem seconded. "And letting go of the past."

Ifusi snorted derisively.

"Is there a problem, Oyolu?" Gast challenged him.

A'Barra attempted to answer for him. "My aide means no disrespect, I'm sure." He turned a stern gaze on the younger Oyolu. "Is that not so, Ifusi?"

"I am sorry, sir, but . . ."

"You will control yourself or you will be silent. Am I understood?"

"No," Tem said, stepping forward. "If the youth has something to say, let him say it. We can make no progress in the days ahead if we shrink from hard truths." He faced Ifusi. "Speak your mind, Oyolu. You took exception to my toast?"

Ifusi hesitated only momentarily, glancing uncertainly at A'Barra before answering.

"Oh, they were fine words, to be sure, but coming from the Scourge of Azoza? Forgive me if I found that difficult to swallow."

A gasp escaped Gast and even Riley appeared taken aback that Ifusi had called Tem that to his face. Kirk recalled the origin of the epithet from his briefings. During the early years of the nativist uprising, Oyolu insurgents had seized control of the Pavakian trading district in the city of Azoza, holding several Pavakian merchants and their staffs and families hostage, while also putting Pavakian ships and warehouses to the torch. In response, the Pavakian military, commanded by General Tem, had imposed a strict blockade on the entire city to bring the insurgents to heel, preventing shipments of food, fuel, medicine, and other vital necessities from making their way into the besieged metropolis. The defiant insurgents had eventually chosen to execute their hostages and commit mass suicide rather than surrendering, but not before hundreds of Oyolu had perished from starvation, disease, and exposure. Many Oyolu still considered Tem a war criminal.

Apparently Ifusi was among them.

Tem flinched and Kirk thought he saw a flicker of guilt ripple across the man's gaunt, furry face, but the general quickly reassumed a reserved, stoic expression.

"Those were trying times," he said. "Hard choices had to be made." Regret colored his voice. "Mistakes were made as well."

"'Mistakes'? You call the slow, agonizing death of hundreds a 'mistake'?" Ifusi mocked the general's words. "And 'letting go of the past' . . . you'd like us to forget what happened, wouldn't you? If there was any justice, you'd be on trial for your crimes right now, not sampling delicacies on a starship!"

"As opposed to the terrorists who butchered innocent civilians and turned their own planet into an abattoir?" Gast retorted. "When, pray tell, do they face justice for their numerous atrocities?"

"You dare compare patriotic Oyolu soldiers to the Scourge?" Ifusi angrily scratched at the floor with his hoof. "No one would have been hurt if you had just minded your own business and stayed on Pavak where you belonged. We were fighting to take back our planet and our rights!"

Attracted by the commotion, Chekov strode over from the buffet, followed by Sulu and Uhura. He discreetly signaled two lurking security officers, who moved in closer, just in case they needed to break up a fight. Kirk was pleased to see that Chekov was taking his duties as security chief seriously, although he hoped the precautions wouldn't be necessary.

"That will be enough, Ifusi," A'Barra said, intervening before Security had to. "Do not forget that we are guests here." His hand went to his truncated right horn, which he fingered pensively. "This is neither the time nor place to settle old scores."

"I couldn't agree more," Kirk said. "Please confine your battles to the bargaining tables as long as you're aboard this ship."

"Yes," McCoy added. "I don't know about the rest of you, but I've seen enough casualties of your war already. I'd just as soon none of you end up in my sickbay."

"Bluntly put, Doctor," Riley said, "but I agree with the sentiment. We're trying to end a war here. Let's not start one . . . at least not at such a lovely reception."

"Of course, Ambassador," Tem said, nodding stiffly at Riley. "I had hoped merely to clear the air, not escalate the hostilities. Let us drop the matter, for the time being."

Judging from the baleful look in Ifusi's eyes, the captain doubted that Tem's past "mistakes" and their festering legacy could remain off the table indefinitely, but Kirk would settle for another temporary cease-fire if it meant they could get through the reception without a physical altercation. The hot-tempered Ifusi struck Kirk as rather too easy to bait, and Colonel Gast as far too ready to push his buttons. It was a volatile combination, like matter and antimatter, which held the distinct possibility of blowing up in everyone's faces.

"I'm tempted to make another toast," Kirk said, "but

perhaps that would be pushing my luck." He noticed that Chekov had a glass of what was almost certainly vodka, courtesy of Mother Russia. "Would you care to try your hand, Commander?"

"My pleasure, Captain." He lifted his glass, only to sneeze explosively before he could get another word out, in Russian or in English. "Excuse me, everyone," he said, sniffling. "I'm not sure where that came—" Another sneeze cut off his apology.

McCoy's brow furrowed. "Are you feeling all right, Pavel?"

"I'm fine, Doctor," he insisted. "Just a bit stuffy, is all." Watery eyes blinked to clear themselves. "I think maybe I caught a little bug during that shore leave at Ishtar Station."

"Perhaps a visit to sickbay is in order," McCoy suggested.

"No, really," Chekov said. "Please don't concern yourself. I'm sure it's nothing serious . . . or contagious." He sniffled again, visibly struggling to contain another sneeze. He backed away to avoid any further embarrassment. "Don't mind me."

McCoy was not so easily dissuaded. "I'm serious, Chekov. It couldn't hurt to—"

His voice trailed off as the doors to the lounge slid open and Lenore Karidian entered, fashionably late and clad in an elegant lilac gown that she had probably borrowed from the theater's costume closet. All eyes turned toward her as she hesitantly stepped inside, looking more than a little apprehensive. The doors slid shut behind her as she took a deep breath and strode toward Kirk and his party.

Riley nearly choked on his drink. "What the hell? Is that—"

"Miss Lyla Kassidy," Kirk said quickly before Riley could blurt out Lenore's true identity. "An old acquaintance we ran into on Oyolo earlier today. She's one of the many selfless volunteers assisting in the relief efforts on the planet."

She joined them before the viewports. If Riley's shocked reaction upset her, she concealed it admirably. No surprise there, Kirk reflected; she had always been adept at keeping her true self hidden, as both an actress *and* a murderess. *Lord knows she fooled me long enough.*

"Good evening, everyone. I hope you don't mind if I intrude. Captain Kirk was kind enough to invite me to the reception."

"I'm glad you could make it," he said and introduced her to the various delegates. A few meters away, Sulu and Uhura were gaping at Lenore with astonishment as well. They had both obviously recognized her from those dire events two decades ago. Kirk found himself grateful that most of the current *Enterprise*'s crew had not served on his first command and were therefore unlikely to recognize Lenore. "I was just telling our guests earlier about the good work you and your colleagues are doing on Oyolo."

"I'm delighted to make your acquaintance, Miss

Kassidy," A'Barra said, beaming appreciatively at the new arrival. Kirk recalled that the charismatic Oyolu leader was said to be something of a ladies' man, with several wives and mistresses. "What a shame that we are only now meeting for the first time. I have nothing but admiration and gratitude for the generous efforts of you and others like you. Truly, you are an angel in spirit, as well as in form."

"I'm just one of many volunteers, Minister A'Barra," she said.

"But every movement is composed of individuals, and each and every person of goodwill contributes to the greater whole. Never discount the importance of a single dedicated individual, Miss Kassidy." He took her hand in his. "Or can I call you Lyla?"

"Lyla will be fine," she replied. "Thank you."

Riley looked like he had seen a ghost straight out of *Hamlet* or *Macbeth*. His jaw was tightly clenched and his fists were clutched at his sides. Only years of diplomatic training and experience allowed him to maintain a degree of discretion as he quietly pulled Kirk aside. "A word, Captain," he said in a low tone. "Now."

Kirk nodded.

The ambassador's dismay was entirely understandable. Along with Kirk, Riley was one of the last two survivors of the massacre on Tarsus IV—and a former target of Lenore's murderous campaign to eliminate all witnesses to her father's wrongdoing. Not only had Kodos executed Riley's entire family before his eyes, but Lenore had later poisoned Riley during her fateful visit to the old *Enterprise* twenty years ago. Only swift action on McCoy's part had saved the young lieutenant from an untimely demise.

Kirk had hoped to warn Riley in advance of Lenore's impending arrival, but the ambassador had been tied up in conferences, attempting to keep the peace and un-ruffle feathers, right up until Riley had arrived at the reception with the delegates in hand. There had never been an opportunity to speak to him alone.

Until now.

They found a quiet corner in the garden area on the port side of the lounge. Lush greenery from diverse worlds provided a degree of privacy, while a tranquil koi pond belied the choppy waters the captain had just sailed into. Riley wheeled about to confront Kirk, his tongue no longer restrained by the presence of the delegates. His face was flushed and angry. A vein throbbed at his temple. His formerly deferential manner was a thing of the past.

"What the devil is *she* doing here?"

"An unexpected twist of fate." Kirk briefly explained how he and McCoy had accidentally encountered Lenore on Oyolo. "I apologize for not alerting you in advance. Believe me, I was just as startled as you were to run into her after all this time."

"And you thought it was a good idea to bring her aboard the *Enterprise* . . . after everything she did last time? After what her father did?"

"Her father, not her," Kirk stressed. "She wasn't even born during that ugliness on Tarsus Four. And as for her own crimes, she's been pronounced sane and rehabilitated by the proper authorities." Kirk had quickly confirmed this via the ship's computer library immediately upon his return to the ship. "I figure that entitles her to the benefit of the doubt, maybe even a shot at redemption."

He kept his own doubts to himself. Sharing them with Riley would not smooth the waters.

"But what about the peace talks?" Riley protested. "Have you forgotten about those?"

"Not at all," Kirk said. "But the Oyolu and Pavakians have no problematic history with her, as you and I do. They're unaware of her past and have no reason to be troubled by her temporary presence here. And tomorrow morning she will be back on Oyolo, tending to the refugees again, safely away from your negotiations." He glanced back the way they'd come. "In the meantime, it seems to me that we can hardly ask the delegates to bury the hatchet if we're unwilling to do the same."

Riley had no ready rebuttal. He backed off a bit, but remained visibly distressed. "Her father killed my family, Captain." His voice was hoarse with emotion. "Had my mother and father vaporized right before my eyes. Along with thousands of other innocent people."

"I know," Kirk said gently. "I was there. But Kodos paid for his crimes—at Lenore's hands. The way I see it, there's already been more than enough tragedy to go around."

Riley stared down into the sparkling pond, as though gazing back through the years. He had only been four years old when Kodos executed his parents. Kirk had once had to talk him down to keep him from taking the law into his own hands and killing "Anton Karidian" with a phaser. Riley had been younger and more impetuous then, but Kirk doubted that his memories of Tarsus IV were any less vivid or painful. Some horrors, once seen, could never be forgotten.

Which was why "moving on" was often easier said than done.

"This is on you, Captain," he said finally. "Just keep her out of my way."

He turned his back on Kirk and marched out of the garden.

Six

Kirk returned to the reception to discover that Lenore was gone.

"What happened to Miss Kassidy?" he asked.

"She left rather abruptly right after you and Ambassador Riley wandered off," A'Barra said with obvious disappointment. The delegates remained clustered with Riley and Kirk's senior officers. "A shame, really. She seemed quite enchanting."

Riley let that pass without comment.

"Perhaps I should check on her," Kirk said, concerned about her sudden departure for more reasons than one. The prospect of Lenore Karidian at loose aboard the ship gave him pause. "If you'll excuse me."

He hurried out of the lounge into the corridor, hoping to catch her, but she was already gone. A solitary security guard was posted outside the lounge to provide an extra degree of protection for their VIP guests. "Did you see an attractive blond woman leave here just a few minutes ago?" Kirk asked.

"Aye, sir," the guard answered. "She was heading for the aft turbolift."

"Thank you, Lieutenant."

Kirk weighed his options. For a moment, he considered alerting security to be on the lookout for Lenore, but he decided that would be premature. There was no reason, other than her *modus operandi* long past, to assume that she was up to foul play. Chances were, she had simply removed herself from a profoundly uncomfortable situation. She was hardly an escaped fugitive.

Instead he tried to anticipate where she might seek sanctuary aboard the ship. No shuttles were scheduled to depart for Oyolo until tomorrow morning, so she would be seeking some place where she could be alone with her thoughts and perhaps avoid running into Riley or any other disapproving specters from her past. Somewhere quiet and unintimidating.

Of course, he thought as a likely candidate came to mind. If nothing else, it was as good a place as any to look for her.

Leaving Riley and the others to entertain their distinguished guests, Kirk walked briskly to the nearest turbolift and stepped inside. The doors whooshed shut behind him.

"P Deck," he instructed the lift. "Express."

A quick ride brought him to a lonely corridor in the ship's secondary hull, several decks below the saucer section where the reception was being held. The corridor's lighting had been dimmed to simulate nighttime conditions; such measures were known to help the crew maintain their natural circadian rhythms.

Striding down the hallway, Kirk had to decide whether to turn left or right at the first juncture. Choosing right at random, he made his way to the starboard observation gallery overlooking the shuttlecraft landing bay one deck below. As he entered the gallery, he saw at once that he had come to the right place.

"I thought I might find you here."

Lenore turned away from the panoramic ports permitting an impressive view of the spacious bay. She did not seem surprised that he had found her.

"Call me sentimental," she said. "This is one of the few places on the *Enterprise* about which I have largely pleasant memories."

She didn't need to explain why. Back on the original *Enterprise*, they had shared some romantic moments in the observation deck overlooking the shuttlebay. Granted, those moments had not been entirely free of darker agendas. In retrospect, she had already been plotting his death and he had been using her, at least in part, to find out the truth about her reclusive father, but even so, there had been some genuine passion in their embrace, or so he liked to think.

"I remember it well," he said.

"I'm glad. One wouldn't want to be forgotten, no matter what happened later."

"That was never a possibility." He approached her slowly. As in the upper-row seats at the amphitheater before, they had the gallery to themselves, while the roomy landing bay below was relatively quiet as well.

Copernicus sat on the floor of the bay, waiting for its next run back to Oyolo. Its sister, *Galileo,* remained on Pavak with Spock and Scotty. He hoped they were having a less intense time of it.

"I'm not entirely sure I believe that," she replied, "but my ego isn't going to argue the point."

He turned his back on the observation window, leaning against it as he stood beside her. The lights from the shuttlebay cast shadows across the floor of the dimly lit gallery.

"You left the reception rather quickly. Minister A'Barra was disappointed."

She sighed ruefully, hugging herself.

"This was a mistake. There are too many memories here. Too many people who remember what I did. Who I used to be."

"Like Riley?"

She nodded. "The look on his face when he saw me . . ." She shuddered at the memory. "He was making an effort to hide it, but I could see it in his eyes. The hatred, the disgust. He's neither forgotten nor forgiven, that much was clear."

Kirk wished he could tell her otherwise, but there had been enough lies between them.

"I should have reminded you he'd be here, but I assumed you knew. Or perhaps I was simply reluctant to mention it for fear you wouldn't come."

"I think I had heard that an Ambassador Riley was representing the Federation in the peace talks, but I never made the connection until tonight." She chuckled and shook her head. "Young Lieutenant Riley a Starfleet ambassador . . . who would have thought it?"

"Look at the bright side," Kirk said. "At least you got to see for yourself that Riley's had a long and accomplished life despite—"

He paused, unsure how to tactfully finish the sentence.

"Despite me poisoning him." She gazed up at the ceiling, as though peering up through the decks to the reception where Riley was. "Small wonder he wasn't exactly pleased to see me."

That's putting it mildly, Kirk thought. "He'll get over it. Trust me, he's got a lot bigger and more pressing matters on his mind these days."

"Yes, of course, the peace talks. I can see where that might almost trump running into the woman who nearly killed you." She glanced at the exit. "Do you need to get back to the reception?"

"Eventually, I suppose, but there's no hurry. I trust Riley and my senior officers to keep a lid on things until I return. Besides, I'm the one who invited you, so that makes you my personal responsibility."

"Oh, really? Are you afraid I'll be up to no good if you don't keep an eye on me?"

Kirk congratulated himself for making the right call and *not* sending Security after her. "That's not what I meant. I simply meant that you're my guest and, as your host, it's my obligation to make sure you're at ease."

She chuckled bitterly. "I'm not sure I've ever been truly at ease, at least not since I found out who my father really was, and certainly not since I came to grips with what I did to seven innocent people."

"Tell me about it."

She turned to look at him more closely, her hazel eyes scrutinizing his features.

"Why do you care? Should I be wary of ulterior motives?"

"Not this time, no."

Her suspicions pricked his conscience, which, to be honest, was not entirely clean where she was concerned. Lenore had been only nineteen years old when they'd first met at that cocktail party, and, yes, he had deliberately romanced her as a means of finding out more about her father, whom he had come to suspect was Kodos. Even though she had ultimately proved to have an even more sinister objective than his own, it was still not one of his finer moments. He had let his desire for justice—or maybe just revenge—drive him to emotionally manipulate a young woman.

"So why?" she asked again.

"Let's just say," he said honestly, "that I'm not particularly proud of what transpired between us, back then, and the way I failed to follow up later on. Maybe it's too little too late, but I really would like to know how you're faring these days."

She contemplated him curiously. Her eyes scanned his face.

"You're different than before. Not quite the brash young Caesar I remember. Time has made you more reflective, I think, and do I detect a touch of melancholy?"

Her assessment cut rather too close to the bone for comfort.

"Well, I like to think that I'm not King Lear," Kirk quipped before getting more serious again. "But, yes, I probably have more regrets than I did before."

She nodded.

"I heard about your ship . . . and your son. My condolences."

Kirk was not surprised that she knew about David's death. The Genesis affair, and its tumultuous aftermath, had sparked a major diplomatic incident that had attracted significant media attention throughout the quadrant. And his subsequent trial for stealing the *Enterprise* had been big news as well.

"Thank you," he said sincerely. "What about you? Do you have any children?"

He had not had a chance to research her recent history in any detail. He had only been able to confirm that she had in fact been released from a Federation mental institution on Gilead III nearly five years ago. What she had been doing with her freedom ever since was still a question mark.

"Heaven forbid," she scoffed. "Being heir to Kodos the Executioner is not a burden I would wish on anyone. Better that my notorious bloodline ends with me."

Kirk observed the shadows spread across the floor before them. It wasn't as visible, but he felt as though the shadow of Kodos was still hanging over them even after all these years. No doubt Riley would agree.

"You can't blame yourself for what your father did," he said, repeating the argument he had used on Riley less than half an hour ago. "You weren't born until *after* he faked his death on Tarsus Four and reinvented himself as Karidian. You had nothing to do with the massacres."

"But I am my father's daughter." She held up her hand to the light. "'Here's the smell of blood still. All the perfumes of Arabia will not sweeten this little hand.'"

Spoken like an actress, he thought. "But Lady Macbeth lost her sanity. You seem to have regained yours."

"'Seem'?"

"Bad choice of words," Kirk said. "Personally, I like to think that our past mistakes do not define us, even if we do carry them with us as we go." He had debated the topic with Spock's renegade brother not so long ago. "Our pasts, our regrets, are forever part of who we are, but they don't determine our futures. We can still chart our own destinies. You're living proof of that."

She gazed at him, listening intently. "Do you truly believe that?"

"Spock likes to say that there are always possibilities," Kirk said with a smile. "Who am I to disagree?"

"And is that why you invited me aboard?" she asked.

"To prove to yourself that the past is not always prologue?"

He recognized the timely allusion to *The Tempest*. "To some degree, maybe, or perhaps I simply thought that you and I deserved a chance to make amends for how we hurt each other before. No grand abstract principle to prove, just two people with some unfinished business between them."

"I see," she said coyly. "And precisely what sort of business are we talking about here?"

Kirk could see where his remark was open to interpretation. He gazed upon the beautiful and enigmatic woman beside him, who was just as striking now as she had been the last time they found themselves alone above a shuttlebay. He smiled wistfully. The brash young captain she remembered would have probably swept her into his arms by now, rushing in where angels feared to tread, and certainly he still felt a spark between them, despite everything, and yet . . . there were enough painful memories—and bodies—between them to make him think twice about rekindling old flames. He'd broken enough hearts in his time and vice versa. He was in no hurry to repeat past mistakes.

"Just a heart-to-heart talk," he clarified, "to give us both a little closure, as you said."

"Probably just as well," she agreed, sounding both relieved and disappointed, "and more, honestly, than I ever hoped for." She placed her hand over his. "For what it's worth, this means a lot to me, Jim, knowing that you've forgiven me for what went on before, and that you seem to be genuinely rooting for my redemption."

"'Seem'?"

She chuckled. "Bad choice of words. Seriously, I'm truly grateful for you not holding my bloodstained past against me. It's more than I deserve."

"Sounds to me like you've earned it . . . or at least you're trying to. And, for my part, I like knowing that you've turned your life around and that what happened back then wasn't the final act." A horrific image flashed through his brain, of Lenore as he last saw her years ago: crazed and delusional, with wild eyes and hair, sobbing and babbling over the lifeless body of her father. "Tragedies are all very well and good onstage, but I prefer happier endings in real life."

"Let us hope I can oblige you," she said, seeming altogether saner and more collected than that delirious madwoman from decades past. "But it's getting late and I've occupied far too much of your valuable time." She withdrew her hand and stepped away. "You should get back to your reception. People will talk."

"People will always talk," he said, shrugging. "Scuttlebutt is a universal constant, like gravity." But she was right that they should probably head back to the lounge. Riley and McCoy were surely wondering what had become of them, if they didn't think that Lenore had killed him by now. He held out his arm. "Shall we?"

She shook her head. "I appreciate the offer, but this

has all been a bit much. Present company excluded, I think I've looked yesterday in the face quite enough for one evening. If you don't mind, I'm inclined to play Cinderella and call it a night." She smiled wanly. "And I suspect that Ambassador Riley would also prefer that I make myself scarce."

"Don't worry about Riley. He's too much the diplomat to make a scene."

"I'm sure, but I'd rather not force my unwelcome company upon him, especially when, as noted, he has more pressing matters to attend to. I owe him that much at least."

"Fair enough," Kirk said, understanding her reluctance to brave the lion's den once more. "The *Copernicus* is scheduled to depart for Oyolo at zero-seven hundred tomorrow. In the meantime, I've arranged guest quarters for you on D Deck. It's not a VIP suite, but I think you'll be comfortable."

"Compared to bunking down in a refugee camp? I'm sure it will be heavenly." She smiled warmly. "Thank you, Jim. That's very thoughtful. I confess I won't mind a real bed for once, instead of a cot or sleeping bag."

"Do you need an escort to your room?"

"That won't be necessary. I'm certain I can find my way. This isn't my first *Enterprise,* you know." She gave him a playful shove. "Now go. Before everyone thinks I murdered you."

That the same thought had crossed his mind was not something he cared to admit. McCoy was probably sweating bullets, however, if he wasn't on the verge of sending out a search party.

"All right then. Perhaps I'll see you in the morning before you leave."

"I'd like that." She came forward and kissed him lightly on the cheek before retreating a few paces back. "It is good to see you again, Jim. It wasn't *just* a ruse . . . before." A wistful expression glided over her face like a passing breeze. "I wasn't pretending that night on the observation deck."

"Neither was I," he confessed.

He exited the gallery before he fell back into old habits. The door swished shut behind him, leaving him alone in the corridor outside. He strode back toward the waiting turbolift, even as, inevitably, a few tantalizing second thoughts dogged his heels. Images of Lenore, past and present, lingered in his mind's eye.

Damn. He knew he was doing the right thing, that some old flames were best left unlit, but being older and wiser had its drawbacks sometimes. *Speaking of regrets,* he thought, *I hope I'm not kicking myself somewhere down the road.* Lenore had seemed so sincere and approachable tonight, more like the charming young actress he'd met on Planet Q, not the deranged killer she'd turned out to be. Had she truly exorcised the demons that had driven her insane before? To his surprise, he'd found her good company and easy to talk to. At times, it had been almost too easy to forget the trail of corpses she'd left in her wake . . . and Thomas

Leighton's widow sobbing on Kirk's shoulder after her husband's body was found. Kirk and Lenore had been taking a romantic stroll in the purple twilight when they came upon the corpse.

Kirk entered the turbolift. "C Deck. Observation Lounge."

There are always possibilities, he thought. *The trick is to know which to explore . . . and which to stay clear of.*

Meanwhile, duty called . . . and he had a party to get back to.

Seven

The reception concluded without actual bloodshed, which Kirk took as a minor victory. Relations between the Oyolu and Pavakian delegations remained frosty, to put it mildly, but one could hardly expect a few drinks and a sumptuous buffet to overcome years of bitter enmity. Kirk had half-considered breaking out some bootleg Romulan ale, which the *Enterprise* "may" have happened to have tucked away in the galley, but he realized that this might put Riley in an awkward position, given that he was formally representing the Federation and its policies. It was enough, Kirk decided, that the delegates had a chance to cool down a bit before going back to the bargaining table tomorrow.

Here's hoping it helps, he thought.

Riley kept casting wary glances at the lounge's entrance, but he relaxed somewhat as it became evident that Lenore would not be making a return appearance. There was still, however, a certain edge to his voice when he bid good night to Kirk, who took it in stride. This unexpected brush with the past had been hard on Riley, Kirk knew; he resolved to make it up to the younger man at some point.

I owe him one.

The buffet had been cleared away and the bar had served its last cocktails. The overhead lights flickered, signaling that the party was over, and the lounge gradually emptied out. As the delegates took their leave, heading back to their respective quarters, McCoy took Kirk aside. He looked as though he had been waiting impatiently to speak his mind.

"You took your sweet time coming back to the party," McCoy said. "Where the heck were you?"

"Just making sure that everything was in order where 'Lyla' was concerned."

"And?" McCoy pressed.

"Nothing to go to Red Alert about. We chatted awhile and she eventually decided that it might be wiser if she didn't return to the reception with me."

"Well, I could have told you that, especially with Riley here. What were you thinking, Jim, inviting her aboard the ship like that?"

About making peace with the past, Kirk thought, *and not merely turning my back on it anymore.* But he didn't feel like getting into all that with his friend right now. "What can I say? It seemed like a good idea at the time."

McCoy's attitude shifted from exasperation to empathy as his bedside manner came to the fore. "And was it?" he asked gently.

"Maybe." Kirk glanced around to make sure that

none of the cleanup crew was listening. They sought out a quiet corner of the lounge and he lowered his voice. "Lenore and I had a long-overdue talk. We said things that probably needed to be said, cleared the air a bit, and I got a better sense of who she is today."

"Do you want to talk about it?" McCoy nodded at the bar. "I could always liberate a bottle of the good stuff, for medicinal purposes, naturally."

"No, thanks, Bones. I appreciate the offer, but perhaps another time." He guided the doctor toward the exit. "You should turn in and get a good night's sleep. We have another long day tomorrow, and the way things are going, you could still end up with one or more of the delegates in your sickbay, especially if Gast and Ifusi keep going at it."

"No kidding." McCoy vented his exasperation. "How in blazes did those two get picked for a *diplomatic* mission? They've all but spit on each other since they beamed aboard."

"As I understand it, Gast has been General Tem's number one aide for some time now, and Ifusi is A'Barra's personal protégé and, rumor has it, possibly his son, although that's never been officially confirmed." Kirk had reviewed the files on all the delegates prior to their arrival. "And, frankly, I suspect that at this point it would be hard to find any Pavakian or Oyolu who *isn't* harboring a generous store of suspicion and resentment toward their lifelong foes. Ifusi and Gast may not be all that remarkable in that respect."

"Now *there's* a discouraging thought," McCoy said. "On that note, I think I will pack it in." He turned to go but lingered to look back at Kirk. "That offer to talk still stands, whenever you feel like it." Compassionate eyes viewed Kirk with sympathy. "I know that you really cared for her . . . before."

"Good night, Bones," Kirk said. "I'll keep that offer in mind."

Having said his piece, McCoy departed, leaving Kirk to wander pensively through the nocturnal corridors. He knew he should turn in himself, but he suspected that sleep would not come easily tonight, so he took a stroll around the deck to clear his head. Night shift crew members going about their business passed by him occasionally, but the corridors were relatively empty at this time of night, at least compared to the usual bustling activity. The ambient thrum of the ship's engines provided a welcome degree of white noise. He briefly flirted with the idea of poking his head onto the bridge, just to check on things, but that hardly seemed necessary. The *Enterprise* was patrolling the buffer zone. If any unusual circumstances occurred, the bridge crew would be quick to alert him. Kirk trusted them to do their jobs without him looking over their shoulders. Instead he let his mind drift as it processed the day's events.

If Ifusi and Gast were having difficulty letting go of old grudges and tragedies, they were hardly the only ones. That was a failing they shared with pretty much any sentient being who had survived harrowing events.

"Each of us hides a secret pain," Sybok had said, and while Spock's messianic half-brother had been wrong about a lot of things, he had probably been onto something. Kirk thought again of Thomas Leighton, one of Lenore's final victims. Long before she had silenced him on Planet Q, Leighton had been tormented by his memories of the slaughter on Tarsus IV, which had left him both physically and psychologically scarred. And even Kodos himself, aka "Anton Karidian," had been somewhat of a haunted, tragic figure consumed by guilt when Kirk encountered him again aboard the *Enterprise*, decades after the massacre. The revelation that his daughter had killed repeatedly on his behalf had practically destroyed the man; his death, mere moments later, had been a mercy.

Kirk remembered wrestling with his own conscience back then, trying to chart a course between justice and revenge. The difference had been far from easy to distinguish, so could he truly blame Ifusi and Gast for tightly holding on to old scores? To many Oyolu, General Tem was "the Scourge of Azoza," a monster on the order of Kodos, while most Pavakians surely considered A'Barra an incendiary terrorist who was largely to blame for the violence that had consumed Oyolo. Scores of Pavakian civilians and military personnel had been killed or maimed by the insurgency, including the hostages slaughtered at Azoza. Much blood had been spilled on both sides of the conflict, the memories of which were no less seared into Gast and Ifusi than

Kirk's own troubled recollections of Tarsus IV . . . and Lenore's descent into madness.

Each of us hides a secret pain, all right. Except sometimes it's not all that hidden or secret.

Lost in thought, Kirk made his way toward his own quarters on E Deck. He found himself wishing that he had taken McCoy up on that offer to liberate a bottle from the bar. He wasn't looking forward to his dreams tonight. He still had nightmares about Tarsus IV occasionally.

"Captain Kirk?"

He turned to see Colonel Gast approaching him. He was surprised to see the Pavakian officer still up and about. He slowed to let her catch up with him.

"Colonel?"

"Excuse me, Captain. Do you have a moment?"

Kirk wondered what this was about. "Certainly. How can I help you, Colonel?"

She faced him in the empty hallway, her posture ramrod-straight, her hands clasped behind her back. For a moment, she seemed unwilling to meet his gaze, but then she lifted her chin, looked him squarely in the eyes, and addressed him in a rather formal tone.

"I wish to apologize for my possibly . . . undiplomatic . . . remarks at the reception. We were indeed your guests and my behavior was perhaps not befitting that of an officer. You should know that I have great respect for Starfleet and your own distinguished career in particular. I would not want you to think poorly of me."

Kirk was impressed by her willingness to take responsibility for her lapses. Perhaps General Tem had known what he was doing when he selected her for this assignment after all. Kirk chose to take this as an encouraging sign where the peace talks were concerned.

"Apology accepted, Colonel," he said graciously. "And don't be too hard on yourself. I understand how difficult it can be to put aside past differences. Trust me, I know."

"Thank you, Captain." A slight smirk lightened her stiff military bearing. "Mind you, this doesn't mean I intend to be any less resolute at the bargaining table when it comes to—"

A high-pitched siren cut off her words and sent a jolt of adrenaline through Kirk's system. He rushed to the nearest wall-mounted comm unit. "Kirk to Security! Report!"

Chekov's voice responded immediately. Kirk assumed he had been burning the midnight oil in his office, possibly reviewing the security arrangements for the ongoing peace talks. More receptions and tours were on the agenda.

"Unauthorized weapons fire on D Deck," Chekov reported. *"In General Tem's stateroom!"*

Gast overheard the report. Shock showed upon her tawny features. "The general?!"

Kirk was equally alarmed. "On my way," he barked into the comm. "Kirk out."

He dashed to the nearest turbolift, with Gast keeping

pace beside him. The siren, keyed to go off whenever an energy weapon was fired without authorization aboard the ship, blared in their ears as the lift carried them up one deck to where the VIP staterooms were located. Sprinting, they arrived outside Tem's quarters just as Chekov and a full security team reached the scene. The alarm had also drawn Riley and the Oyolu delegates from their respective quarters. They spilled into the corridor, some still in their bedclothes, and looked about in confusion and alarm. Lenore emerged hesitantly from a smaller stateroom, intended for visiting aides and hangers-on, located between those assigned to the Oyolu and Pavakian delegations. She pulled a modest silver nightgown tightly shut as she joined the others in the hallway. Her eyes were wide awake and alarmed.

"Jim?" she asked worriedly. "What's happening?"

He didn't have time to respond to her or the Oyolu at the moment.

"Everybody, stay back!" he ordered as he commandeered a phaser from a security guard. He nodded at Chekov, who overrode the lock on the door. Phasers drawn, they charged into the deluxe stateroom to find a severed right arm lying on the floor of the work area—and the charred silhouette of a humanoid figure scorched into the carpet nearby. Command stripes on the sleeve and a furry brown hand made it clear at a glance that the limb had belonged to General Tem. The rest of the Pavakian military leader had apparently been vaporized by a disruptor blast.

"Bozhe moi!" Chekov exclaimed, reverting to his native Russian.

Kirk knew how he felt. He looked around warily but did not spot any lurking assailant. The security officers fanned out, clearing the stateroom corner by corner. The phaser alarm kept on wailing, making it hard to think. "Somebody kill that damn siren."

"Aye, sir," Chekov said, locating a control panel on the wall. He entered the access code to silence the alarm. "That should do it, sir."

The siren mercifully abated, but a high-pitched whine immediately drew Kirk's eye to a disruptor pistol resting atop a desk in front of a computer terminal. There was no mistaking the bloodcurdling sound of a disruptor on overload. Smoke rose from the pistol. The smell of overheated circuitry alerted Kirk's nostrils. The weapon sounded as though it was only moments away from an explosion that could take out a good portion of the deck.

Kirk reacted quickly. Setting his own phaser to disrupt, he fired at the screeching pistol. A brilliant azure beam vaporized the disruptor before it could detonate. Kirk let out a sigh of relief, glad to have averted the explosion in time, even as he recognized that he had probably just eliminated a key piece of evidence.

So much for the murder weapon, he thought. *Damn.*

To add insult to injury, the weapons alarm went off again, triggered by Kirk's own blast. Chekov hastily deactivated the siren before he issued the order. Kirk appreciated it.

"Excellent reflexes, Captain." Chekov gazed at the spot where the overloading pistol had been only seconds before. A scorch mark marred the surface of the desk. "That was rather too close for comfort, if you don't mind me saying so."

"I quite agree, Mister Chekov," Kirk said, scowling. An uncomfortable sense of déjà vu was already sending a chill down his spine, but he forced himself to focus on the apparent murder of General Tem instead. "Any other trace of the general?"

Chekov conferred with his team, then shook his head. "Negative, Captain." He stared bleakly at the lifeless arm on the floor, which appeared to have been cauterized at the shoulder as though by an energy beam, as well as at the charred silhouette on the carpet. He sniffled, beginning to sound a little stuffy again. "I think that may be all that's left of him."

Kirk was thinking the same thing.

"Let me through! I demand to see—"

Colonel Gast barged into the stateroom, forcing her way past an officer at the door. Kirk moved to block her view of the remains, but it was already too late. She froze in place, brought up short by the horrific sight. A strangled gasp escaped her throat. She clutched her chest.

"I'm very sorry," Kirk said. "Rest assured, we'll find out who is responsible for this."

"Who?" she asked scornfully. "Can there be any doubt?" Rage contorted her features as she wheeled about to confront the Oyolu, who were crowded in the foyer with Riley and the others, just outside the study area. "You! You did this!" she accused, pointing at A'Barra and Ifusi. "Murderers! Assassins! We were fools to think we could ever trust you!"

"But I know nothing of this!" A'Barra insisted. He turned anxiously toward his aide. "Ifusi?"

"I swear to you, Great Defender, this is not my doing!" The younger Oyolu's face hardened as he gazed upon the severed arm and the blackened silhouette. "Not that any of our people are likely to mourn the Scourge of Azoza. This looks like justice to me."

"Justice?" Gast snarled. "I'll show you justice, you barbaric animal!"

She lunged at Ifusi, but Chekov and his squad moved quickly to restrain her. "Please control yourself, Colonel," Chekov said. "Do not force us to take you into custody."

"I am not the criminal here," she protested. "The true villains are right in front of you!"

"That remains to be proven," Kirk stated.

"Are you blind?" She stopped struggling against the guards' grip, but her chestnut eyes continued to shoot photon torpedoes at the Oyolu. "Who else could have committed this heinous act?"

Riley glanced suspiciously in Lenore's direction, and Kirk knew that they had another tense discussion in their future. He had to admit that the same thought had crossed his mind as well, especially after that business with the disruptor pistol . . .

Twenty years ago, Lenore had tried to kill Kirk by planting an overloading phaser in his quarters aboard the old *Enterprise*. Alerted by its telltale whine, he had barely disposed of it in time. A few more moments and he would have been blown to atoms . . . just like tonight.

"I assure you, Captain Kirk, Ambassador Riley," A'Barra said, "we are innocent of these charges. I am as dismayed and baffled by this shocking event as you are."

"Liars!" Gast hissed. "You wouldn't know the truth—or basic decency and honor—if we bombed your entire wretched planet with it."

"You call us liars?" Ifusi said, predictably taking offense. "How dare you doubt our word?" He threw out his arm and pointed indignantly at the grisly evidence on the floor. "This is some duplicitous Pavakian ruse to soil our good name and exact unfair concessions from us. It has to be!"

Kirk realized that he needed to stop things from escalating more than they already had.

"That's enough, all of you," he said firmly. "This is a crime scene and I need everyone to clear out immediately." He gestured toward the exit. "Mister Chekov, please see to it that the delegates are escorted back to their quarters . . . separately."

"Yes, Captain." Chekov signaled his people to release Gast, who refrained from launching another physical attack even as she practically radiated an icy fury. He personally took charge of the surviving

Pavakian delegate. "Please come with me, Colonel. Your cooperation will be greatly appreciated."

He reached for her arm, but she yanked it away.

"This isn't over, Kirk," she said coldly. "My government will hear of this."

Kirk had no doubt of that. "Please express our most sincere condolences. I will keep you informed of the investigation."

"This way please, Colonel," Chekov insisted. "Let Captain Kirk do what he has to." He turned his head to one side as he sneezed loudly. "Excuse me."

Kirk barely noticed. At the moment, Chekov's stuffy nose was the farthest thing from his mind. He contemplated the gruesome remains on the floor and examined the stateroom. An assortment of data disks were piled at the work station by the computer terminal, as though the general had been busy earlier, while the bed in the adjacent compartment was unmade, suggesting that Tem had not yet retired for the evening when he was attacked. Kirk crouched to inspect the severed arm. Fingerprints and DNA could be used to verify that the arm had indeed belonged to Vapar Tem, but Kirk suspected that would be a mere formality. Aside from Gast, Tem had been the only other Pavakian aboard.

I'll have the arm sent to sickbay, he thought, *not that McCoy will have much to autopsy.*

"Kirk."

He looked up to see that Riley had lingered behind after the others left. The ambassador looked understandably perturbed. Although he was missing his jacket and shoes, he was still fully dressed in a dark shirt and trousers, having apparently not hit the sack yet. His expression was hard, his fists clenched at his sides. Glancing past Riley, Kirk saw that Lenore had apparently retreated back to her own quarters at some point.

Probably not a bad idea, under the circumstances.

Kirk rose to his feet. "I'm sorry, Ambassador. It looks like both our jobs just got a lot more complicated."

"And you don't find anything, well, suspicious about the fact that this attack took place not long after you brought a certain multiple murderer aboard the *Enterprise*?" He didn't wait for an answer before beginning to lay the case for the prosecution. "I'm told you found a disruptor pistol, set to overload, on this site when we arrived?"

"That's right," Kirk confirmed, knowing where Riley was going with this.

"An apparent murder. An overloading pistol. Does any of this sound familiar to you?"

Yes, Kirk thought. *Too much so.*

Eight

It was still daylight on Pavak as Brigadier-General Pogg escorted the two *Enterprise* officers into the enormous aboveground silo Spock had noted before. More than ninety meters tall, the ominous gray structure had been constructed expressly for the purpose of eliminating the protomatter missiles in a (hopefully) safe and efficient manner. Its seamless outer shell reportedly boasted several layers of dense shielding to contain the protomatter in the event of an accident. Spock considered this a prudent precaution. He knew better than most how dangerously unstable the substance was.

Armed guards were posted all around the silo and at every entrance. Even with Pogg accompanying them, both Spock and Scott were scanned to confirm their identities before being allowed inside the facility, the interior of which was lined with several levels of catwalks and scaffolding overlooking a king-sized transporter pad some six meters in diameter, atop which a towering gantry had been erected. Busy Pavakian soldiers and technicians swarmed the walkways, preparing for the disarmament process to begin. An elevated monitoring station located near the top of the silo appeared to offer an excellent view of the operations below. As worked out in advance, the plan was for each missile to be beamed, one by one, onto the pad from various sites across the planet. Upon arrival, each missile would be inspected and identified before being disintegrated. After each such operation, the transporter buffers would be purged to prevent the missiles from being rematerialized here or elsewhere.

"As you can see," Pogg said, "we have spared no expense or effort to carry out this process. It has been an ambitious, laborious, and frankly expensive operation involving dedicated teams of Pavakian engineers all over the planet . . . lest anyone doubt our commitment to peace."

"Very impressive," Spock replied. "I applaud your obvious industry and diligence."

"Aye," Scott agreed, looking happy to have come in from the cold. He craned his head back to take in the imposing structure. "Ye've put a lot of quality work into this facility, I can tell." He rapped a riveted support beam with his knuckles. "And sturdy, too."

"I am pleased that it meets with your approval." Pogg's flat tone made it difficult to determine if he was being sarcastic or not. He guided them toward a waiting elevator. "This lift will take us to the primary control room, where you will be able to oversee the operation as agreed."

"All in good time, Brigadier-General," Scotty said.

"If ye don't mind, I'd like to make a hands-on inspection of the first missile before we get fully under way."

"That hardly seems necessary," Pogg protested. "All the documentation will be made available to you."

"I have no doubt," Scott said. "Just the same, I'd prefer to conduct a physical inspection myself. In my experience, paperwork and sensor readings are no substitute for checking things out with your own eyes. After all, we wouldn't want people to think that maybe a counterfeit or decoy had been destroyed instead, would we?"

Pogg bristled indignantly. "Are you suggesting deception on our parts?"

"Not at all," Spock insisted. "But there is an old Vulcan saying: Trust, but verify." He spoke calmly and diplomatically. "No accusation is intended, but it is vital, for all concerned, that there be absolutely no room for doubt. We must avoid even the possibility of fraud or the exercise is pointless."

Pogg mulled this over. "So be it, if you insist. How do you wish to proceed?"

Scott peered up at the looming gantry. "Let's start with the first warhead, shall we?"

"Very well." He led them into the elevator, which was of the cage variety, and pulled the door shut behind them. "I will accompany you to the appropriate level, although I assure you that this degree of scrutiny is unnecessary."

"Let us be the judge of that," Spock said. "A preliminary physical examination is indeed advisable before we relocate to the control room, where I will naturally wish to familiarize myself with your transporter mechanisms and displays."

Full access to the transporter data was also essential to their mission. It was still necessary to confirm that any "disintegrated" missiles had not instead been beamed to another location. Spock declined to spell out his specific concerns, however, in order to avoid provoking Pogg.

"Naturally," Pogg said sourly. "Perhaps we can also provide you with a complete list of all our military codes and passwords, as well as the home addresses of all our top commanders?"

"I do not believe that will be necessary," Spock replied. "Shall we proceed to the inspection?"

The elevator carried them to the top of the gantry, where they stepped out onto a platform that Spock estimated to be approximately sixty-point-five-eight meters above the reinforced transporter pad below. Vulcans were not notably subject to an irrational fear of heights, and Spock himself had spent much of his childhood exploring Vulcan's steep hills and mountains, but the vertiginous drop caused Spock to briefly think of the thruster boots he had worn while visiting Earth's Yosemite Park with Captain Kirk and Doctor McCoy. Such boots would be a useful safety precaution at this altitude. Pavak's gravity was no less forgiving than that of any other Class-M planet.

It was, as they said, a long way down.

No missile occupied the gantry at present, although a small team of Pavakian technicians was already present on the upper platform. They regarded the Starfleet visitors with various mixtures of curiosity, suspicion, and resentment, which Spock chose to studiously overlook. It was clear, however, that he and Scott were not universally welcome here—which came as little surprise. Military personnel seldom approved of outsiders taking away their weapons.

"Time passes and there is much to accomplish," Spock observed. "Shall we commence?"

"By all means." Pogg raised a wrist-communicator to his lips. "Begin procedure."

"Affirmative," a voice from the control replied. *"First unit arriving."*

The pad below lit up and the familiar whine of a transporter in operation filled the silo. A shimmering pillar of light, some seventy meters high, appeared atop the pad. The glare was bright enough that Pogg and Scott averted their eyes, but Spock's inner eyelids protected him from the intense brilliance. The towering matter stream solidified before his eyes and, as the glare faded, the first missile appeared on the pad.

Spock recognized the weapon from its specifications. Precisely sixty-six-point-five-zero meters in height, the gleaming black missile consisted of a pointed warhead mounted atop a huge impulse booster capable of delivering the missile's formidable payload to Oyolo in approximately thirty minutes, depending on the position of the planets relative to each other. Spock noted that the reinforced transporter pad supported the missile's considerable weight without buckling. Pavakian engineering continued to impress.

Despite his Vulcan reserve and emotional discipline, he felt something of an inward shudder at the sight of the weapon. Just one such missile, he knew, was capable of raining unimaginable devastation down upon Oyolo, enough so that the crude photonic missiles that had already wreaked havoc on the planet would seem like a gentle rain by comparison.

Serial numbers in Pavakian script were embossed on the missile's glossy ceramic casing. Pavakian technicians read off the numbers, checking them against the records on their data slates.

"Unit PMTT-1000000-3XV-001," a young tech called out. "Verified."

"Not so fast, laddie." Scott came forward to inspect the newly arrived missile, which had theoretically been beamed to the site from its original location. "Aye, that looks like the real McCoy," Scott said, "with all due respect to a certain chief medical officer."

Pogg did not ask him to clarify that last remark. "Well?" he asked impatiently. "Are you quite satisfied, Commander Scott?"

"Not yet." He scanned the nose cone with his tricorder. "Everything seems to be in order, but I still need to take a peek under the hood." He gestured at the nose cone's outer casing. "Open her up."

Pogg fumed visibly, but assented. "Do as he says," he instructed the technicians, who complied by unlocking a seal to reveal the warhead within. An opaque containment vessel shielded the protomatter core of the weapon, but the mechanics matched the specs unearthed by Oyolu intelligence and provided to Starfleet for the purposes of this inspection. Spock conducted his own scan of the warhead and found the readings consistent with the presence of protomatter . . . to an unsettling degree.

The Genesis effect relied on protomatter, he recalled. He owed his own resurrection, in part, to the very substance that made this warhead such a dreadful instrument of annihilation. It seemed a waste that such a remarkable material was so readily subverted to warlike ends, but, as he'd observed in the past, historically it had always been easier to destroy than to create. *More's the pity.*

Scott seemed to share his aversion.

"Aye, that's the genuine article," he said with obvious distaste. "Nasty stuff, that."

"But you are satisfied that the warhead is authentic?" Pogg pressed.

Scott nodded. "Aye."

"And you, Captain Spock?" Pogg asked.

"Affirmative," Spock said. "You may proceed with the disposal of the weapon."

"Good," Pogg said curtly. He spoke into his wrist-device again. "Continue."

The transporter operator responded with admirable speed. The transporter fired up again and the missile dissolved into atoms, which quickly dissipated to leave an empty pad behind. Spock experienced a very human sense of relief as the weapon—and its malignant warhead—vanished from existence. He reminded himself to conduct a thorough review of the transporter's memory banks later.

"One down," Scott said. "And a good many more to go."

"Then let us waste no further time." Pogg contacted the control room. "Receive the next unit."

"*Affirmative.*"

This time, the men availed themselves of tinted safety goggles as a dazzling pillar of energy delivered another missile to the pad. Aside from its serial number, it appeared identical to the missile that had just been disintegrated. The technicians once again checked and double-checked the serial numbers on the weapon's casing. Satisfied, Pogg raised his communicator to order the missile's destruction.

"No," Scott said. "Let's check this one's innards as well."

"What?" Pogg said, raising his voice. "This is intolerable."

"Is it?" Scott asked. "And how are we to know that ye didn't try to pull a fast one by making sure that the *first* missile to be inspected was genuine . . . but slipping in a dummy missile later on?"

Spock had to concur with Scott's reasoning. He'd had enough experience with humanoids such as the nefarious Harry Mudd to be familiar with the concept of a "shell game."

"But do you realize how much time this will take?" Pogg asked, growing steadily more vexed. "There are over a thousand missiles to be destroyed. Are you intending to personally inspect every one?"

"No. Just a random spot check, every now and then, to keep us all honest."

This clarification did little to mollify the indignant Pavakian.

"And precisely how many spot checks do you have in mind? Every fifth missile? Every tenth?"

Scotty took the other man's choler in stride. "Ah, that would be telling."

Pogg unhappily consented to another physical inspection, which yielded results identical to the first. As the second missile dissolved into nothingness, Spock allowed himself to hope that perhaps the lengthy disarmament process could be carried out without significant complications or obstructions. A third missile materialized upon the transporter pad. Pogg challenged Scott with a surly look.

"Well? Must we waste time opening up this unit as well?"

"No," Scott replied. "I suppose we can speed things up a wee bit, as long as we reserve the option to conduct random checks without warning."

The engineer's stubborn persistence on this point clearly tested Pogg's patience, but he was more than willing to keep the process moving. Hours passed and the system proceeded like clockwork, pausing irregularly so that Spock and Scott could again verify that the warheads were genuine. Spock was about to suggest that they relocate to the control room when a Pavakian colonel rushed onto the platform, accompanied by a half-dozen soldiers armed with phaser rifles.

"Brigadier-General!" she said urgently. "We've just received word. General Tem has been assassinated . . . aboard the *Enterprise*!"

"What?" Pogg reacted in shock. "Is this confirmed?"

"Affirmative, sir! The news comes straight from High Command."

Hostile eyes turned toward Spock and Scott as the tense atmosphere took a sudden turn for the worse. Rifles were pointed in their direction and Spock found himself acutely aware of the precipitous drop surrounding them. That both he and Scott were completely unarmed added to the probability of this unexpected development having adverse, and possibly fatal, consequences.

Pogg wheeled about to confront them. "What do you know of this?"

"I possess no more information than you do," Spock insisted. "This regrettable news surprises me as well."

Indeed, even as he assessed the difficult position he and Scott now faced, his mind was already considering

the larger ramifications of General Tem's apparent assassination. The killing of the Pavakian delegate—
aboard the *Enterprise,* no less—had the potential to
throw the entire peace process into jeopardy, if not
terminate it abruptly. Despite his own predicament,
he did not envy Captain Kirk or Ambassador Riley.

"You don't act surprised," Pogg accused him.

"I am Vulcan," he reminded Pogg. "We are not
known for noticeable displays of emotion. But I assure
you that I find this tragic news most distressing."

"Aye!" Scott said, much more emotively. "This is
a bad business, which we most certainly did not see
coming!"

Pogg eyed them dubiously as he pressed the nameless colonel for more information. "Has the assassin
been apprehended or identified?"

"I do not believe so, Brigadier-General," she stated.
"Reports are still coming in. Details are sketchy . . . but
it must have been the Oyolu! Who else could it be?"
She glared at Spock and Scotty. "Unless Starfleet was
conspiring with our enemies to kill the general!"

Judging from the vengeful looks on the faces of her
fellow soldiers, she was not alone in her suspicions—
and perhaps her desire to act upon them. Spock perceived the odds of his and Scott's survival shrinking by
the moment. One trigger-happy soldier, or perhaps an
"accidental" plunge from the gantry, and this peacekeeping mission would end in a distinctly less than
satisfactory manner.

"Don't be ridiculous," Scott said. "I have no idea who killed the general, but I give ye my word that Captain Kirk and Starfleet had nothing to do with it!"

"And yet Tem was killed aboard your ship," Pogg said harshly, "while under your protection."

"I can offer you no explanation at this juncture," Spock said evenly. "But I urge you not to react in haste or emotion. We are in perilous waters here, and it behooves us to proceed with caution."

Time itself seemed to warp as a worrisome moment stretched subjectively for what felt like a much longer interval. Spock realized that their future was in Pogg's hands now, provided the Pavakian officer was able to maintain control of his aggrieved troops. Spock's short acquaintance with Pogg did not provide sufficient data to predict the other man's behavior under these circumstances with any degree of reliability. Spock could only wait to see how events would play out.

I must have faith, he thought, *that the universe will unfold as it should.*

Pogg himself seemed uncertain as to how to respond. He deliberated longer than Spock would have preferred before brusquely reaching a decision.

"Escort our guests back to the officers' barracks," he ordered. "These inspections are done for the day."

Spock had to wonder if they would ever resume.

Nine

"Are you sure you and your people are safe on Oyolo?" Kirk asked Tamris via a long-distance link to the planet. "Perhaps it would be prudent to bring you aboard the *Enterprise* for the time being, at least until tensions have died down a little?"

"*Thank you, Captain, but I must decline your generous offer.*" The Andorian's careworn face occupied the viewscreen on the far wall of the briefing room. "*We cannot abandon our work here. Too many suffering people require our assistance.*"

"Are you quite certain of that?" Kirk asked from his seat at the conference table, facing the viewer. Riley sat across from Kirk, his chair also toward the screen. "The situation on both planets has become much more volatile, to say the least."

It was the morning after General Tem's apparent assassination and the news had already reached Oyolo and Pavak, causing considerable uproar. Tem's mutilation and death had provoked riots and demonstrations on Pavak, along with formal protests from the Pavakian High Command, while jubilant public celebrations on

Oyolo had only exacerbated the crisis. Accusations were flying back and forth like missiles. Kirk had planned to make a courtesy call on Pavak today, but things had obviously changed.

"I appreciate your concern," Tamris replied, *"and I'll grant that we're all a bit on edge today, much more so than when you visited us yesterday, but my decision stands. My people understand that our work often puts us in potentially dangerous environments."* She shrugged philosophically. *"If we pull up stakes every time there's a security issue, we might as well stay home."*

"I understand." Kirk nodded, respecting her decision. "Risk is your business. But please don't hesitate to call for help if you think you need it. There's a fine-but-crucial line between courage and foolhardiness, as Doctor McCoy is often quick to remind me."

Tamris chuckled. *"Have no fear, Captain. I haven't lasted in this game this long by not knowing when to cut and run when needs be. If our situation becomes untenable, you'll be the first to know."*

"Just try not to call it too close. We're not within transporter range after all."

"Point taken," she said. *"In the meantime, might I ask when Lyla will be returning to Oyolo? I understand that you have many other things on your mind right now, but I feel a responsibility to keep tabs on my volunteers."*

Kirk felt Riley's baleful gaze upon him.

"We're still conducting our investigation of last night's tragic events, so we've asked Miss Kassidy to remain aboard until we can take her statement," he replied. This was the truth, more or less, although the situation was a good deal more complicated than that. "I'll let you know when she is free to resume her duties on Oyolo."

"*Of course, Captain,*" Tamris said. "*You can count on Lyla to cooperate fully with your investigation. She's a very dedicated and responsible person, as I'm sure you're well aware.*"

Riley coughed skeptically, but otherwise refrained from commenting. Kirk admired his restraint. Diplomacy was clearly his proper line of work.

"Miss Kassidy's singular qualities are well known to me," Kirk said. "But I won't keep you from your work any longer. Please take care and keep your eyes and ears open."

"*And my antennae as well,*" she promised. "*And good luck with your investigation . . . for everyone's sake.*"

The screen went blank as she cut off the transmission at her end.

"Well, that's that," Kirk commented. "I hope we don't regret not evacuating those people. Not to mention Spock and Scotty."

Concerned over the unrest on Pavak, he already had contacted the weapons-inspections team, both of whom had volunteered to continue their mission on the planet, despite—or even because of—the escalating tensions caused by General Tem's assassination. Kirk had trusted their judgment and respected it. If anything, destroying those missiles had become more important than ever.

"Spock and Scott are on a secure military base," Riley noted. "They should be safe from any riots in the streets. Whether they're safe from the Pavakian military is another question." He scowled behind his beard. "I've been in touch with my contacts at the capital. The Pavakians are, understandably, not happy about what happened to Tem while he was under our protection. This could scuttle not just the peace process, but Pavak's relations with the Federation for years to come."

Kirk could believe it. An already challenging situation was going south in a hurry.

"I've placed Chekov in charge of collecting evidence," he said. "The sooner we get to the bottom of this, and find out who is responsible for the attack on Tem, the better."

"I'm not sure we need to look all that far." Riley fixed his gaze on Kirk. "Do I need to spell it out for you again?"

Kirk knew what he was getting at. "You think it was Lenore."

"And you don't?" Riley did not hold back. "You bring a known murderer aboard the *Enterprise* and hours later a man is dead. And the killer left behind an overloading energy weapon just like she did all those years ago." He contemplated the coffee cup resting on the table before him. "I suppose I should keep a close eye on what I drink while she's aboard."

Lenore had attempted to kill Riley by slipping a near-lethal dose of tetralubisol, a volatile industrial lubricant, into a glass of milk. The young lieutenant had barely survived the experience.

"I agree it looks bad," Kirk said. "But there was a reason, however twisted, for why she killed back then. What motive would she have for murdering Tem? As far as we know, they'd never even met before last night."

Kirk couldn't recall anything ominous or even unusual about Lenore's brief encounter with Tem at the reception. A'Barra had been clearly enamored with her, but Tem, as far as Kirk could recall, had been his usual reserved self. He and Lenore had barely exchanged more than a few pleasantries before Kirk and Riley had gone off on their own. Could something have happened between Tem and Lenore in the few minutes that he and Riley had been away? If so, Kirk wasn't aware of it.

"She's insane," Riley said. "Who knows what kind of deranged motive possessed her? Maybe she'd heard too many horror stories from the Oyolu about the Scourge of Azoza? Maybe Tem reminded her of Kodos and it struck a nerve? Maybe she even thought she was doing the right thing, atoning for her past by slaying another infamous mass-murderer? The point is, she's done this before, as you and I are both aware. For all we know, she staged your 'accidental' meeting down on Oyolo just to get to the general. Or maybe it was a spur-of-the-moment thing, a crime of opportunity? Frankly, I don't care *why* she might have done it. I just know that she's our prime suspect."

"But she was pronounced sane," Kirk pointed out.

"McCoy is trying to obtain her full medical records as we speak, but I've already confirmed that responsible authorities judged her no longer a danger to herself or others."

"Doctors can be wrong," Riley said. "And what about that overloading pistol? You can't believe that's simply a coincidence!"

"I don't know," Kirk said. He'd be lying if he didn't admit that the parallel troubled him as well. "But doesn't that seem almost too pat for you? As though, perhaps, someone was trying to frame her?"

"Like who? As far as we know, nobody in this system aside from you and me and a few veteran members of your crew are familiar with her past. What motive would the Pavakians or Oyolu have to frame her?"

"To cover up their own involvement in the murder," Kirk suggested. "Certainly there's no shortage of people who might have wanted General Tem dead, including most of the population of Oyolo."

"So you're suggesting that A'Barra or Ifusi was responsible?"

"I'm simply suggesting that we not rush to judgment, regarding Lenore or anyone else."

The intercom on the desk chimed, interrupting the discussion. Kirk leaned over to answer the prompt. "Kirk here."

"Sorry to disturb you, Captain," Uhura said. *"But our guests are demanding to speak with you and Ambassador Riley."*

"I imagine they are." Kirk figured they couldn't put off meeting with the delegates any longer. "Have Security escort the Oyolu to the briefing room, and please inform Colonel Gast that we will meet with her shortly."

"Aye, Captain. I'll see to that at once. Uhura out."

Riley peered at Kirk from across the table. "Why the Oyolu first?"

"We already know that Gast is going to accuse the Oyolu of complicity in the murder. I want to hear their story, get their account of last night's events, before we talk to her."

Riley nodded. "That makes sense. We might as well be prepared for the inevitable." He signed wearily. "From what I gather, the majority of Pavakians are convinced that A'Barra is behind the assassination."

Just like you're convinced Lenore is responsible, Kirk thought. He braced himself for the tense confrontations ahead. "You ready for this?"

"I have to be," Riley said. "The whole peace process could depend on it."

Don't remind me, Kirk thought.

Security made good time escorting the Oyolu delegates to the briefing room. Within minutes, the door slid open to admit A'Barra and Ifusi, both of whom looked somewhat less disheveled, if no less worried, than they had the night before.

"Thank you for seeing us, Captain, Ambassador," A'Barra said. "I am eager to get this distressing matter cleared up as swiftly as possible, as you must surely understand."

"Absolutely," Riley replied. "We appreciate your patience." He gestured at the remaining seats around the table. "Please make yourself comfortable."

A'Barra took a place at the far end of the table and Ifusi sat down beside him. The younger Oyolu had yet to utter a word, but he already looked as though he was spoiling for a fight. His beefy arms were crossed atop his chest and he glowered at Kirk and the others. No doubt he expected to be accused of the murder at any moment.

And not without reason, Kirk thought. Ifusi made a decent suspect as well. *He made no secret of his hostility toward Tem last evening.*

Kirk got right to the point. "You're aware of course that many Pavakians are already blaming you for General Tem's murder."

"As was to be expected," A'Barra said gravely. "And I won't deny that I have more than my fair share of Pavakian blood on my hands, but I assure you, gentlemen, that I played no part in this particular killing. And I'm confident that my aide is innocent as well."

"Not that I'm sorry the Scourge is dead," Ifusi growled. "If it was up to me, his assassin would be awarded a medal."

"Yes," Kirk said. "You made that quite clear last night. Can I ask you what you did and where you went after the reception?"

"Are you questioning my word?" He rose angrily to his feet. "I knew you would attempt to implicate me! But do not think that I will be made to pay for another's deed!"

"Sit down, Ifusi," A'Barra said sternly, "and calm yourself. The captain is merely doing his duty."

"That's quite right," Kirk said. "We're questioning everyone about the events of last night, and we're not accusing anyone just yet."

He had already decided to take the lead when it came to interrogating the suspects. The peace talks were one thing, but in this case it was probably better that Riley not be placed in such an adversarial posture regarding the various delegates. Kirk was perfectly happy to play "bad cop" if it meant not souring Riley's diplomatic relations with both delegations.

And the murder took place on my ship, Kirk thought, *so I'll be damned if I'm going to sit back and let someone else ask the tough questions.*

Ifusi sat back down at the table. He glared sullenly at Kirk. "What do you want to know?"

"What you did last night after the reception," Kirk asked again.

"I spoke briefly with Minister A'Barra in his stateroom before retiring to my own quarters."

"I can confirm this," A'Barra said, "at least in part. Ifusi and I had a discussion about his behavior at the reception, after which I dismissed him and told him to get a good night's sleep."

"And this would have been . . . ?" Kirk asked.

"I'm not sure," Ifusi said. "Approximately twenty-three thirty by your clock. But I did as my leader suggested and went straight to bed." A bellicose stare dared Kirk to dispute him. "You must take my word for this."

It wasn't much of an alibi, Kirk noted. The delegates were hardly under lock and key, let alone twenty-four-hour observation. The time of death was presumably when the weapons alarm went off, at exactly five minutes after zero hour, but it would have been easy enough for Ifusi—or A'Barra for that matter—to return to his quarters on the same deck before Kirk or the security team arrived on the scene.

And the same applied to Lenore.

"What about you, Minister?" Kirk asked.

A'Barra answered without hesitation. "After bidding Ifusi good night, I sat up reading for a time, the better to digest the many gustatory delights I consumed at the reception. I had just gone to bed—alone, sadly—when that ear-piercing siren went off and the quiet of the night gave way to the turmoil that followed." He sighed. "I wish I could provide you with a better alibi, Captain Kirk, but you have to believe that I would *never* endanger the peace talks in this manner, not even to avenge the restless dead of Azoza. My people have endured enough conflict and sorrow. Oyolo deserves a chance to rebuild."

"I couldn't agree more," Riley said. "Which is why it is vital that we not let this shocking crime, no matter how appalling, derail the peace process. And, forgive me, Minister, the celebrations on Oyolo are not helping matters. The Pavakians are upset enough about General Tem's death without seeing broadcast images of your people rejoicing over the assassination."

Kirk had seen some of the same broadcasts. Tem's death had been greeted by fireworks, jubilant crowds, patriotic anthems, and dancing in the streets, particularly in the hard-hit regions around Azoza. He could only imagine how such images were playing with Colonel Gast and her fellow Pavakians. It would be like watching the Klingons celebrating the destruction of the *Enterprise*.

"I have already issued a statement unequivocally condemning the attack on General Tem," A'Barra said, "and affirming Oyolo's commitment to peace. But there is only so much I can do to control the reaction in the streets and, truthfully, I cannot entirely fault my people for taking some satisfaction in the demise of an individual who brought so much pain and grief to so many." His hand went again to his damaged right horn. "Look to your own history, Ambassador. Was not the passing of, say, Osama bin Laden or Colonel Green greeted with equal parts relief and celebration? The heart craves justice as well as peace. And not always in equal amounts."

Kirk thought of Kodos, whom A'Barra could have just as easily cited. "Justice . . . or revenge?"

"Who is to say where the difference lies," A'Barra

said, "or if such a difference truly exists? Greater minds than ours have grappled with that perennial dilemma and come no closer to a solution." He let go of his broken horn. "In any event, you can rely on my full cooperation regarding your investigation. I am willing to submit to whatever test or examination might dispel any doubt of my innocence. And I speak for Ifusi as well." He gave his protégé a sideways glance. "Is that not so?"

Ifusi scowled. "If you insist, Defender."

"Thank you, Minister," Kirk said. "I may be taking you up on that offer. I appreciate your willingness to assist in our investigation."

"It is not a choice. It is a necessity." He leaned forward for emphasis. "You *must* identify the true killer, Kirk, or any hope of a lasting peace will die with General Tem. There is no other way."

Kirk nodded. "I understand."

Not for the first time, he wished that Spock was here to lend his prodigious intellect to the task. He had seriously considered recalling Spock from his vital mission on Pavak to take over the investigation, but dismantling Pavak's stockpile of protomatter missiles was arguably just as crucial to preserving the peace. Chekov, in his role as security chief, would just have to pick up the slack.

Don't let me down, Pavel. A lot is riding on this.

Namely, peace between two worlds.

Ten

Kirk waited until the Oyolu had been safely escorted back to their quarters before meeting with Colonel Gast. The last thing anyone needed was an angry confrontation in the corridors. Matters were explosive enough already.

"Thank you for your patience," Riley said as she joined them in the briefing room. "Once again, my sincere condolences on your loss."

"I would prefer justice to platitudes," she said sharply. "And action to equivocation."

Kirk noted that she was showing signs of strain. Her chestnut eyes were bloodshot and she dropped into her seat rather heavily, without quite as much of the crisp military bearing he associated with her. He guessed that she had not slept much since the assassination, if at all. Doctor McCoy would probably prescribe a sedative, but Kirk suspected that Gast would refuse any such treatment. She had other things on her mind beyond taking care of herself.

Her superior officer was murdered only hours ago, Kirk thought. *She's entitled to be a little overwrought.*

"General Tem's death was a great shock to us all," Kirk stated. "Those responsible will be found and held accountable."

"I doubt you need look much further than the Oyolu," she said. "The only question is whether one or both of them were involved and how many others might have helped plot this craven act." She sniffed disparagingly. "I would not be surprised if the general's assassination was conducted with the full knowledge and complicity of the entire Oyolu upper ministry."

"Let's not jump to conclusions," Riley cautioned her. "I assure you that we are pursuing every possible line of investigation . . . and the true identity of the assassin remains to be discovered."

It occurred to Kirk that Riley would doubtless prefer the killer to be Lenore, and not simply because of any personal vendetta. Pinning the assassination on a lone outsider like Lenore would simplify matters considerably and possibly allow the peace process to move forward. For better or for worse, Lenore made a highly convenient scapegoat.

"And who else could be responsible?" Gast asked. "Surely you don't intend to cast suspicion on the crew of the *Enterprise*?"

"Of course not," Kirk said, feeling obliged to defend his people. "I have the utmost faith in the honor and integrity of this crew, some of whom have served with me for decades. The very idea that one of my people could have committed this crime is inconceivable."

He spoke with conviction. He hoped he never lived to see the day that a Starfleet officer under his command would take part in anything so nefarious.

"Your loyalty to your crew does you credit, Captain, and I am inclined to take you at your word where your people are concerned. Starfleet has an impeccable record after all." She placed her palms down on the table. "But that brings us back to the Oyolu, does it not? Who else could possibly be to blame?"

Kirk glanced at Riley, worried that he might be tempted to throw Lenore under the shuttle for the sake of the peace talks, but, to Kirk's relief, the ambassador was more careful than that.

"Our investigation is still in its preliminary stages," he stated. "We will naturally keep you fully apprised on any significant developments."

"I expect no less," she said. "Indeed, given that a Pavakian citizen has been murdered, I would prefer that we take charge of the investigation. Give the word and I can have an entire forensic team from our top criminal justice agency en route to the *Enterprise* before the hour is out."

"I'm afraid that's not an option," Kirk said. "The *Enterprise* is neutral territory, beyond your jurisdiction, and bringing more Pavakian authorities aboard would violate the terms of the peace talks. Moreover, the Oyolu would surely insist on dispatching their own investigators . . . and would probably reject any findings from your detectives, especially if they implicated the

Oyolu delegation." Kirk had already thought about this; the prospect of rival law-enforcement agencies fighting a turf war aboard the *Enterprise* was something to be avoided at all costs. "An independent investigation, conducted by my people, is in everyone's best interests, if we want both sides to accept the results."

"I feared that would be your attitude," Gast said. "Rest assured that we will revisit this issue if and when the precise identity of the perpetrator becomes obvious to all but the most willfully blind. The Pavakian people will accept nothing less than the immediate extradition of all those responsible for the general's death. Justice demands it."

There's that word again, Kirk thought. *I'm starting to dislike it.*

"Let's cross that bridge when we come to it," Riley suggested. "In the meantime, can I ask what your government's position is regarding the peace talks, in light of recent events?"

"My superiors are obviously reluctant to dispatch another emissary to the *Enterprise* since it is clear you cannot guarantee their safety. However," she said sourly, as though the words tasted bad in her mouth, "I have been instructed to proceed with the negotiations until such time as the identity of the assassin is determined conclusively, at which point justice for General Tem will become paramount. Furthermore, we insist that the Oyolu delegates not be allowed to return to their planet . . . or be granted sanctuary aboard the *Enterprise*."

Kirk let Riley split these hairs.

"Again, it's premature to discuss hypotheticals, but I can assure you that the Oyolu delegation have no intention of departing the ship at this juncture. Minister A'Barra insists that he remains fully committed to the peace process."

"Despite the brutal murder of his enemy," Gast said sarcastically. "How magnanimous of him."

"And what are your views on the peace talks, Colonel?" Kirk asked. "Do you agree with your government's decision to continue the negotiations, even after what happened?"

She paused before answering.

"My instructions are clear," she said eventually. "And it is what the general would have wanted. I feel it is my duty to finish what he started, if it is at all possible. You will forgive me, however, if I am rather more skeptical of making peace with the Oyolu than I was before."

That was hardly a ringing endorsement, Kirk observed, but it was probably the best they could hope for under the circumstances. At least the Pavakians weren't walking away from the table just yet. But what if one or more Oyolu did turn out to be guilty? Then the cease-fire was likely to be as good as dead.

"It speaks well of Pavak," Riley said, "that your people remain intent on peace even after suffering this terrible tragedy. And I have to agree with you. We owe it to the general to see that his death was not in vain."

Nicely put, Kirk thought. Better that Tem became

a martyr to peace than yet another cause for conflict. They needed to break the cycle of revenge and retaliation. "And you can count on us to ensure your own personal safety while you remain aboard the *Enterprise*. I'll have security assigned to you for your personal protection."

"A wise, if belated, precaution," she said. "I don't suppose such concern would also extend to providing me with a weapon?"

"I'm afraid not," Kirk said. Given the tensions aboard, and Gast's own conviction that the Oyolu were behind the assassination, providing her with a phaser sounded like an incredibly bad idea. "But our security forces are well-equipped to keep you safe."

"And in one piece, I hope." She smiled mirthlessly. "Unlike General Tem."

Kirk remembered Tem's severed arm lying on the carpet. He suspected the grisly image was burned into Gast's brain as well, probably for the rest of her life. One more not-so-secret pain, from the very recent past, to carry into her future. That the rest of Tem had presumably been vaporized was possibly a mercy.

"That's the basic idea, yes," Kirk said. "The general's stateroom remains a crime scene, by the way, but please let me know if there are any materials related to the negotiations that you need to retrieve from his quarters. Commander Chekov can arrange for a security detail to accompany you on a supervised visit to the site."

"Thank you, Captain, but I believe I already have

everything I require to deal with the Oyolu. Except, as I said, a weapon."

"Which will not be necessary, Colonel," Kirk said. "You have my word on that."

"Very well. It seems I have little choice but to place my safety, and the search for the general's murderer, in your hands, at least for the moment." She rose, somewhat unsteadily, from her seat. Kirk got the impression that she was holding herself together through sheer force of will. "Now then, if you have no further questions, I need to update my government on this meeting."

Kirk briefly considered asking her about her whereabouts last night, then he recalled that she had been with him, one deck below the VIP quarters, when the weapon alarm went off. He was her alibi for the murder.

"No," he said, "that will be all for now. Once again, please accept our sincere condolences . . . and try to get some rest."

A bitter chuckle escaped her lips.

"Rest? There will be no rest for me until the general's death is avenged. Nor for any of us, I suspect." She turned and marched toward the exit. "Good day, gentlemen."

The door opened for her. A security officer was waiting outside to escort her back to her quarters. Kirk had no intention of letting her suffer the same fate as Tem. His promise to keep her safe was one he took very seriously.

"Well, that actually went better than I was expecting," Riley observed after she left. "Not that that's really saying much." He turned toward Kirk and his face hardened. An edge crept into his voice. "You know who's next, don't you?"

Kirk didn't need to be prodded. He leaned forward and activated the comm unit.

"Kirk to Uhura. Please have Miss Kassidy brought to the briefing room."

Let's get this over with, he thought. *One way or another.*

Eleven

Lenore entered the briefing room, looking understandably apprehensive. She had exchanged her party gown for an everyday outfit that Kirk assumed she had brought with her from Oyolo. Her pale features were strained and she faltered briefly when she saw Riley waiting for her. As with Gast, Kirk assumed that she had not slept well.

"I take it I will not be catching a shuttle to Oyolo in the immediate future?"

"Given the volatile situation on both planets," Kirk said, "it's probably best that you remain aboard the *Enterprise* until this matter is cleared up. For your own safety, of course."

"Of course," she echoed. "But my work on Oyolo . . . ?"

"I've already explained the situation to Doctor Tamris," Kirk said.

"The whole situation?"

"Only that we needed your statement regarding last night's events," he clarified. "Nothing more."

She sighed in relief, clearly in no hurry to share her checkered past with her fellow relief workers. "Thank you, Captain."

"Let's get on with it," Riley said brusquely. He gazed at Lenore with a stony expression, as though she was a Klingon spy caught in the act. His eyes were hard as polished dilithium. He gestured at the empty chair Gast had just vacated. "Please be seated."

Lenore sat down at the end of the table. She took a deep breath and faced Riley.

"Before we begin, Ambassador, I want to take the opportunity to apologize for trying to hurt you so many years ago. There was no good way to broach the subject at the reception last night, but you have to believe me that I sincerely regret what I did to you."

If her apology moved him, his face and voice gave no indication of it.

"The events of twenty years ago are a matter of public record and do not need to be recapitulated. Everyone in this room knows who you are and what you are capable of." Riley plowed ahead, taking the lead. Unlike with the delegates, he obviously wasn't going to sit back and let Kirk be the "bad cop" where this particular suspect was concerned. "For the record, would you prefer to be addressed as Lyla Kassidy . . . or as Lenore Karidian?"

For the moment, her alias remained more or less intact. Kirk had quietly instructed both Sulu and Uhura to keep mum about her true identity for the time being. Chekov had not yet signed on aboard the old *Enterprise* when the Kodos affair took place, but Kirk had taken the security chief into his confidence as well. Matters

were dicey enough without either the Oyolu or Colonel
Gast discovering Lenore's history of homicide. There
would be time enough to drop that bombshell if and
when it became unavoidable.

"What's in a name?" she replied, shrugging. "Considering our shared past, is there any point in me stating
that I had nothing to do with this particular murder?"

"That's what we're here to decide," Riley said. "Where
were you last night when the weapon alarm went off?"

"In my room." She glanced at Kirk. "Alone."

"That's not much of an alibi," Riley said.

"I had no reason to suspect that I would need one."
She appealed to Kirk, a quaver in her voice. "I promise
you, Captain. I'm not the assassin, not this time. Why
on earth would I want to kill General Tem?"

"The Scourge of Azoza?" Riley said. "Who didn't
want to kill him?" His eyes narrowed suspiciously.
"Perhaps he reminded you of someone else. Your father, maybe?"

"But that makes no sense," she protested. "I loved
my father, not wisely but too well, despite his crimes.
I never wanted to kill him." Her voice cracked as she
struggled visibly to maintain her composure. Her hands
trembled. "And even if I had wanted to kill General Tem,
how could I have planned this? I didn't even know that I
would be coming aboard the *Enterprise* until yesterday,
let alone that I would be in proximity to the general?"

Riley had already anticipated this argument.

"Maybe it was a murderous impulse," he speculated,

"or perhaps your 'accidental' encounter with Captain Kirk wasn't actually a matter of chance. Maybe you arranged it somehow, knowing that you could finagle an invitation to visit the *Enterprise* if you played on your past relationship to the captain . . ."

Kirk opened his mouth to object to the implication, but he realized there was no point in denying that he had once had feelings for Lenore. Pretending otherwise would not bring them closer to the truth.

Lenore, on other hand, appeared stricken by the accusation. She turned toward Kirk, seemingly overcome with emotion. Moist eyes searched his.

"Is that what you think, Jim? That was I manipulating you?"

You have before, he thought, rather uncharitably, but resisted the possibility. *I don't want to believe that.*

"We just need to clear things up, that's all." He maintained a cool, professional tone, as much for Riley's sake as Lenore's. The situation was charged enough as it was. "We're talking to everyone who might have had motive and opportunity to get at the general last night."

"But I'm the only known serial killer in the vicinity, right?" She chuckled bleakly. "I suppose I can hardly blame you for suspecting me. I almost suspect myself."

Kirk hoped she wasn't unraveling under the strain. This ordeal had to be taking a toll on her hard-won sanity.

"The sooner we can eliminate you as a suspect, the better for all of us. Help us clear your name."

"And which name is that—'Lyla Kassidy' or 'Lenore Karidian' . . . or Lady Macbeth, for that matter?" She held up her hands and examined them. "Sometimes I wonder who I really am. Who knows, maybe I really am the killer and don't even know it."

Riley seized on her remark. He leaned forward intently. "Is that a confession?"

"That would make things easier for you, wouldn't it? For all of you?" Her eyes searched Kirk's. "Is that what you want, Jim?"

Kirk didn't like the plaintive, defeated tone in her voice. He feared she was on the verge of confessing regardless of her guilt or innocence.

"What we want is the truth," he said emphatically. "Nothing more, nothing less."

"But truth is often just a matter of appearances. All the world's a stage, remember, and all we men and women merely players." She kept staring at her raised hands. "If I am typecast as a killer, what does it matter who I truly am behind the greasepaint . . . or what parts I might have foolishly dreamed of playing?"

Kirk frowned. He thought he understood the pressure she was under, but Lenore was not helping her case by indulging in such dramatics. Actress or not, she needed to sound more down-to-earth and less theatrical. Then again, he recalled, she'd always been prone to colorful flights of fancy in her language. It had been charming . . . before.

"It matters here and now," Kirk stated. "We need to

identify the actual assassin, not just pin the blame on the first convenient suspect."

Riley stiffened, as though suspecting that Kirk's remark might have been partially aimed at him. And he wouldn't have been entirely wrong about that.

Good, Kirk thought. *He got the message.*

The intercom chimed again and Kirk responded, grateful for the interruption. "Yes?"

"It's Mister Spock," Uhura said. *"He's hailing us from Pavak."*

Kirk was eager to confer with Spock as well. "I'm afraid we'll have to continue this discussion another time, if that's acceptable to you, Ambassador?"

"Quite acceptable. The situation on Oyolo demands our attention, too." He peered icily at Lenore. "Although I'm certain we'll have more questions for Miss Karidian as the investigation develops."

"And I hope you will believe my answers," she said, regaining her composure to a degree. She rose from her seat. "Please extend my apologies to Doctor Tamris, Captain, as it appears I will be detained a while longer. Shall I report back to my guest quarters . . . or to the brig?"

"Your room will be sufficient," Kirk assured her. "Although I'm going to ask that you be escorted to sickbay first. Doctor McCoy is expecting you."

"To conduct a psychiatric evaluation."

Pretty much, he thought, *among other things.* "Just to make sure you're holding up okay. This whole business has surely been more than you bargained for."

"I confess that I rather wish that I had declined your gracious invitation and remained on Oyolo. Then matters might not be quite so muddy, at least as far as your investigation is concerned." She gazed wistfully at Kirk and sighed. "Perhaps someday we can enjoy a pleasant evening without a dead body turning up."

That would be preferable, Kirk thought. "We'll speak again later."

"After I've had my head examined, of course." She turned to leave. "Till then, gentlemen."

Riley watched her exit. "Well, she knows how to make an exit. I'll give her that."

But this drama was hardly over, Kirk realized. Indeed, he had the unsettling feeling that it was only beginning. There was still a murderer aboard the *Enterprise,* hiding in plain sight. Kirk couldn't help flashing back to Lenore's first visit to his ship, years ago, and the play she had performed in less than twenty-four hours ago. Shakespeare's chilling words echoed at the back of Kirk's mind.

What's past is prologue . . .

Twelve

Despite Pavak's frigid climate, news of General Tem's death had ignited a veritable firestorm upon the planet. A viewscreen on the wall of the guest quarters assigned to Spock and Scott conveyed muted images of riots and demonstrations breaking out across Pavak, as outraged civilians and politicians demanded justice for Tem and retaliation against the Oyolu. The visiting weapons inspectors didn't need to rely on the planet's global media to assess the situation, though. The view from the barrack's windows offered direct visual evidence of the planet's mood. Crowds of angry demonstrators, bearing signs and slogans, had gathered outside the fort's fences, chanting and throwing rocks. Spock was unclear whether the demonstrators wanted him and Scott turned over to the mob or simply banished from the planet, but it was clear that an even greater percentage of the populace now opposed the disarmament efforts and were perhaps prepared to halt it by force of arms if necessary. What was significantly less clear was how much such sentiments were held by Brigadier-General Pogg and his troops, and whether the Pavakian military could truly guarantee his and Mister Scott's safety. At the moment, the fort's guards were keeping the irate crowds at bay, but Spock knew better than to assume that they could rely on this protection indefinitely. He had not forgotten the disruptor rifles that had been turned on them in the immediate aftermath of Tem's murder. *We were hardly among friends before the assassination,* he thought, *and considerably less so now.*

"This is a fine kettle of fish we're in," Scott said, pacing restlessly back and forth across the main living area of the suite. Having shucked his heavy field jacket, he wore his engineer's vest over a standard-issue white turtleneck. He scowled at the chanting demonstrators outside. "I can't believe it. An assassination aboard the *Enterprise* of all places!"

"Sadly, not without precedent," Spock observed. He was seated at the computer terminal conducting a thorough review of the transporter records from the interrupted disarmament procedure. Despite the present crisis, he had been allowed continued access to the data. Precisely 16.08 hours had passed since word of the general's murder had reached Pavak, and he had made good use of that time. "Need I remind you of the Babel conference of years gone by?"

"No." Scott sank glumly onto a couch. "But that was aboard the old *Enterprise.* I had hoped that this new ship might stay unbloodied." He peered up at the ceiling as though he could spy the *Enterprise* far beyond the orbit of Pavak. "Do you think the captain needs us back on the ship? I can't imagine that he and Ambassador Riley are having an easy go of it."

"You are no doubt quite correct in that supposition," Spock said. "I confess to being torn myself as to where our presence is most needed at the moment. Yet we have an important duty here on Pavak, perhaps even more so than before, now that tensions between Pavak and Oyolo have increased dramatically. With the ceasefire in danger, eliminating the remaining protomatter weapons becomes even more imperative."

"But do you really think the Pavakians are going to want to continue with the process," Scott asked, "after all that's happened?"

"That remains to be seen, Mister Scott. But we cannot simply abandon the mission without making every effort to see it through, despite your very valid concerns."

"I suppose not," Scott said. "In for a penny, in for a pound." He sighed heavily. "I just wish they'd catch the bloody-handed villain who caused this ruckus."

"As do I, Mister Scott. As do I."

An emphatic rap at the door heralded the arrival of Brigadier-General Pogg, who let himself into the quarters without further ado. Spock and Scott rose to greet Pogg, whom they had not seen since the weapons inspections had been curtailed abruptly. Despite their inquiries, little information regarding their status had been forthcoming from the Pavakians. Spock was, in fact, slightly unclear on whether he and Scott were currently guests or prisoners or something in between. Several armed guards and layers of security separated them from the *Galileo,* which remained on the landing pad within the fort. *So near and yet so far,* Spock reflected.

"Gentlemen," Pogg greeted them stiffly. "I regret leaving you waiting, but, as you can surely imagine, the murder of General Tem has provoked considerable turmoil, which has fully occupied the attention of myself and my superiors."

"So we gather," Spock said, indicating the silent news broadcasts on the viewscreens. "We quite understand how busy you must be under the circumstances, but may I ask whether any decision has been made regarding the disarmament process?"

Pogg nodded solemnly. "I am here to inform you that all such operations have been placed on hold indefinitely." He strode over to the window and gazed out at the growing mob of demonstrators beyond the gates. "Furthermore, as the commander of this base, I suggest that you might be safer back aboard the *Enterprise.*"

Scotty took mild umbrage. "Is that a threat, sir?"

"A courtesy," Pogg said. "If I truly believed that Starfleet had deliberately played some part in the general's death, you would be in the brig now . . . or facing a firing squad."

"I appreciate you giving us the benefit of the doubt," Spock replied, "but I am reluctant to call short our mission just yet, particularly in light of a certain irregularity that has come to my attention."

Pogg frowned. "Irregularity?"

Spock gestured at the computer terminal. The data on the screen, which was highly technical in nature, was hardly self-explanatory, so Spock attempted to summarize his discovery.

"I have been examining the data from your transporter silo, paying particular attention to the energy readings for each operation, and I have encountered some curious discrepancies with regards to one particular missile. Unit number PMTT-1000441-6XV-057, to be precise."

Pogg stared at the bewildering columns of figures on the computer screen. His brow furrowed. "What kind of discrepancies?"

"Discrepancies in the quantities of energy required and produced by both the initial transportation of the missile and its eventual disintegration," Spock explained. "Although the basic process is the same whenever a transporter energizes a solid object, and when the process is reversed, different objects require and expend varying amounts of energy. This is only logical when you think about it; different objects and materials have different masses, as well as atomic bonds of varying strength. Converting a feather to energy is hardly equivalent to doing the same with a block of solid duranium. And the resulting matter stream will vary as well, as I'm sure Mister Scott can attest."

"Aye, that's the truth of it," Scott said. "More energy in, more energy out, depending on the mass and composition of the item being transported."

Pogg nodded slowly. "So?"

"You would expect that all the missiles, being identical in size and substance, would display the same energy signatures, within a reasonable margin of error, but Unit Zero-Five-Seven, if I may abbreviate its serial number, registers differently . . . perhaps because it lacked a true protomatter warhead?"

Spock's exceptional memory recalled nothing distinctive about that particular missile, except that it had *not* been subjected to one of Scott's random physical inspections. If his theory was correct, *someone* had played the odds . . . and won. A dummy warhead had passed through the process without being detected, which left at least one protomatter warhead unaccounted for.

"You must be mistaken," Pogg insisted, instantly grasping the implications of Spock's discovery. "There is some error in the data or your calculations."

"Unlikely," Spock stated. "The same discrepancy appeared both when the missile was transported to the site *and* when it was subsequently disintegrated. And the variation, compared to the other missiles, is well beyond the margin of error." He spoke deliberately to be certain he was understood. "The conclusion is unmistakable: One of your warheads is missing."

Pogg's sable countenance kept him from visibly flushing or going pale, but the Pavakian officer was clearly troubled by the revelation. He froze in place. "I don't believe it. It can't be possible."

Spock extracted a microtape disk from the computer and handed it to Pogg.

"Here is the relevant data, which I urge you to verify for yourself. In the interim, I believe it best that Mister Scott and I remain on hand until this matter is resolved. I am not comfortable returning to the *Enterprise* while even one protomatter warhead remains at large, particularly when there is a disturbing indication of deception on the part of whoever substituted the counterfeit warhead for the real one. This concerns me greatly, Brigadier-General, as it should concern you."

"I—I must look into this immediately," Pogg stammered. He tucked the disk into his breast pocket and hurried for the door. "If you will excuse me."

He paused in the doorway and looked back at Spock and Scott.

"A word of advice, gentlemen. Please remain within your quarters . . . for your own safety's sake."

"We are not going anywhere," Spock assured him. "For better or for worse."

Thirteen

"Do you think the Oyolu are responsible, Commander?"

Lieutenant Debra Banks was assisting Chekov in his investigation of the assassination. A lanky, energetic redhead with a buzz cut and freckles, she had been Chekov's assistant in Security for some time now. A thick accent betrayed her roots in America's Deep South; Chekov found the accent somewhat comical, but he had come to rely on her keen instincts and enthusiasm.

"That is what it is imperative that we determine," he said. "As soon as humanly possible."

Chekov knew that Captain Kirk was counting on him to help identify the assassin before the entire peace process collapsed. Acutely aware of the responsibility that had been placed on his shoulders, the *Enterprise*'s chief of security was determined to unravel the mystery, just like the famous Russian detective Porfiry Petrovich.

At the moment, he and Banks were conducting a thorough sweep of the crime scene. The general's arm had been carted away to sickbay for examination, but otherwise the luxurious stateroom remained just as it had been when he and Captain Kirk had arrived on the scene last night. The VIP suite, which was distinctly larger and more impressive than Chekov's own quarters on E Deck, consisted of roughly three compartments. Tem's remains had been found in the largest area, which included a work desk, computer terminal, personal communications station, and dining module, along with various storage cabinets and closets. A retractable partition divided the living area from the adjacent foyer and bedroom. Bathroom facilities, including a sonic shower, were in a separate compartment on the opposite side of the foyer.

Despite their diligent efforts, little in the way of evidence had been found so far. Tricorder scans had detected traces of Pavakian, human, and even Oyolu DNA, but given the confusion last night, that was to be expected. In the chaos, A'Barra and Ifusi had made their way into the stateroom to find out what was happening, which offered a plausible explanation for the Oyolu DNA found in and around the foyer. Chekov regretted that he had not maintained tighter control of the crime scene, but, at the time, there had been other matters to attend to, such as that overloading disruptor and the possibility of an all-out brawl breaking out among the surviving delegates.

No use crying over spilled DNA, he thought. *Live and learn.*

Not for the first time, he wished that the captain had not been forced to disintegrate the murder weapon, but at least Kirk's quick thinking had preserved the rest of the crime scene.

And kept the rest of us from being blown to atoms as well.

"Nothing too interesting here, sir," Banks reported after personally inspecting another cabinet. "Any idea what exactly it is we're looking for?"

"Besides a signed confession from the assassin?" he asked. "Anything that will help us reconstruct the events leading up to the disruptor being fired."

The entrance to the stateroom had shown no evidence of being forced, which suggested that Tem had willingly admitted his attacker or perhaps done so at gunpoint. Chekov contemplated the circular dining table in the northeast corner. A single glass of ice water and a half-eaten biscuit hinted at the general's ascetic ways while giving no indication that he was entertaining company prior to his death. Chekov glanced around the stateroom, seeing no sign of a struggle either. The assassin appeared to have struck quickly and with little warning.

"Why did the killer leave the arm?" Banks asked out loud, gazing at the spot on the carpet where the grisly remains had been found. "Why not just vaporize all of him?"

Good question, Chekov thought. "To disarm the general, no pun intended, before he could defend himself? Or perhaps to leave us conclusive proof of his assassination?" An autopsy conducted by Doctor McCoy had confirmed that the arm had been severed by an energy beam while the general was still alive. "I suspect the killer meant to send a message of some sort."

"They couldn't use subspace like everyone else?" Banks quipped.

"That would be too easy," Chekov said, wandering over to the computer terminal. Judging from the neatly stacked piles of data tapes, Tem had been working at some point after the reception. The fact that his arm had still been in the sleeve of his uniform also suggested that he had not been abed when the assassin arrived. Chekov wanted to collect the disks for review, and search the terminal's memory as well, but, according to Ambassador Riley, there were certain political obstacles to consider. The general's personal files and communications were protected under diplomatic seal. Indeed, as Chekov understood it, even searching Tem's quarters in this manner tested protocol, although there was no way around it if they wanted to conduct any sort of proper investigation. Nevertheless, Chekov felt as though he had one hand tied behind his back so that he only had one arm to work with.

Not unlike the general before he was disintegrated . . .

And to make matters worse, Chekov's nose and eyes were acting up again. Sniffling, he plucked a handkerchief from the pocket of his maroon jacket. His eyes watered and an irritating itch tickled the back of his throat. If he didn't know better, he'd swear he was suffering from Aldebaran hay fever, although he hadn't set foot in the *Enterprise*'s botanical gardens in weeks, and it was hardly the right season anyway. He dabbed at his runny nose while attempting to stifle a sneeze.

"Are you all right, sir?" Banks asked, as observant as ever.

"Just a little stuffy, Lieutenant." He stepped into the foyer to avoid contaminating the crime scene. "It comes and goes . . . and always when most inconvenient."

"Perhaps you should visit sickbay," she suggested.

Doctor McCoy had advised the same, but Chekov was reluctant to take time out from the investigation to deal with a mild, if annoyingly intermittent, case of the sniffles. There were far more urgent matters to attend to, like catching a killer and preserving the peace.

"Maybe later, after we have the assassin in the brig."

She joined him in the foyer. "With all due respect, sir, you won't be doing anyone any good if you come down with a bad case of the Triskelion flu or whatever." She gestured at the remainder of the stateroom. "I can finish up here, not that, honestly, I expect we're going to find a smoking gun . . . or disruptor. The killer has done too good a job of covering their tracks."

Chekov was inclined to agree. The stateroom had yet to yield any incriminating evidence.

"Then perhaps we need to expand our search," he said, "and treat the *Enterprise* itself as the crime scene."

"The entire ship, sir?" Banks sounded understandably daunted. The *Enterprise* was more than three hundred meters long and had over twenty decks. "I wouldn't know where to begin."

"At zero-five last night. We know precisely when and where the murder occurred. What we do not know is what transpired immediately before and after the killing. A forensic review of what was transpiring aboard the ship during that interval might offer a clue as to the assassin's movements and identity. That is where we should concentrate our efforts next."

"A very logical plan of attack, sir. Mister Spock would be proud, if you don't mind me saying so." She snapped to attention. "I'll get right on it, as soon as I finish scouring this stateroom, that is. In the meantime, you head straight to sickbay and get that stuffy nose checked out. A sick detective is a distracted detective."

Chekov surrendered to the inevitable. He wondered if he was ever this pushy when he was an up-and-coming young officer.

No, he decided. *I was probably worse.*

Eager to get McCoy's evaluation of Lenore's mental state, Kirk swung by sickbay after conferring with Spock. The situation on Pavak sounded worrisome and the matter of the missing warhead even more so.

Entering from the corridor, he found McCoy temporarily occupied with Chekov, who was sitting atop an examination table one room over while McCoy surveyed him with a handheld med scanner. The Russian's legs dangled over the edge of the table.

"Well, Doctor, what is your diagnosis?" Chekov asked. "Am I going to live?"

"As long as you stay away from angry Klingons and overloading disruptors, absolutely." McCoy consulted the results of his scan, which were displayed upon a wall-mounted medical monitor. "Nothing to worry about. As nearly as I can tell, you're just suffering from a minor allergic reaction."

"Allergic?" Chekov echoed. "To what?"

"That's going to take a little longer to determine. You been exposed to anything unusual lately?"

"Aside from cold-blooded murder?" Chekov shook his head. "I had some sushi and caviar at the reception last night, but that's never bothered me before."

McCoy collected more data with the scanner.

"I'll run some tests and simulations to try to isolate the specific allergen," McCoy promised, "but in the meantime, here's a general antihistamine." He handed Chekov a vial of pills. "Use this to treat any symptoms as needed, and let me know if your condition worsens."

"Thank you, Doctor." Chekov accepted the medication. "My apologies for bothering you over such a trivial matter, especially at a time like this."

"That's what I'm here for," McCoy assured him. "To tell the truth, it makes a pleasant change from the usual phaser burns, exotic viruses, and alien parasites."

Kirk entered the examination room from the doorway. "Not to mention the odd murdered delegate and severed arm, I imagine."

"Captain!" Chekov hopped off the table onto his feet. He appeared slightly embarrassed to be caught in sickbay while the investigation into the murder was still under way. "I did not hear you come in."

"At ease, Commander," Kirk said. "Glad to hear you're not seriously under the weather." Chekov had taken plenty of lumps in recent years, from Ceti eels to a serious fall from a twentieth-century aircraft carrier; Kirk was sincerely pleased to know that Chekov was only suffering from allergies this time around. "How goes your investigation into the assassination?"

"It is in progress, Captain, which means, honestly, that I have little to report yet."

Kirk appreciated his candor. "Keep at it, and let me know the minute you turn up anything."

"Aye, sir," Chekov said. "I am pursuing a new line of investigation and hope that it will yield results soon." He turned to McCoy. "If I may be excused, Doctor?"

"Get back to work, Chekov." McCoy crossed the room to place the blood sample on a counter. "I'll be in touch when I've identified the allergen."

"Thank you, Doctor." He nodded at Kirk. "Captain?"

"You're dismissed, Commander. I need to talk to Doctor McCoy anyway."

Chekov hurried off to resume his investigation. Kirk thought again about summoning Spock back to assist in solving the mystery, but he decided to give Chekov a little more time to track down some leads. Chekov had been something of a protégé of Spock's back in the old days, when the intrepid Russian was just a green young ensign with a knack for science, but Pavel had come into his own through the years. Kirk had faith that Chekov would get the job done.

"Let me guess," McCoy said. "You're here to get my assessment of Lenore?"

Kirk was glad to get to the point. "And . . . ?"

"Give me just a moment." McCoy crossed sickbay to reach the lab section and transferred the readings from the scan into the medical computer. "Conduct full diagnostic analysis to determine primary allergen," he instructed the computer. "With emphasis on biomes visited by *Enterprise* within the past seventy-two hours and working backwards from there."

"Acknowledged," the computer replied. *"Commencing analysis."*

Confident that the procedure was under way, McCoy stepped away from the lab.

"All right. Let's get to it."

They relocated to McCoy's office, which was just off the lab area. McCoy sealed the office door behind them so they could speak freely. There were no patients currently recuperating in sickbay, but it was always possible that a stray nurse or orderly might walk by. It occurred to Kirk that McCoy had learned his lesson from that time he had accidentally mentioned Anton Karidian's true identity where a young Lieutenant Riley could overhear. Out for vengeance, Riley had nearly taken the law into his own hands.

"So, Doctor," Kirk asked, "what is your professional opinion?"

"Based on a general examination and brief consultation, she seems sane enough to me, albeit under severe stress and a bit prone to melodrama." McCoy sat down behind his desk and called up a file on his computer terminal. Kirk caught a glimpse of a photo of a somewhat younger Lenore wearing a brown coverall. "She allowed me to access her confidential medical files, which I've had a chance to review. She was indeed institutionalized at the Federation mental treatment center on Gilead Three for fifteen years, and she spent another year under probation at a colony for recovered criminal offenders before being released on her own recognizance."

Kirk nodded. This was what he had already verified in broad strokes. He wanted a fuller picture now. "Why was she released?"

"After many years, she responded positively to an aggressive regimen of therapy, counseling, Vulcan meditation techniques, and medication. In particular, she benefited greatly from regular doses of zetaproprion."

It took Kirk a minute to recognize the name. "That's the same drug that cured Captain Garth, isn't it?"

Garth of Izar was a legendary starship fleet captain who went insane after suffering a serious injury, exacerbated by some well-meaning Antosians who endowed him with the ability to alter his body's cellular structure. Confined to a rehab colony on Elba II, Garth had been a dangerous lunatic until the *Enterprise* succeeded in delivering the then-revolutionary new drug to the asylum. Kirk had personally witnessed the zetaproprion's dramatic effect on Garth, restoring his sanity after years of madness. He wasn't surprised to hear that it had helped Lenore as well.

"Bingo," McCoy said, "although the effect wasn't quite as immediate in Lenore's case, given their very different pathologies. Garth's issues were primarily organic—brain damage complicated by that damn 'cellular metamorphosis' trick the Antosians taught him—so it was just a matter of correcting his brain chemistry. But Lenore's psychological scars went much deeper and needed more than just a quick biochemical fix. The zetaproprion couldn't undo her troubled past, or relieve her guilt over killing her father and all those others, but it *could* help dispel her delusions so that she could remember that past and begin to come to terms with it. Once she was able to face reality, with the help of the drug, therapeutic breakthroughs became possible and she could finally make real progress."

Kirk remembered Lenore mentioning that it had taken years of treatment before she could acknowledge what she had done. Apparently the zetaproprion had played a big part in that.

"I see. And do you agree with her doctors' ruling that she no longer poses a threat?"

"Hard to say," McCoy said. "Psychiatry is not an exact science, even today. She's still taking regular doses of zetaproprion for maintenance, which seems to be doing the trick. Then again, we all missed her pathology the last time around . . . and she *is* quite the actress. For all we know, her 'sanity' is just another brilliant performance."

Along with her claims of innocence, Kirk thought. "No offense, Bones, but I would've preferred a more conclusive diagnosis."

"I'm not a mind reader, Jim. That's Spock's department. And before you ask . . . no, I can't in good conscience sanction a Vulcan mind-meld in this instance. Her psyche is far too fragile for that kind of invasion, even if she consented to it willingly. You know how intense a meld is. We both do. Given her history of mental instability, it would be criminally irresponsible to subject her to that."

Kirk knew where McCoy was coming from. They'd both been on the receiving end of mind-melds on occasion, so Kirk knew Bones wasn't exaggerating when he stressed just how unsettling it could be to let another person go rooting around in your mind. It was a troubling experience at the best of times, let alone for someone like Lenore who had spent years struggling to regain her mental equilibrium. A mind-meld could very well undo her hard-won sanity.

"Point taken," he said. "And I suppose the same applies to using a psychotricorder to probe her memory of the last twenty-four hours? Or even monitoring her brain waves to see if she's telling the truth?"

"More or less," McCoy said. "Those are not quite as invasive, but, given her history, the results would be inconclusive anyway. Her thought processes and psychology are already suspect. She might not react the same way a fully sane person would."

So much for that idea, Kirk thought. He had already decided to ask the Oyolu to submit to computerized lie-detector tests and had hoped to do the same with Lenore, but apparently it was more complicated than that.

"Let me ask you something, Bones. Could she have conceivably committed the murder without retaining any memory of it?"

"I can't rule out that possibility," McCoy said. "Her records *do* indicate a past history of disassociation and denial. As we've discussed, it was years before she could even accept that her father was dead, let alone that she had killed him."

"While trying to kill me," Kirk said. "How do we know she's not repressing the memory of having killed General Tem as well?"

"We don't, not one hundred percent. But her previous issues were years ago, *before* she responded to treatment. In theory, the zetaproprion helps her keep her grip on reality and holds any delusions at bay."

That's not always a blessing, Kirk thought. *Personally, I'm dealing with rather too much reality right now.*

"Understood, Doctor. You've given me a lot to think about."

"Sorry about that," McCoy drawled. "Comes with the job, I'm afraid."

"Yours or mine?"

McCoy shrugged. "Take your pick."

"Moving on to other matters," Kirk said, "I'd still like to run lie-detector tests on A'Barra and Ifusi, so I'm going to need your assistance getting that set up, hopefully in the next day or so. I assume we're going to have to recalibrate the program to accommodate Oyolu physiology? Their basic metabolism and characteristics?"

"Just give me a chance to do a little homework," McCoy said. "But even if the Oyolu come through with flying colors, will the Pavakians accept the results as decisive? Or will they claim that the tests were rigged or that the evidence is inadmissible according to their laws?"

"All very good questions," Kirk conceded. Different planets had different legal systems and ideas about what constituted proof of guilt or innocence. And the Pavakians had every reason to reject any test that cleared the Oyolu of wrongdoing. "I just wish I had more answers than questions."

McCoy sighed. "Don't we all?"

"You found something?" Chekov asked.

Lieutenant Banks had summoned him to the forward end of Q Deck, where the secondary hull's emergency transporters were located. She was standing before the transporter control console, examining various readouts with a look of great concentration, when he arrived on the scene. To his relief, he felt no desire to sneeze. The doctor's antihistamine appeared to be working.

"Possibly," she reported. "I was following your advice and reviewing the ship's computer records in and around the time of the murder and I found something peculiar. According to the logs, one of these emergency transporters was activated approximately fifteen minutes before the murder took place."

"But there was no emergency that night," Chekov said. "At least not until the weapon alarm went off."

"Exactly," Banks said. "That's what seemed so puzzling. Granted, this might not have anything to do with the assassination, but . . ."

"No," Chekov said. "I think we are onto something." *But what?* he wondered.

The emergency transporter facility was one of two such units positioned on either side of the central intermix chamber in Engineering. They were intended as a means of quickly evacuating personnel from the secondary hull in the event of a disaster. In theory, endangered crew members could be beamed to the primary transporter facility in the saucer section or, if possible, to a nearby vessel, planet, or space station. They were a safety precaution, to be employed only in dire circumstances. He could think of no reason why they would have been used last night.

No legitimate reason, that was.

"Could the assassin have beamed aboard right before the killing?"

"Unlikely," she replied. "I checked the proximity scanners and there was no vessel within transporter range at that time. And a cloaked vessel would not have been able to activate their transporters without being detected."

Chekov had to agree. One of these days somebody was going to invent a cloaking device that allowed a ship to activate its weapons or transporters while cloaked, but, thankfully, that day had yet to arrive. Unless they were dealing with an enemy possessed of some radical new technology.

He nodded at the control panel. "What do the transporter records say?"

"Nothing," she said glumly. "The data has been completely scrubbed from the terminal and the pattern buffer is empty as well." She stepped away from the console. "A thorough forensic analysis of the hardware might turn up something, but that's going to take a while. In the meantime, there's no way of knowing who used the transporter or why."

Chekov nodded. "And I take it there's no authorized usage on record?"

"I'm afraid not. This was not ordered by anyone in charge." She stepped away from the controls. "Maybe the killer used the transporter to beam directly into General Tem's quarters, bypassing the locked door?"

"A very risky strategy," Chekov said. Intraship beaming was a highly hazardous feat to be avoided except in the most extreme emergencies. The odds of accidentally beaming into a bulkhead or some other solid object, with fatal results, were considerable. "It hardly seems worth the danger to life and limb just to get past a lock."

"Unless we're looking for a fanatic . . . or a lunatic."

Chekov thought of "Lyla Kassidy," a.k.a. Lenore Karidian. He had not been aboard the old *Enterprise* when the visiting actress had been exposed as a deranged murderer, but Captain Kirk had discreetly alerted him to the suspect's history. Kassidy/Karidian had once been diagnosed as criminally insane; she was allegedly saner these days, but maybe she was still crazy enough to beam herself into the general's quarters? Then again, Tem had been the Scourge of Azoza after all. Who knew how far the Oyolu would go to avenge the many victims of his infamous blockade?

He peered at the empty transporter pads. It was all too easy to imagine any one of their suspects there.

Armed with the disruptor they used to vaporize General Tem.

"What are you thinking, sir?" Banks asked.

"I am thinking that you may have uncovered a significant clue. Excellent work, Lieutenant."

"Thank you, sir, but what does it mean?"

Chekov wished he knew.

Fourteen

"So there's no way to tell who used the emergency transporter right before the murder?"

"Apparently not, Captain," Chekov reported. "Lieutenant Banks is going through the console's circuits with a fine-tooth comb, but I cannot promise that they will cough up anything anytime soon . . . or ever."

"Understood," Kirk said. "Thank you for keeping me informed."

Another day had passed since General Tem's assassination, and the killer's identity remained a mystery. Kirk and Riley had reconvened in the briefing room in hopes of possibly clearing the Oyolu's names at least. McCoy was also on hand to help administer the lie-detector test. A witness seat equipped with a biological sensor mechanism had been installed at one end of the table, while the computer had been programmed to monitor the Oyolu's brain waves and physiological responses in order to tell whether they were lying or not. The program was not one hundred percent accurate, especially where different varieties of humanoids were concerned, but it might help them rule out A'Barra and Ifusi as suspects.

That would be good news for the peace talks, Kirk reflected, *but look bad for Lenore.*

Granted, there was always the possibility that the Pavakians would reject the findings of the test, but at least the results might point the investigation in the right direction. At this point, Kirk was willing to try most anything to cut through the fog surrounding the general's murder.

"We ready to go?" Kirk asked McCoy.

"As ready as we're going to be," McCoy answered. "I'm going to want to take some baseline readings of the Oyolu when they get here, but we might as well get the show on the road."

"Very well." Kirk leaned forward to activate the comm unit on the table in front of him. "Kirk to Uhura. Please have the Oyolu report to—"

Before he could finish, Uhura interrupted him.

"Captain! I'm getting reports of a disturbance on D Deck. There's trouble among the delegates."

Kirk and Riley exchanged worried looks. *Now what?*

"On my way. Kirk out!"

The briefing room was abandoned as all present rushed to the corridor outside A'Barra's VIP suite, where they found a furious Ifusi being restrained by a couple of struggling security officers, including the bodyguard Kirk had assigned to Colonel Gast.

"Monster! Demon!" the young Oyolu bellowed as

he strained to get at Gast, who backed away cautiously, looking understandably shaken. Spittle sprayed from Ifusi's lips as he glared furiously at his Pavakian counterpart. His head was hunched beneath his shoulders, as though he was intent on goring Gast with his horns. His hooves pawed at the floor. "You will pay for this, Pavakian! Your entire vile species will pay!"

"Hold on here!" Kirk said, taking charge. "What's this all about?"

"I have no idea, Captain." Gast put more distance between herself and Ifusi. "Except that this barbarian has obviously lost his mind."

"You are the barbarians!" Ifusi shot back. "Perfidious and cruel and completely without mercy!"

"That's enough, both of you!" Kirk waded in between them. "Somebody tell me what started this."

"See for yourself!" Ifusi said, snorting derisively. Unable to break from the guards' grip, he stopped straining and twisting long enough to turn his horns toward the door to A'Barra's guest quarters. "Let your own eyes look upon a great wrong."

A sinking feeling came over Kirk as he realized that A'Barra was nowhere to be seen. Even Lenore had been drawn from her own quarters by the commotion; he spotted her standing off to one side, anxiously watching this latest imbroglio. But the senior Oyolu had yet to make an appearance, despite the noisy, undiplomatic confrontation taking place right outside his door.

This didn't look good.

"Chekov, you're with me." Kirk secured a phaser and headed for the door. "Everybody else, stay where you are." Riley moved to join them, but Kirk shook his head. "That means you too, Ambassador."

Riley started to protest. "But the minister—"

"You'll be the first to know," Kirk promised. He addressed the security officers. "Keep everyone out. Am I understood?"

"Aye, sir," Lieutenant Xadd responded. The burly Zeosian had the build of a barroom bouncer. A stony expression made it clear that nobody would be getting past, including Riley and the feuding delegates. His webbed feet were planted firmly on the floor. "Crystal clear."

McCoy knew better than to try to push past Xadd. "Jim?"

"If I need a doctor, I know where to find you."

Kirk and Chekov approached the door, which slid open before them. Entering cautiously, phasers drawn, they were quickly confronted by what Kirk had feared: A'Barra's body sprawled upon the floor. Glassy eyes stared lifelessly at the ceiling. His face was contorted in a frozen rictus. Dried saliva and bile caked his lips. Kirk didn't need McCoy to tell him that the man was dead.

Unlike General Tem, however, he appeared to be in one piece.

"Damn it," Kirk swore.

Chekov finished clearing the suite. He lowered his phaser. "No one else here, Captain," he reported. "We should be careful to avoid contaminating the crime scene."

"My thoughts exactly, Commander."

He didn't question Chekov's describing the suite as a crime scene. It was possible, Kirk supposed, that A'Barra had died of natural causes, but he didn't believe that for a second. They clearly had another assassination on their hands, even if the cause of death wasn't immediately apparent. Kirk peered down at the body, but he did not spy any weapons burns or obvious wounds. He guessed that Ifusi had discovered the corpse when he'd reported to A'Barra this morning.

Unless, of course, Ifusi was the killer.

"Let Doctor McCoy in," Kirk instructed, "but no one else."

There was no hope of keeping A'Barra's death secret, of course, but Kirk wanted to keep the number of people traipsing through the crime scene to a minimum. The killer had left an entire body behind this time. Kirk could only hope the assassin had also left them a clue to his or her identity.

"Yes, sir." Chekov's nose wrinkled, as though he was holding back another sneeze. "Excuse me just a moment, Captain." He fished the pill vial from his pocket and popped a tablet into his mouth. Chekov sighed in relief as the medication quickly took effect. "Ah, much better. I will be right back with Doctor McCoy, sir."

True to his word, Chekov returned moments later with McCoy, who gasped at the sight of A'Barra's body.

"Good God," the doctor said softly. "Not again."

"Looks like it," Kirk responded. "I need you to tell me what killed him, as quickly as you can. A tense situation is about to go critical, if it hasn't already, and I need answers, pronto." There wasn't even time to mourn the man's passing and regret the tragic loss of life. "Anything you can tell me about how he died might help me keep a full-scale war from breaking out."

"Understood." McCoy bent to examine the body. A handheld scanner hummed as the doctor passed it over the still and silent form. "I'll do what I can."

Kirk stepped back to let the doctor work, while wondering just how bad things were about to get. By now Ifusi had surely informed Riley and the others of A'Barra's death, which meant the news would be hitting both planets soon. Kirk had to wonder if there was any chance of salvaging the peace talks or if that was already a lost cause. And had this murder been committed by the same assassin—or done in retaliation for General Tem's death? Finding Lenore guilty for both killings was actually the best-case scenario, at least as far as the peace process was concerned, but Kirk found it hard to hope for that outcome.

McCoy rose from the body, a troubled expression upon his face.

"What's the verdict, Doctor?" Kirk asked.

"Poison," McCoy declared. "An overdose of zeta-proprion, to be exact."

The same medication Lenore was on.

"Are you sure, Bones?"

"Pretty much," McCoy said. "I can do a more de-tailed postmortem and tox screen to confirm, but I'm detecting a lethal dose of zetaproprion in his system and the neurological damage is consistent with an over-dose. If it's any consolation, he probably died quickly." He turned away from the body. "I'm sorry, Jim. I know this doesn't look good for Lenore."

That's putting it mildly, Kirk thought. He needed a moment to absorb the disturbing new information, which made him question his gut instincts regarding Lenore's innocence and apparent sanity. Could it be that she hadn't really been "cured" at all? *Did she fool me again?*

"Chekov," he said tersely. "Please admit Ambassa-dor Riley to the foyer, but no further. We need to speak privately, away from the surviving delegates."

"Aye, sir," Chekov said. "I'll be right back."

McCoy gave Kirk a worried look. "You sure you want to share this with Riley, Jim? You know what he's going to think."

"I have no choice," Kirk said, regardless of his own conflicted feelings. "Another key diplomat has been killed under our watch. The Pavakians and the Oyolu are bound to blame each other for the assassinations. Riley needs to have all the relevant facts, no matter who the evidence points to."

"You're right, of course." McCoy put away his gear. "But this isn't going to be pretty."

"I don't expect it to be."

Kirk heard the outer door slide open and went to meet Riley in the foyer outside the main living area. The ambassador waited until the door slid shut behind them, granting them a degree of privacy, before interrogating Kirk.

"Is it true? Is A'Barra dead?"

Kirk nodded. "Doctor McCoy has just completed a preliminary examination of the body . . . and there's something you need to know."

"What?" Riley asked, bracing himself for more bad news. He peered past Kirk at the body lying in the adjacent room. He winced at the sight.

Getting straight to the point, Kirk told him about the zetaproprion in A'Barra's system . . . and its possible connection to Lenore. Riley reacted just as expected.

"Damn it, Captain, I knew she was dangerous, but you didn't listen to me." He kept his voice low to avoid being heard by the delegates outside in the corridor. "It wasn't enough that she poisoned me years ago? Now she's succeeded in claiming yet another victim."

Kirk overlooked Riley's angry outburst. "We can't ignore this information," he conceded, "but we still can't be certain that she committed either murder. Or even that both assassinations are the work of the same killer. It's very possible that A'Barra was murdered to avenge Tem's death . . . by a different killer."

To his credit, Riley considered the possibility. "Are

you suggesting that Colonel Gast might have something to do with A'Barra's death?"

"I don't know," Kirk said. "But she has more of a
motive than Lenore does."

"At this point, I'm not convinced Lenore Karidian
even needs a motive to commit murder," Riley coun-
tered. "Not a sane one anyway."

He has a point, Kirk admitted. Nobody ever said
that murder was always a rational act. Who knew
what homicidal impulses might still be lurking within
her tortured mind and soul? "I'm just saying the case
against Lenore is circumstantial at best. And she's
hardly our only suspect."

"Seriously, Kirk? You're still defending her?" He angrily ran through the evidence against Lenore. "First, the
overloading pistol again. Then another poisoning, using
a drug we know she has access to? This is practically
Lenore Karidian's greatest hits. I have to wonder: Would
you be quite so intent on giving her the benefit of the
doubt if you and she did not share a romantic history?"

Kirk understood Riley's frustration, but he couldn't
let that accusation stand.

"I like to think you know me better than that,
Riley. When Scotty was accused of murder on Argel-
lius, I cooperated fully with the local authorities until
he was proven innocent. I did not attempt to shield
him for personal reasons. Ditto for when Spock's father fell under suspicion for murder during the Babel
conference. My feelings, past or present, for Lenore

Karidian are not relevant to this investigation. My only concern is that we not railroad a possibly innocent woman without more than some suspicious coincidences."

"Innocent?" Riley challenged him. "Lenore Karidian is hardly an innocent. She has the blood of at least seven people on those pretty little hands of hers."

"Now who's letting their personal feelings cloud their judgment?"

"But the zetaproprion . . ." Riley turned toward McCoy, who was lingering outside the doorway. "Just how uncommon is this medication, Doctor?"

"Actually, it's not that rare or experimental anymore," McCoy said. "Zetaproprion, in various doses and formulations, has even been used to treat posttraumatic stress disorders in soldiers and war victims on both Pavak and Oyolo. It's possible the fatal dose could have been obtained at a hospital or refugee camp, or even on the black market."

"Is that so?" Kirk asked, pondering this. "In other words, anyone could have gotten their hands on enough zetaproprion to kill A'Barra."

He thought again of Colonel Gast, only to remember that he had personally assigned a bodyguard to the sole surviving Pavakian delegate. It was hard to imagine how Gast could have poisoned A'Barra while under the watchful gaze of a vigilant security officer, even if she had wanted to avenge General Tem's death. She had an airtight alibi.

"I can't believe I'm hearing this," Riley said. "It's like you're both going out of your way to avoid seeing the obvious. Lenore Karidian is a poisoner. She presumably has this specific drug in her possession. And you still think it's merely a coincidence that A'Barra just happened to be poisoned while she's aboard the *Enterprise*, residing only a few doors away on the very same deck?"

It certainly sounded bad when you put it like that. Kirk recalled A'Barra's obvious attraction to Lenore at the reception. It wouldn't have been hard for her to charm her way into the Oyolu's suite . . . and possibly General Tem's as well?

"The evidence is right in front of your face, Kirk," Riley insisted. "You can't simply ignore it."

"I have no intention of doing so, Ambassador, although I'd hardly call what we have 'evidence.'" He turned to Chekov. "Have Miss Kassidy confined to her quarters for the time being. Consider her under house arrest until further notice."

"Aye, Captain. I understand."

Kirk confronted Riley. "Is that good enough for you, Ambassador?"

"I'd prefer the brig," he said, scowling, "but it will do . . . for now." He took a deep breath, making an effort to compose himself before heading out to deal with the ugly diplomatic fallout from A'Barra's assassination. He adjusted his suit to ensure that he looked properly ambassadorial. "But we *have* to get to the bottom of these killings, provide solid answers for what happened, if we're going to have any hope of preserving the cease-fire, and we have to do it soon before passions on both planets are running too hot to douse. And, like it or not, Lenore Karidian is still our number one suspect."

Or scapegoat, Kirk thought.

Fifteen

"A'Barra, too? I cannot believe it, Mister Spock."

News of the Oyolu leader's assassination had spread rapidly across both planets. Still confined to their quarters on the Pavakian military base, Scott and Spock monitored the global news broadcasts on the viewscreen provided by their hosts. This latest tragedy had provoked reactions that were both equal and opposite to those ignited by the killing of General Tem: tears and anger on Oyolo and jubilant celebrations here on Pavak. Spock could hear the crowd outside the fort cheering and singing. The only positive aspect of A'Barra's murder was that the mob congregating beyond the fences now appeared to be in better spirits, although this was small consolation when considering the larger picture . . . and the diminishing odds for peace.

"Our capacity to believe it is immaterial," Spock observed. "What matters is that Minister A'Barra is indeed dead, which complicates matters considerably."

"That's putting it lightly," Scott said, shaking his head at the disturbing images on the screen. "If this solar system was a warp core, I'd say we'd be approaching a catastrophic breach right now."

Spock had to agree. "All the more reason to locate that missing warhead, which may well have fallen into intemperate hands."

"But do ye really think there is any hope of peace-keeping at this point?"

"There is always hope," Spock said.

"Well, given that you actually came back from the dead, I suppose you know what you're talking about in that respect. But what good can we do when we're cooped up in here? And even if we were to make a break for it, where would we even begin to start looking for that warhead? It could be anywhere on or off the planet by now!"

"Those are excellent questions, Mister Scott, for which I do not yet have ready answers."

A familiar rap at the door preceded the return of Pogg. If anything, the Pavakian officer appeared even more troubled than he had been after their last meeting yesterday. He marched into the room, then he glanced over his shoulder to ensure that the door had slid shut behind him. He wasted no time on pleasantries.

"I've looked into those 'discrepancies' you pointed out to me," he said.

Spock was encouraged to hear it. "And?"

"I didn't want to believe it, but I ran the data past a technician I trust, and she verified your findings." His expression darkened behind his white-and-sable fur. "We have been deceived, and a warhead is un-accounted for."

Pogg's reaction suggested that he was not part of any conspiracy to preserve the warhead, but Spock cautioned himself not to take this assumption for granted. At this point, they had no way of knowing how many individuals had been involved in the deception or how high up the conspiracy went. Pogg could be an honest soldier kept unaware of the plot, or he could be merely feigning innocence.

"In this instance, I regret being proved correct," Spock said. "The alternative would have been vastly preferable."

Pogg nodded. "Very much so, Captain Spock."

"Do ye think this business with the warhead," Scotty asked, "has anything to do with the assassinations of General Tem and Minister A'Barra?"

That possibility had crossed Spock's mind as well. "We can only speculate at this point, but I would not be surprised if there was a connection."

"Nor would I," Pogg confessed. "You must understand, gentlemen, that this discovery shakes me to my core. I had assured you that Pavak could honor its agreements without outside scrutiny, yet now I find that at least some elements of our military have conspired to violate the agreement. That disturbs me deeply."

His words had the ring of sincerity. Spock wanted to believe him.

"Do you have any idea of who might be involved?" he asked.

Pogg nodded grimly. "I have *a* name at least. I did some digging and discovered that Unit Zero-Five-Seven, which was originally located in an underground silo on the other side of the continent, was inspected on that end by a team led by a certain Major Rav Takk."

He extracted a datatape from his breast pocket and inserted it into the computer terminal. His gloved fingers tapped the control panel and a Pavakian face appeared on the screen. Velvety gray fur barely softened the man's granite expression. Steely blue eyes betrayed nothing of what was going on behind them. Takk appeared both fit and formidable.

"What do you know of this Major Takk?" Spock asked.

"Disturbingly little. Much of his 'official' military record is redacted, vague, or obviously fabricated, which is usually an indicator of, well, dubious missions best left unspecified, if you understand my meaning."

Spock did. Covert operations, often of a morally questionable nature, were an unfortunate reality through the galaxy. "And where precisely is Major Takk now?"

"That's the most unsettling part," Pogg said. "Takk has been reassigned, but I'm having a devil of a time finding out where. My legitimate queries are being ignored, rebuffed, or met with evasion and runarounds." He slammed a gloved fist into his palm. "Frankly, the whole thing stinks of conspiracy."

Spock agreed. "And what do you intend to do about it, Brigadier-General?"

"I only wish I knew, Captain Spock," Pogg said. "Believe me."

Spock hoped he could.

Sixteen

A missing warhead?

Kirk brooded upon the bridge, mulling over the latest communication from Spock, which was troubling in the extreme. With tensions between the two planets nearing a boiling point, the last thing they needed was a protomatter warhead floating around somewhere. Kirk had his own reasons to be leery of anything involving the banned material. His son, David, had experimented, illegally, with protomatter. . . .

"Captain," Uhura said from the communications station. "I've been monitoring the situation on both planets, and I think you need to see this. It's a global news broadcast on Pavak."

Kirk trusted her judgment. "On screen."

A stern-looking Pavakian woman in civilian attire appeared on the viewer. She stared directly forward and spoke gravely as she delivered the news:

"Reliable sources report that a Terran calling herself Lyla Kassidy, attached to the so-called relief efforts on Oyolo, has been conclusively identified as Lenore Karidian, a convicted mass murderer and assassin."

Twin images of Lenore filled the screen. The one on the left depicted her as she appeared twenty years ago, around the time of her killing spree. The one on the right showed Lenore as she appeared now. That they were the same woman was unmistakable.

"*It has been confirmed that Karidian, who has a documented history of homicidal mania, was aboard the Federation* Starship Enterprise *at the time of General Vapar Tem's assassination. Furthermore, she remains aboard the vessel at this time. The daughter of a notorious genocidal despot, she is also rumored to be a former paramour of Captain James Tiberius Kirk, who is currently spearheading Starfleet's investigation into the general's brutal death, leading to concerns that he may be protecting her from prosecution . . .*"

The broadcast elicited a few gasps from the crew members unfamiliar with Lyla's true identity and colorful history. A few even snuck curious glances in Kirk's direction before studiously turning their attention back to the screen or their stations. Not that Kirk blamed them; that was quite a bombshell to absorb. The crew had to be wondering how much of the report was accurate and what this meant for their mission.

"It's all over the Oyolu news feeds as well, Captain," Uhura informed him.

Damn, Kirk thought. As if the current situation wasn't precarious enough, somebody had obviously leaked Lenore's true identity to the press. But who had done so . . . and how had they found out about her in the first place?

The turbolift door slid open and Riley barged onto the bridge. "Have you seen—?" he began before spotting the Pavakian broadcast on the main viewer. He came to a halt at the rear of the bridge.

Kirk signaled Uhura to mute the sound on the transmission. He'd gotten the gist of it.

"I've just been informed," he told Riley. "Obviously, this complicates matters."

"Yes, Captain, it does." Riley joined Kirk in the sunken command well. "I'm already getting extradition demands from both planets. The Pavakians and Oyolu both want to try her . . . for the murders of General Tem and Minister A'Barra, respectively."

Kirk was afraid of that. Now that Lenore's cover was blown, Riley wasn't going to be the only one suspecting her of the murders. And to be honest, he had his doubts about her innocence as well.

"You're the diplomat," he said to Riley. "Where do you stand on extradition?"

Kirk half-expected Riley to throw Lenore to the wolves without hesitation, but the ambassador surprised him by mulling things over for a few moments before answering. He stroked his beard thoughtfully.

"It's complicated," he said finally. "Lenore is a Federation citizen and both murders took place on the *Enterprise,* which is outside the jurisdiction of both worlds, at least as long as we remain in the buffer zone.

In addition, it could be argued that my presence aboard the ship, in an official capacity, renders the *Enterprise* an embassy of sorts, and therefore Federation territory. Not that this line of reasoning is likely to go over well on Pavak and Oyolo."

"Probably not," Kirk agreed. "But, frankly, I'm somewhat surprised that you're not in a hurry to offer Lenore up to them as a peace offering of sorts."

Riley chuckled mordantly. "I wish it were that easy. But even if I wanted to hand her over, there's the issue of who gets dibs on her first. Politically, we're in a bind here. We can't deliver her to either planet without provoking the other, but the longer we hang on to her, the more we appear to be harboring a known assassin."

"That's a problem," Kirk conceded. "Sounds like a diplomatic *Kobayashi Maru*."

"A no-win scenario?" He turned toward Kirk. "So what do you advise, Captain?"

Kirk thought it over. "I think we need to talk to our prime suspect again, Mister Ambassador."

Lenore's quarters were smaller or more modest than the VIP staterooms, comparable to those enjoyed by the *Enterprise*'s junior officers. A combined living area and bedroom abutted a compact bath and shower compartment. The accommodations were intended for the aides and staff members of more high-ranking visitors. Kirk had chosen to interview Lenore here rather than have her paraded through the corridors before gawking eyes. That would have been uncomfortable for everyone.

"Who else knew about your past?" Kirk asked, concerned with identifying the source of the leak. "Is there anybody on Oyolo—or Pavak—who could have tipped off the press to your true identity?"

"Not that I know of." She sat with her back to a built-in dresser and wall mirror, facing Kirk and Riley, who stood before her. She wrung her hands in agitation. "I didn't tell anyone, not even Doctor Tamris. I wanted to put that all behind me." Her voice quavered. "I thought I was done with this . . ."

"Yet you admit you have zetaproprion in your possession," Riley said.

"Of course. I never go anywhere without it." She extracted a hypospray from a dresser drawer and showed it to the two men. "A week's supply, just in case I was delayed. But you can see that it's still mostly loaded. There's not enough missing to kill someone."

Kirk accepted the device, but realized it hardly proved anything. They had no way of knowing how much of the drug she had originally brought aboard with her.

Riley didn't even inspect the hypospray. "So you still maintain that you had nothing to do with either murder?"

"Maybe. I don't know anymore." She turned and stared at herself in the mirror. Dark circles shadowed her eyes, hinting at another sleepless night. Her haunted, haggard expression reminded Kirk of her father. "I don't think I hurt anyone . . . this time . . . but who knows? My memory has tricked me before and my mind is an insubstantial pageant faded, full of sound and fury but signifying . . . what? I can't even be certain who I am anymore, or what role I am meant to be playing."

She spun around to face them again. Moist eyes sought out answers.

"Perhaps it would be easier for everyone if you simply let me stand trial for the murders. Better that I take the blame than for peace to be sacrificed on my behalf. I'm not certain my battered conscience could endure that. . . ."

"No," Kirk said. He wasn't about to sacrifice due process for the sake of expediency. "The only one responsible for endangering the peace is the actual killer. We find out who that is, *then* we can talk trials and extradition." He glanced sideways at Riley. "Are we on the same page here, Mister Ambassador?"

Riley frowned, but he did not contest the point. "We all want the truth, and not just the most convenient one. But I'm not sure how long the Pavakians and Oyolu will wait for us to provide them with answers." He stared coldly at Lenore. "And that we're not looking at the 'actual killer' this very minute."

Lenore flinched.

"You see, everyone thinks I'm guilty anyway . . . and they always will. Why not just get it over with and let me throw myself on this sword? I'm already guilty of more than enough murders. What's two more deaths laid at my feet if it will preserve the peace and save countless lives?"

The needs of the many, Kirk thought, *outweigh the needs of the one.* There was a cruel logic to Lenore's proposal, but it was deceptive as well. Letting Lenore assume the role of martyr might be politically convenient in the short term, and help assuage her guilty conscience, but it would possibly leave the real killer free to strike again.

"This isn't just about peace," he said. "It's about justice. And I doubt that the former can be achieved without a healthy respect for the latter. Just putting out the fire isn't enough, not if we don't know what really started it."

"And how many innocent souls will burn while you protect me?" Tearful eyes entreated him. "Please, Jim, let me do this . . . for your sake as well as everyone else's."

The intercom whistled for his attention. Kirk strode over to the wall unit, grateful for the interruption. "Kirk here."

"Sorry to be the bearer of more bad news, Captain," Uhura reported, *"but I think you and Ambassador Riley are needed on the bridge. There's a crisis on Oyolo . . . and hostages have been taken."*

Kirk put two and two together.

"The relief workers. Tamris and the others."

"*That's correct, Captain. Angry locals have seized control of the refugee camp and captured the GRC workers. They're demanding that we turn over Lenore Karidian in exchange for the hostages.*"

Lenore gasped. She looked at Kirk with anguished eyes.

"*It seems the fire is spreading, Jim. What will you do now?*"

Kirk wished he knew.

Seventeen

"Lenore Karidian," Scott said, wonderingly. "Now there's a name I've not thought of in many a year."

"Indeed," Spock replied. "I've had no occasion to think of her as well, until the present occasion."

Along with nearly everyone else on Pavak, the two men had been closely following the global news reports concerning the true identity and background of "Lyla Kassidy" and her possible involvement with the murders of General Tem and Minister A'Barra. Public opinion on Pavak appeared to be tending very much in the direction of her guilt, with the only question being whether or not she had killed Tem on behalf of the Oyolu or on her own. The precise nature of Captain Kirk's relationship with the accused was also a matter of intense speculation as far as the local media was concerned.

"Do ye think she did it, Mister Spock?"

"I cannot say," Spock said. He remembered the Kodos affair vividly, but, in truth, he'd had very little personal contact with the younger Karidian at the time. He had been concerned with determining the true identity of her father; that Lenore herself was a killer had eluded his detection until the truth had ultimately been revealed. "That she once was capable of murder is a matter of record, but that was two decades ago. Who knows what changes rehabilitative treatment might have wrought on her character and behavior?"

It did not escape the Vulcan that attributing both murders to Lenore might well be advantageous to the peace process, provided it could be convincingly demonstrated that she had acted alone. Many of the loudest voices accusing her belonged to public figures on both planets who were strongly in favor of peace. Pinning the blame on a lone madwoman, who was neither Pavakian nor Oyolu, would resolve the political crisis, at least in the short term. But that, of course, would leave the real assassins at large and unaccounted for.

Not unlike a certain protomatter warhead.

"I confess I barely recall the lass," Scott said, "just the commotion afterwards." He contemplated the suspect's image on the viewscreen. "Ye don't suppose it's true what they're saying about her and the captain . . . ?"

"I sincerely doubt it," Spock answered. While well aware of Kirk's past romantic exploits, particularly in the captain's younger days, Spock considered it highly unlikely that Jim Kirk would be quick to resume a relationship with a woman who had once attempted to kill him, particularly in the middle of a delicate diplomatic mission. "I suspect the captain has more important matters to occupy him."

"Aye, that's for sure," Scotty agreed. "But this doesn't look good."

"No, Mister Scott, it does not."

The door whisked open and Pogg returned. He glanced briefly at the viewscreen, which was still displaying coverage of the Karidian revelation. "I see you gentlemen are already familiar with recent developments."

"Regrettably so," Spock said. "But to spare you the effort of asking, neither Mister Scott nor I were aware of Miss Karidian's presence in this solar system, let alone aboard the *Enterprise.* Neither of us has laid eyes on her for approximately twenty years."

"But is it true what they're saying about her?" Pogg inquired. "Could she be the assassin?"

"We were just asking ourselves that same question. Unfortunately, we did not arrive at a conclusive answer."

"That is unfortunate," Pogg said. "In any event, I regret to inform you that, in light of this new information, I have received word from my superiors that you and Mister Scott are to be detained on Pavak—for your own protection—until such time as the suspect, Lenore Karidian, is delivered to Pavak to be interrogated by the proper authorities."

"The hell you say," Scott blurted. "We're hostages now, is that it?"

"So it appears," Spock said, none too surprised. He had been anticipating this response, which, in fact,

merely made official a preexisting state of affairs. They
had been potential hostages ever since news of General
Tem's assassination had first reached Pavak. The pro-
verbial other shoe had finally dropped.

"My apologies, gentlemen. You'll recall I urged you
to leave earlier."

"So you did," Spock said, "but our reason for remaining has not changed." If they were truly trapped
on Pavak for the duration, he intended to make fruitful
use of their time there. "Regardless of whether or not
Lenore Karidian committed the murders aboard the
Enterprise, she was most certainly not responsible for
the theft of the missing warhead. May I ask if you have
made any progress in locating the elusive Major Takk?"

"I have," Pogg said grimly. "It wasn't easy, and I had
to call in more than a few old favors, but it seems that
Takk has been assigned to pilot a supply ship, *Outward
Six,* making deliveries to a remote science outpost on
Sumno. He left approximately seventy-two hours ago."

Sumno was one of the system's outer planets: a
lifeless ball of rock and ice that remained largely un-
inhabited. It struck Spock as a curious place to send
a military officer suspected to specialize in covert
operations. "And what is your take on this discovery,
Brigadier-General?"

"It sounds damn fishy," Pogg admitted. "Why would
an advanced weapons specialist, which is what Takk is
officially listed as, be dispatched on a routine supply
run . . . and during the middle of a major disarmament

operation no less." He snarled angrily. "It stinks to high heaven if you ask me!"

"I concur," Spock said. "I believe we should operate on the assumption that Major Pakk is currently in possession of the warhead."

"But why haul it out to the edge of the system?" Scott asked.

A logical question, Spock thought. "Perhaps to hide it until the peacekeeping operations are concluded and the *Enterprise* has departed from the buffer zone? But, in that case, is the intent merely to preserve it for possible future use . . . or do the conspirators have a more specific and immediate purpose in mind?"

The latter possibility was ominous in the extreme. Even a single protomatter warhead could inflict untold damage on Oyolo and terminate any hope of peace between the two worlds.

"We can't take any chances," Scott concluded. "We need to go after that supply ship before it's too late!"

"I quite agree," Spock said, "but we are not currently at liberty to do so, unless the brigadier-general is inclined to take action to alleviate our situation."

Pogg stiffened at the suggestion. "My orders are clear. You are to remain in custody pending extradition of the Karidian woman. You cannot ask me to overlook that."

"That is precisely what I am asking, sir," Spock said sternly. He looked Pogg squarely in the face. "It has become increasingly evident that certain parties,

including a faction in your own military, are out to
disrupt the peace process by any means possible . . . and
that they may even be planning to unleash a weapon
of mass destruction on an unknown target, in clear
violation of the cease-fire. Given those facts, you must
ask yourself where your true duty lies."

Pogg did not want to hear it. "I have my orders . . ."

"And you have a responsibility to avert a potential
catastrophe and save two planets from the horrors of a
never-ending war." Spock regretted putting Pogg in this
position, but he saw no other alternative. "We cannot
do this without your assistance."

"Listen to him, man," Scott said. "You know what
that warhead is capable of. Millions of lives may be at
stake!"

"I—I do not have the authority to make such deci-
sions. This is beyond my rank."

"Fate has decreed otherwise, Brigadier-General.
You must rely on your own judgment now, not the
chain of command, which may well be corrupted."

Pogg's face twisted in indecision, his training and
discipline obviously warring with a truth he could
not readily dismiss. He spun about on his heels and
headed for the exit, retreating from the dilemma. "You
will remain in custody, as ordered, until further notice.
I will . . . update . . . you after I have given this matter
further examination."

"Do not take too long," Spock advised him. "Major
Takk—and perhaps the warhead—already have a

substantial head start on us. Every moment we remain here, that weapon may be getting farther away."

Pogg looked back at Spock, acknowledging the other man's warning, but left without another word. The door closed behind him, but not before Spock caught a glimpse of Pavakian soldiers posted outside their quarters. He did not bother trying the door, which was surely sealed from the outside.

"Do you think you got through to him, Mister Spock?"

Spock wanted to think so, but he was all too aware that sentient beings were known to be stubbornly unpredictable. They had just asked Pogg to go against his lifelong habits and code for the sake of a greater good. Calculating the energy signature of a disintegrating protomatter missile was easier than estimating the probability that Pogg would reach the correct decision in time.

"We can only hope, Mister Scott."

Eighteen

"The leader of the protesters, a Mister W'Osoro, is hailing us, Captain. He's demanding to speak to you directly."

All concerned had convened on the bridge to deal with the hostage crisis on Oyolo. The rival delegates occupied opposite sides of the bridge, keeping their distance from each other, while additional security stood by to guarantee that everyone minded their manners. Riley and McCoy shared the command well with Kirk, who was seated in the captain's chair. Lenore, flanked by two watchful security officers, stood over by the security station, out of sight of the forward viewscreen. Riley had initially protested bringing her to the bridge, but Kirk had wanted her on hand just in case the protesters demanded proof that she was still aboard the *Enterprise*.

Besides, this affected her, too.

"Thank you, Uhura," Kirk said. "Put him through."

A male Oyolu, who looked to be around the same age as Ifusi, appeared on the viewer. Rangy by Oyolu standards, W'Osoro had a lean, undernourished look.

His pocked yellow skin was more sallow than citrusy, and a bald pate further distinguished him from the likes of Ifusi and A'Barra. Coarse, fraying civilian attire made him look more like a disgruntled refugee than an authorized representative of the Oyolu government or military. Baleful, unforgiving eyes gazed out from behind a distinctly saturnine expression. Guards toting disruptor rifles stood at attention in the background, in front of a draped Oyolu flag, which featured a pair of stylized golden horns against an emerald background. W'Osoro's own horns looked freshly sharpened.

"*I am W'Osoro and I speak for all patriotic Oyolu,*" he said gruffly. "*We demand justice for A'Barra. Deliver his assassin, the foreign she-devil known as Lenore Karidian, and we will release the hostages.*"

Preliminary reports indicated that Tamris and the others were being held in the very same amphitheater that had hosted Lenore's production of *The Tempest,* which had since been taken over by the protesters and converted into a makeshift fort. The weatherproof force field kept anyone from beaming in or out of the theater, while armed guards were reportedly stationed in the tiered bleachers overlooking the stage. Kirk had to applaud the protesters' choice of venue. The intact theater was probably the most defensible structure in the immediate vicinity of the refugee camp.

"This is Captain James T. Kirk of the *Starship Enterprise.* Release the hostages first and then we can talk."

"*You expect us to trust you? After you stood by and*

let your bloodthirsty lover slay our Great Defender?"
W'Osoro snorted in derision. *"You will play by our
rules. Give us the Karidian woman or suffer the consequences."*

Kirk took care not to ask what those consequences
might entail; he didn't want to provoke W'Osoro into
making bloody threats he couldn't back down from
later. The last thing they needed was to draw any irre-
vocable lines in the sand, not with more than a dozen
lives at stake.

"The identity of Minister A'Barra's killer has yet to
be determined," Kirk attempted to point out, despite
the fact that Lenore had been all but convicted by the
planet's media. "An investigation is under way, but—"

"We have no faith in your farce of an 'investigation,'"
W'Osoro interrupted. *"This is an Oyolu matter . . . to
be dealt with by the Oyolu people. Only we can provide
justice for A'Barra and see to it that his assassin pays in
full measure for her crime."*

So much for a fair trial, Kirk thought. Clearly, Lenore had already been judged guilty, at least as far as
W'Osoro and his fellow protesters were concerned. Realizing that any lectures on due process and the pre-
sumption of innocence would likely fall on deaf ears,
Kirk tried another tack.

"How do we know the hostages are safe? Let us see
and talk to them before we go any further."

Kirk wasn't simply stalling for time. He was genuinely anxious to find out whether Tamris or any of her

people had been harmed. *Damn it,* he thought. *I should have evacuated them when I had the chance!*

"*Do not fear for the hostages,*" W'Osoro said. "*Rest assured that they are safer with us than A'Barra was upon your deathtrap of a vessel.*" He leaned forward, filling the viewer. "*Understand me, Kirk, we have no grudge against the hostages nor any desire to harm them. But they will not be released until A'Barra's killer is in Oyolu hands.*"

Kirk took some comfort from the other man's words, but he knew that he couldn't necessarily count on the Oyolu's promises to keep Tamris and the others safe. This was a volatile situation and passions were running high. Things could easily go south in a hurry, with deadly consequences for the hostages. The sooner he got them out of there, the better.

"Let's talk about this," Riley said, adopting a diplomatic tone. "Perhaps if you were to release *some* of the hostages, as a show of good faith . . ."

"*There is nothing to discuss,*" W'Osoro declared. "*This is not a negotiation. You will give us Karidian . . . or the hostages will remain our prisoners for as long as it takes.*"

Lenore stepped forward, perhaps intending to sacrifice herself, but Lieutenant Banks restrained her. An agonized expression betrayed Lenore's dismay and anxiety, unless, of course, it was simply another brilliantly convincing performance.

"It's not that simple," Kirk protested, speaking up

before Lenore could. "Be reasonable. Is this what Minister A'Barra would have wanted? There must be some compromise—"

"*Do not presume to tell* us *what the Defender wanted!*" W'Osoro snarled. "*His martyred spirit cries out for vengeance. We will not be denied!*"

The transmission ended abruptly. The empty void of the buffer zone replaced W'Osoro upon the viewscreen.

"Uhura!" Kirk said. "Get him back if you can."

"I'm trying, Captain. But he's not responding to our hails."

I was afraid of that, Kirk thought. *Not that we were making much progress anyway.*

"Guess he meant what he said about not wanting to talk," McCoy said. "Honestly, he didn't exactly strike me as the most reasonable of fellows."

"That was my impression, too," Riley said, "which doesn't bode well for negotiating the hostages' release."

"Please," Lenore said, "just give me to them. My life's not worth risking so many others for. And this isn't just about Doctor Tamris and the other volunteers. What about all the suffering refugees in the camp and medical center? Who is taking care of them while this is going on?"

Kirk feared that ship had sailed. Even if the protesters released their prisoners, he wasn't sure it would be safe for the GRC to resume its relief efforts on the planet. The twin assassinations had brought the hot zone to a boil on both worlds.

"It's not that simple," Riley said, perhaps a tad regretfully. "It's against policy for Starfleet to surrender to terrorist demands. Handing you over under these circumstances, no matter how tempting that might be, would encourage similar incidents and endanger Federation citizens throughout the galaxy." He looked at Lenore as though she was a mine he couldn't step off without detonating. "And don't forget: The Pavakians *also* want to get their hands on you—for the murder of General Tem—which complicates matters further."

"I am gratified that you remember that, Ambassador," Colonel Gast stated. Gripping the safety rail on the port side of the bridge, she peered across at Lenore. Red-rimmed eyes betrayed the strain she was under. "Our claim on the suspect is equally pressing and no less important to us, even if we would hardly resort to such blatant terrorist tactics." Her nose wrinkled in disgust. "But what else can one expect of the anarchic hordes of Oyolo?"

Ifusi predictably took the bait. "Take care, Pavakian . . ."

"That's enough," Kirk ordered, even as Chekov's security team tensed for action. "I remind you both that you're here as a courtesy, and in the hopes that we can work out a peaceful solution to the present crisis. Save your bickering for some time when no innocent lives are at stake."

"Of course, Captain," Gast said. "I merely meant to assure you that you need not fear a similar incident on

Pavak. Your personnel are safely under the protection of the Pavakian military."

Which makes Spock and Scotty potential hostages as well, Kirk noted, unsure how exactly to take Gast's remark. That his friends remained on Pavak, investigating the missing warhead, only added to Kirk's worries. *Was that supposed to be genuinely reassuring . . . or a veiled threat?*

This ambiguity was not lost on Ifusi. "One is hardly 'safe' in the custody of Pavakians," he said mockingly. "As my people know too well. They've spent decades crushing our liberties in the name of 'protecting' us from the violence they provoked. If I were you, Captain Kirk, I'd worry more about your men on Pavak than the unfortunate hostages on Oyolo!"

Kirk tried to head off another airing of old grievances. He looked to Ifusi. "What is your take on the protesters and their demands?"

"I confess to having mixed emotions regarding this matter," the Oyolu said. "I too crave justice for A'Barra, but not at the expense of innocents. That the GRC has done much good for my people cannot be denied; it pains me that they have been caught up in this conflict."

"And what of your government?" Kirk asked. "Can't they intervene on behalf of the hostages?"

"Their hands are tied, I'm afraid." Ifusi sounded faintly embarrassed by this admission. "Although the capture of the relief workers was not authorized by my government, the protesters have many sympathizers among the people, our armed forces, and even high-ranking elements of our leadership. In addition, the loss of A'Barra has left a vacuum at the top of our government, which various factions are now vying to fill. With the new administration in flux, no one in authority is going to defy the protesters for the sake of a handful of outworlders, whom many deem guilty by association. It is a pity, but freeing the hostages is not good politics at present."

"I see," Kirk said. He had to wonder just how "unauthorized" the attack on the camp had been. Had it truly been a spontaneous uprising, catching the distracted Oyolu government by surprise, or had certain authorities instigated the crisis while carefully looking the other way? In any event, it seemed that they could not count on the Oyolu government to rescue Tamris and the others. "And if we were to attempt to liberate the hostages by force?"

Ifusi answered carefully. "It would be better if I were unaware of such things."

"I understand," Kirk said, appreciating the delicate position the Oyolu was in. Plausible deniability, it seemed, went both ways. He rose from his seat to address the delegates. "Colonel Gast, Mister Ifusi, I thank you for your input. Despite our differences, I'm sure we're united in our desire to resolve this situation in a peaceful manner. Now, if you don't mind, I'd like to confer with my staff in private. If you could kindly return to your quarters."

Security personnel escorted the delegates toward the rear of the bridge. Kirk was grateful that this *Enterprise* had both port and starboard turbolifts on the bridge so that Gast and Ifusi could exit via separate lifts. Gast paused before entering the port turbolift.

"I remind you, Captain, Ambassador, that Pavak will not look kindly on an attempt to appease the Oyolu terrorists by exchanging the suspect for the hostages." Icy brown eyes locked onto Lenore. "Pavak may not be governed by an unruly mob, as is Oyolo, but we expect justice as well."

"Point taken, Colonel." Kirk worried again about Spock and Scotty and their safety on Pavak. "Believe me, we have no intention of playing favorites here."

"I will hold you to that, Captain," she said. "Although, to be fair, it does seem as though Pavakians and Oyolu have equal opportunity to be murdered aboard this vessel. That's something, I suppose."

She exited without another word, giving Kirk no opportunity to reply. Not that there was much he could say to refute her charge. Gast had every reason to be displeased with what had transpired on the *Enterprise* since her arrival. They were going to have a lot of diplomatic damage control to do if and when the current crises were over. For now, however, rescuing the hostages had to take priority.

"I suppose you want to return me to my quarters as well," Lenore said after the delegates had departed. She began to make her way toward the turbolifts, accompanied by the security officers keeping tabs on her. "Exit stage left."

Kirk shook his head. "Actually, I'd prefer if you remained on the bridge for the time being."

This elicited puzzled looks from both Lenore and Riley. The latter scowled at Kirk, already primed to protest this latest offense. His voice held a tone of warning.

"Captain?"

"Miss Karidian knows the hostages and the location they are being held at better than anyone else aboard," Kirk explained. "That inside information could prove extremely valuable."

"Of course," she volunteered. "If there's anything I can do."

Riley emitted a bitter chuckle. "Chances are, you've already done more than enough."

Lenore retreated from his withering tone. Her gaze dropped to the floor.

"Let's focus on the task at hand," Kirk said. Determining Lenore's guilt or innocence could come later; at the moment, they needed to concentrate on the hostage crisis. He raised his voice to address the entire bridge. "Talk to me, people. I need options."

Riley stared at the starry blackness upon the viewscreen. "I just wish we could've gotten a glimpse of the hostages, to check on their conditions."

"I may be able to help you there," Uhura said. "It took some effort, but I've managed to tap into some communications and weather-monitoring satellites in

orbit around Oyolo, not to mention some illegal Pavakian spy satellites. I've also managed to trace W'Osoro's
transmission back to its source in order to get a lock on
the arena where the hostages are being held. Give me
just another moment and I think I can provide us with
some eyes in the sky."

"Good thinking, Commander," Kirk said. He recalled that Scotty had pulled off a similar trick decades
ago in order to spy on a twentieth-century rocket base
in Florida, during their first run-in with Gary Seven
back in 1968. "Whenever you're ready."

"Aye, sir."

Uhura worked her magic and within moments an
aerial view of the amphitheater and the ruined parklands appeared on the main viewer, unobstructed by
the transparent force field over the arena. At first, the
surveillance was from too high up to make out any crucial details, but she zoomed in on the site until they
seemed to be looking down on it from less than fifty
meters above the stage. Lenore gasped and clasped her
hand over her mouth as the hostages and their captors
came into view.

Tamris and approximately fourteen relief workers,
including the Horta, huddled together in the center
of the stage, surrounded by scowling Oyolu bearing
disruptor rifles, pistols, and other weapons. The guards'
worn civilian clothing testified to the unofficial status of
the armed protesters, many of whom looked as though
they had been drawn from the ranks of the refugees

themselves. Kirk was relieved to see that the hostages appeared more or less unharmed, although they were obviously frightened and uncomfortable. He recalled the hot, humid climate he'd experienced before and felt an extra twinge of sympathy for the sweaty, miserable-looking hostages. By his calculations, it was midafternoon in that time zone.

Could be worse, he thought. *At least it's not fall or winter in that region.*

He had no intention of letting them stay captive long enough to see the seasons change.

"I don't understand," Chekov said. "How are they holding the Horta hostage? Couldn't he just burrow out of there if he wanted to?"

As Kirk knew from experience, sustained phaser fire could eventually penetrate a Horta's rocky, all-but-indestructible carapace, but Chekov was right in assuming that the Horta could probably make his escape before sustaining any serious injuries. All he'd have to do would be to bore straight down and deep below the planet's crust.

"He's probably concerned with the safety of his friends and colleagues," Kirk guessed. "The protesters may have threatened to harm the other hostages if he didn't cooperate."

"Absolutely," Lenore said. "Jorgaht would never abandon the others, or risk them being punished for his escape."

Kirk trusted her assessment of her colleague. He

had yet to meet a Horta who was not a model of integrity. They had a truly admirable culture that produced many remarkable individuals.

"This is obscene," McCoy said, understandably offended by the distressing scene of the viewer. "Those people have dedicated their lives to helping strangers. They don't deserve to be treated like bargaining chips." Indignation mixed with compassion on his careworn countenance. "We can't just sit here and let them be held captive by an armed mob. We have to do something!"

"I quite agree, Doctor," Kirk said. "The only question is what."

"We could try the direct approach," Chekov suggested. "I'm betting the *Enterprise*'s phasers could easily overpower that theater's rudimentary force field. Then we just beam in a tactical team—or lock onto the hostages directly."

"I wish it were that easy," Kirk said, assessing the situation. "But we don't know how long it would take to knock out the force field, and the protesters might take action against the hostages before we could remove them from jeopardy. More importantly, we're not within transporter range of Oyolo, which means we'd have to leave the buffer zone and proceed to Oyolo before we could launch an assault on the force field, which might also alert the protesters to our intentions. They could easily harm or move the hostages before we got into position."

"Forget it," Riley said, shaking his head. "Departing the buffer zone and going into orbit around Oyolo is simply not an option, diplomatically. That would be a deliberate incursion into Oyolu space and a clear violation of the terms of our peacekeeping mission."

The captain had to agree. "It's vital that we rescue the hostages, but we have to keep one eye on the big picture as well. We're here to stop a war, not start one."

Sulu sighed. "So I guess that rules out knocking out the whole vicinity with a wide-dispersal phaser blast, like we did that time on Iotia?"

"I'm afraid so," Riley said. "Even if we could get within firing range of Oyolo, I absolutely cannot sanction a Federation starship launching a phaser attack on the planet. There's no way the regrouping coalition government on Oyolo could regard that as anything except a brazen act of war."

"What about the Oyolu government?" Kirk asked. "Is what Ifusi said true, that we cannot expect them to rein in the protesters or take action to free the hostages?"

"That's a fair assessment," Riley confirmed. "According to my sources, there's a lot of support for the protesters, overt or otherwise, at every level of government, from global to municipal. Speaking frankly, we cannot trust the Oyolu authorities with whatever we're planning. They're just as likely to tip off the protesters as cooperate with us on any rescue operation."

"So we're on our own," Kirk said, "and sending in the *Enterprise* is off-limits."

Riley nodded. "That's the long and the short of it, yes."

"Then we're talking about a fast, surgical strike," Kirk said. "Get in, get the hostages, and get out, preferably without any serious casualties on either side." He looked at Riley. "That work for you, Ambassador?"

"The Oyolu government will doubtless protest any unilateral raid on their planet, but this may be a case where it's better to ask for forgiveness than permission." He smiled wryly at Kirk. "A strategy I learned from you, Captain, back in the day."

Kirk recalled his occasional bouts of insubordination, always for the best of reasons, of course. "I'm sure I have no idea what you're talking about, Ambassador."

Riley tactfully refrained from citing chapter and verse.

"If you are going to stage a rescue mission, Captain, I'd like to volunteer to take part." Riley squared his shoulders. "I know it's been a few years—more than a few, really—since I've had any combat duty, but—"

"I appreciate the offer, Ambassador, but no dice." Kirk had no doubts regarding Riley's abilities; as a Starfleet officer, Lieutenant Riley had proved himself on any number of landing parties in the past, but Kirk still shook his head. "You're too valuable to risk. The hostages are important, but so is our larger mission. We're going to need you to smooth things over if everything goes as planned . . . and even more so if it doesn't."

Riley grudgingly conceded the point. "There is that, I suppose."

"In fact," Kirk suggested, "maybe it would be more politic if you stepped outside as well. Plausible deniability and all that."

"Not a chance," Riley said firmly. He stared intently at the hostages on the screen. "Diplomacy has its limits. I'll stay behind, but I won't be kept in the dark."

"Fair enough," Kirk said. "Now we just need to settle on a plan, pronto."

Chekov scratched his head. "Perhaps if we create a distraction . . . ?"

"Please tell me you're not thinking about another fan dance," Uhura said, rolling her eyes at the memory. "I'm all for being a team player, but once was enough."

"That won't be necessary, Commander," Kirk assured her. Another plan was coming together in his mind as he contemplated the occupied arena on the screen. He turned toward Lenore. "How much can you tell me about that amphitheater?"

She looked back at him, her gaze steady.

"What do you need to know?"

Nineteen

The shuttlecraft descended through the cloudy night sky.

"This is the *Copernicus,* coming in for a landing," Sulu said, piloting the shuttle. "We are delivering the prisoner, Lenore Karidian."

"We read you, Starfleet," a sullen voice replied from the planet below. *"Proceed."*

Chekov listened attentively to the exchange as the shuttle touched down on a muddy field within walking distance of the occupied amphitheater. The landing site had been selected in advance as part of the arrangements to exchange Lenore for the hostages. Chekov turned to his companion, who was seated beside him in the passenger cabin, which they had entirely to themselves. In order to save room for the hostages, no other personnel had accompanied them on this mission. He glimpsed an armed mob waiting outside. Triumphant shouts and angry jeers greeted the shuttle's arrival.

"Are you sure you want to do this?" he asked her.

She tucked a loose blond hair into place and smoothed out the wrinkles in her practical civilian attire. For this role, she had donned a conservative tan suit and slacks. Despite a flicker of trepidation, determination showed in her hazel eyes. She rose from her seat like an actress preparing to make her entrance.

"It's too late to turn back now," she said. "Let's go meet my adoring public."

"Very well." Chekov braced himself for what was to come. A lot was riding on Captain Kirk's plan. It was crucial that they all played their parts to perfection. He headed for the exit. "I'll go first, as planned."

"Break a leg," she said.

Chekov did not find that expression particularly reassuring. He signaled Sulu and the starboard hatch slid open, letting in a gust of warm night air and another furious chorus of shouts and jeers. Dozens of irate Oyolu surrounded the shuttle, armed with everything from disruptor rifles to wooden planks studded with nails. Floodlights lit up the improvised landing site, practically blinding Chekov. He raised a hand to shield his eyes from the glare.

"That's my cue." Chekov nodded at Sulu. "Keep the motor running."

"Absolutely," Sulu promised. "Good luck."

We're going to need it, Chekov thought as he cautiously emerged from the shuttle, holding up empty hands to show that he came in peace. Per the agreements worked out earlier, he was completely unarmed, which did not make facing a hostile mob any easier on the nerves. Chekov swallowed hard. Despite his training and faith in the captain, he knew only too well the risks that such missions entailed; over the years, he had been on the receiving end of everything from plasma bolts to serious cranial fractures. Doctor McCoy sometimes kidded him about being an injury magnet, and job security for a ship's surgeon, but Chekov was in no hurry to end up in sickbay again—or worse.

Speaking of which, I wonder how the captain and the doctor are doing?

The door slid shut behind him. Bolstering his courage, Chekov strode forward to meet the mob. The thick mud squelched beneath his boots. He squinted into the glare of the floodlights.

W'Osoro waited at the forefront of the crowd. He eyed Chekov suspiciously, as though anticipating a trick. A disruptor was tucked into his belt, while a few dozen armed supporters backed him up. Chekov felt more than a little outnumbered.

"Name yourself, Starfleet."

"Commander Pavel Chekov of the U.S.S. *Enterprise.*" He kept his empty palms raised. "I have custody of the prisoner."

"Where is she?" W'Osoro demanded. "Give her to us."

Not so fast, Chekov thought. The captain's plan required him to drag this out. "Where are the hostages?" Looking past W'Osoro, he saw only an excess of angry Oyolu. "Let me see them, as a show of good faith, and we can proceed with the exchange."

"Good faith?" W'Osoro spit upon the ground. "Was Starfleet acting in good faith when it allowed the great A'Barra to be murdered aboard the *Enterprise*? And by your captain's maleficent lover?"

Chekov took offense at the fallacious attack on Captain Kirk's honor, but he managed to control his temper.

"Slander will not get us anywhere. Release just one prisoner."

W'Osoro's sour expression darkened, which Chekov would not have thought possible. He stomped his hoof impatiently.

"Do not think you can dictate terms to us. Give us Karidian now."

The crowd closed in menacingly, brandishing their weapons. Bellicose mutterings rippled through the mob, whose mood was getting uglier by the moment. Flushed yellow faces advertised the crowd's intentions. Hammers, shovels, picks, and machetes waited to be employed to bloody ends. Assessing the situation, Chekov concluded that he had stalled as long as he could. He needed to appease W'Osoro and his supporters before matters took a serious turn to the worse.

"No need for things to get unpleasant," he assured W'Osoro. Slowly lowering one hand, so as to avoid provoking the crowd, he took hold of his communicator and raised it to his lips. "Chekov to *Copernicus*. Send her out."

"*Copy that,*" Sulu said. "*Here she comes.*"

The hatch opened again and she stepped out into the light. Like Chekov before her, she held up her hands to show that she was unarmed. The crowd erupted in angry shouts and boos at the sight of her. Furious voices accused her of everything from cold-blooded murder to conspiring with Pavak. It was unclear which charge was considered most hateful.

"All right," she called out. "You want me? Here I am!"

The impatient mob surged forward to seize her. For a few heart-stopping moments, Chekov feared for the worse. Reports of wartime atrocities committed against both Pavakians and those accused of collaborating with them rushed through his mind. What if the crowd decided to exact vengeance for A'Barra's murder right here on the spot? Unarmed, there was little he could do to protect the defenseless target of their hate.

"Are you in control here?" he challenged W'Osoro. "Show me!"

W'Osoro's scowl deepened, but he raised his voice above the tumult.

"Bring the assassin forward!"

The crowd dragged its prisoner over to where Chekov and W'Osoro were standing. The Russian officer was relieved to see that the mob had not been too rough on her yet, but he wondered how much longer the aggrieved Oyolu would show such restraint. There were far too many agitated people—and too many weapons—in play for his liking. It was irrational, he knew, but he actually found the nail-studded planks and crude home weapons more disturbing than the phasers and disruptors. A nice clean energy beam struck him as preferable to blunt-force trauma. He tried to head off any such unpleasantness.

"There," he said. "We have fulfilled our end of the bargain. Please release the hostages into my custody."

"All in good time." W'Osoro examined his captive. "You are Lenore Karidian, alias Lyla Kassidy?"

"I am," she said.

"Daughter of Kodos the Executioner and foul poisoner of A'Barra?"

"Yes to the former. No to the latter." She projected her voice across the field. "I am innocent where the death of your revered leader is concerned. I have surrendered myself only out of concern for the safety of the hostages."

W'Osoro lifted her chin, the better to inspect her features.

"Hold a moment," he said suspiciously. "I saw you perform on this very stage, playing the sorceress in that Terran theatrical. You look different to me now."

She shrugged. "I am an actress. I play many parts."

He appeared unconvinced. He plucked a hand-held electronic device from his belt and called up the images of Lenore, past and present, that had recently been splashed all over the media of two worlds. His gaze shifted back and forth between the images on the device and the woman standing before him. Chekov shifted uncomfortably.

"I assure you," Chekov said. "This *is* Lenore Karidian, just as you requested."

"Prove it." W'Osoro crossed his arms atop his chest. "Recite your lines from the play."

She balked at the command. "Now is hardly the time for Shakespeare, and I'm not remotely in character."

"The lines," he demanded. "Speak the lines . . . now."

"I'm not sure I remember them exactly."

"After only a few days?" W'Osoro asked skeptically. "I find that hard to believe. And it is my understanding that *The Tempest* is regarded as a timeless classic among your people. Are you truly asserting that the part has slipped your mind entirely?"

"You try reciting Shakespeare when you're surrounded by an angry mob," she shot back, "not to mention falsely accused of murder. My mind is not exactly on literature at the moment!"

"I do not have to prove my identity," W'Osoro said. "You do."

She looked to Chekov, who had little help to offer her. "This cross-examination is uncalled for," he protested. "I insist that you release the hostages without further delay."

"Silence!" W'Osoro drew his phaser pistol and aimed it directly at Chekov's face. "No more stalling. If you are indeed Karidian, let us have an encore at once . . . or your Starfleet escort will pay for your silence."

"All right, all right," she said. "Let's not do anything hasty." She took a deep breath and furrowed her brow in concentration, as though racking her mind for some immortal passage or soliloquy. "Um, to be or not to be . . ."

Chekov groaned inside. W'Osoro's eyes bulged and his face curdled in rage.

"Oh, hell," Lieutenant Banks said, letting her native accent out of hiding. She shrugged. "What can I say? I'm no Shakespeare buff. Always more of a Tennessee Williams fan, actually."

"Imposter!" W'Osoro grabbed onto her blond locks and yanked the wig from her head. He hurled the offending hairpiece into the mud at his feet. "What manner of trickery is this?"

"Unsuccessful?" Chekov ventured.

He had hoped that the two women would look roughly the same to the Oyolu, but apparently a wig, contact lenses, and an assumed accent had not been enough to pass Debra Banks off as Lenore Karidian for long. *Just our luck that W'Osoro has a good eye for faces.*

"Sorry, Commander," Banks apologized. "I thought I could pull it off."

"Nothing to apologize for, Lieutenant. Truth to tell, I don't know *The Tempest* by heart either. Now Pushkin, on the other hand . . ."

"Still your lying tongues," W'Osoro barked. "Seize them both!"

Oyolu protesters took hold of Chekov, confiscating his communicator. Rough hands searched them both for hidden weapons and found the communicator in Banks's boot. Chekov could only imagine what Sulu had to be thinking as he watched this scene unfold from the relative safety of the shuttle. It had to be killing Sulu not to rush to their rescue, despite the odds against him.

Well, we wanted a distraction, Chekov thought. *Here's hoping this does the trick.*

At least he wasn't sneezing anymore.

Several minutes earlier.

"Ten thousand meters and counting, Captain," Sulu reported from the helm as the *Copernicus* descended through the planet's atmosphere toward the continent below. Kirk estimated that they were only minutes away from the bombed-out city where the hostages were being held. In theory, W'Osoro and his protesters were waiting for them outside the captured amphitheater.

"Thank you, Mister Sulu."

Kirk was seated in the passenger cabin with the rest of the rescue team, which consisted of three armed security officers and one uneasy ship's surgeon. Every member of the team, including Kirk, wore heavy-duty field uniforms comprised of a sturdy sweater, matching pants, and boots. Kirk's gear was a dark matte green, while the other personnel wore brown. A pair of safety goggles hung around his neck. Lemon-yellow face paint and prosthetic horns disguised their non-Oyolu origins in order to help them avoid detection if spotted. The horns itched where they were glued to Kirk's brow, but that was the least of his worries.

"Get ready, everyone," he said. "We're approaching our insertion point."

The team was small by design. This mission was about speed and stealth, not strength of numbers. And, should everything go as planned, they would need room in the shuttlecraft to transport the rescued hostages. As is, it was going to be a tight squeeze.

"I can't believe you talked me into this," McCoy said, shaking his head. "I'm getting too old for this kind of thing."

"It's not too late to back out, Bones." Kirk nodded at one of the security officers. "Lieutenant Del Gaizo is fully trained in field medicine."

"Forget it. If you're going to insist on these daredevil stunts, you'd better have a real doctor along. No offense, Del Gaizo." McCoy double-checked to make sure his medkit was securely strapped over his shoulder. "And those hostages may require medical attention as well."

"It's good you're coming along then," Kirk said. "And, for the record, I'm not getting any younger myself, but don't think that's going to stop me from freeing those hostages."

"That's the spirit, Captain," Chekov said from the front of the cabin, where he was seated with Lieutenant Banks, who had been hastily done up to resemble Lenore. Kirk took a moment to reexamine the woman's disguise, which he hoped would fool the protesters below, at least for a while. Lenore had personally applied the woman's makeup, covering up Banks's natural freckles and doing what she could to heighten the resemblance. A wig and contact lenses added to the illusion. Kirk, who knew Lenore's face better than most, wasn't deceived, but maybe the disguise was good enough to buy them some precious time?

That was the plan at least.

"Thank you for volunteering for this mission, Lieutenant," he told Banks. "Your courage is to be commended."

"Hey, I always liked playing dress-up as a kid," she said breezily. "Whatever it takes to help the hostages."

"I couldn't agree with you more." Kirk was proud of Chekov and Banks, who were about to walk unarmed into the lion's den. Duty or not, he considered that above and beyond. "Good luck, both of you. Be careful. Don't take any unnecessary risks."

"You're a fine one to talk," McCoy muttered.

"Belay that, Doctor. I'm trying to deliver a pep talk here."

"Good luck to you as well," Chekov said. "See you soon . . . I hope."

If all goes well, Kirk thought.

"Insertion point in approximately one minute," Sulu called back to them.

The team gathered at the rear of the shuttle before the aft hatchway, while Chekov and Banks remained strapped in their seats. Kirk positioned his goggles over his eyes. At his signal, the hatch dropped open and a roaring wind invaded the pressurized atmosphere of the shuttle. The wind buffeted Kirk as he shouted above it.

"This is where we get off!"

He took the lead, throwing himself out of the shuttle into the night sky. Despite the seriousness of their mission, Kirk found the high-altitude jump exhilarating. Gravity seized him and the wind whipped past his face as he free-fell for several moments, plunging toward the surface of the planet, before, somewhat reluctantly, activating his levitation boots.

The boosters ignited, halting his precipitous descent. Computerized gyros responded to even subtle bodily movements, allowing him to control his flight. He hovered in the air, more than a thousand meters above the planet, to get his bearings.

High overhead, the *Copernicus* veered off toward the prearranged site for prisoner exchange. With any luck, this mid-air insertion would go undetected by anyone tracking the shuttlecraft. He silently wished Chekov and the others a smooth flight and success carrying out their end of the mission.

This is going to take good timing and teamwork on all our parts.

Glancing back over his shoulder, he saw the rest of the team falling into formation behind him. McCoy needed a few moments to get the hang of navigating in the boots, darting about erratically like a malfunctioning anti-grav lifter, but he eventually stabilized his flight, more or less. Kirk took comfort from the knowledge that the viridium patches sewn into their field uniforms would allow them to track one another, or even be located by the shuttlecraft's sensors, should they get separated.

Here we go, he thought.

Kirk leaned forward and the boots responded to the motion, propelling him through the sky at high speed, with McCoy and the others right behind him. Night-vision lenses in his goggles allowed him to scope out the war-torn landscape hundreds of meters below. Bomb craters, collapsed structures, and charred rubble testified to the brutal toll decades of war had taken on this region. Navigational programs compared the view to Uhura's aerial surveillance to ensure they were flying in the right direction. Kirk deliberately skirted populated areas, sticking to less habitable wastelands, in order to avoid detection. They jetted low above the ground, zipping over and sometimes through shattered skyscrapers and towering heaps of debris until they arrived at their destination.

The abandoned cemetery lay on the outskirts of the ruined city. Fallen gates and demolished monuments confirmed that the graveyard had been forgotten and fallen into ruin and neglect. No lights illuminated the untended grounds, which had been taken over by weeds and creeping vines. No tributes, floral or otherwise, graced the toppled stone markers. If there had ever been a night watchman to guard the cemetery, those days were long gone . . . just as Lenore had promised. She had suggested that the decaying cemetery would be free of inconvenient onlookers, especially after dark, and Uhura's eyes in the sky had verified her description of the site.

So far, so good, Kirk thought.

The team touched down in the cemetery, cooling their rockets. Kirk did a quick head count to ensure that they hadn't lost anyone. McCoy looked happy to be back on solid ground again. "You still with us, Bones?"

"You bet I am," McCoy groused, "no thanks to these infernal boots. If *homo sapiens* was meant to fly, he would have been born a Betelgeusian."

Kirk grinned. Clearly, his friend's cantankerous attitude had come through the flight intact. "Come on, Bones. Where's your sense of adventure?"

"Adventure?" McCoy said, exasperated. He stared at Kirk accusingly. "I should have known. You *enjoyed* that, didn't you?"

Kirk didn't deny it. "You're the one who used to say that I didn't belong behind a desk."

"I didn't mean that you should go jumping out of a speeding shuttle!"

The banter was good for morale, but they needed to hustle if they wanted to rescue the hostages before daybreak. They shed their levitation boots in the interests of stealth and stowed them amid the weeds just in case they found their way back here again. Night-vision led them to a crumbling limestone mausoleum that appeared more structurally sound than its demolished companions. A heavy stone door refused to budge, so Kirk vaporized it with a blast from his phaser. The glow from the beam briefly illuminated the gloomy interior of the crypt before darkness claimed it once more. A gaping maw opened before them.

"This keeps getting better and better," McCoy grumbled. "Why am I having flashbacks to Pyris Seven?"

"You surprise me, Bones," Kirk said. "I never took you for the superstitious type."

"Who said anything about ghosts? It's the rats and spiders I'm not looking forward to."

Kirk shrugged. "Maybe they don't have those lifeforms on this planet?"

"Yeah, we should be so lucky," McCoy said.

Kirk led the way into the murky crypt, which held two matching stone sarcophagi. Despite his optimism, some manner of cobwebs hung from the ceiling while furtive vermin scurried away from the invaders. Desiccated skeletons and mummies, some more intact than others, occupied niches in the walls, while fallen bones littered the floor. A thick layer of dust and soot coated every surface. Kirk assumed the ash had blown in from the fires of war and terrorism. Ignoring the twin tombs, Kirk scanned the floor with a tricorder. The sensors detected a hidden stairway beneath a paving stone at the rear of the crypt. A steel ring was attached to the stone to make it easier to lift.

"Here we are," he declared.

He was tempted to disintegrate the stone as he had the door, but was reluctant to desecrate the forgotten crypt more than they already had. Instead two sturdy security officers, Quinn and Assik, used their old-fashioned muscle power to heft the stone out of the way, exposing dusty steps leading down beneath the cemetery. A musty smell emanated from the stygian depths. Something skittered away from the noise. Dry bones rattled.

Kirk was not surprised to find the steps. According to Lenore, an extensive network of underground catacombs, tunnels, and sewers ran beneath the city, dating back long before the war and the arrival of the early Pavakian traders. Lenore had read about the catacombs while prepping for her volunteer work on Oyolo; for better or for worse, mass graves and other melancholy topics held a certain fascination for her, no doubt because so much of her past and family history was steeped in violent death. She was sometimes drawn, she had confessed, to reminders of mortality.

Her morbid streak had served to their advantage when planning the rescue mission. With luck, the subterranean tunnels would provide a covert route into the city and perhaps even the lower levels of the occupied amphitheater. Even homeless Oyolu supposedly shunned the dismal catacombs, which were widely believed to be haunted as well as dank, unsanitary, and infested with vermin. Gazing down into the unwelcoming shadows, Kirk could see why the Oyolu would prefer to leave such places to the dead.

"I don't know about you," McCoy said, giving the dusty stairs a dubious look, "but I'm starting to wish I had traded places with Chekov."

Kirk feared Chekov and Banks would not feel the same way. Wasting no time, he headed down into the catacombs, counting on his tricorder—and the viridium patches in their fellow officers' attire—to guide their way. His goggles revealed crumbling tunnels lined with funeral niches stretching off into the distance. Cobwebs hung like curtains, shrouding the way ahead. Something crunched beneath his boots. He hoped it was a bone and not a largish insect.

"Step lively," he told the others. "We've got a date at the theater."

Looks like the jig is up, Sulu thought.

He watched with concern from the cockpit of the *Copernicus* as the angry mob outside seized Chekov and Banks. It appeared that the Oyolu had seen through Banks's disguise even faster than anticipated. This was worrisome, but not entirely unexpected. Nobody had ever thought that the proposed exchange would take place without a snag. That was what the rescue mission was all about.

Cries of rage penetrated the shuttlecraft's hull. Outraged by the deception, the surrounding mob charged the shuttle from all directions, intent on capturing the

Copernicus. Energy beams, rocks, and even frenzied bodies bounced off the shuttle's force field, producing bursts of bright blue Cherenkov radiation whenever a threat collided against the shields. Given time, the assault might actually wear down the shuttle's defenses, but Sulu wasn't going to stick around to find out.

Time to go, he realized.

He activated the thrusters on both sides of the shuttle. The landing gear lifted off from the mud as he executed a vertical takeoff in order to avoid slamming into anyone. Determined Oyolu threw themselves at the *Copernicus,* frantic to keep it from taking off, only to be repelled by the deflectors. They splashed down into the mud beneath the escaping shuttle. Within minutes, the craft was high above the ruined parklands, out of reach of the rioters.

Which didn't do Chekov or Banks any good.

Sulu watched from above as the Oyolu dragged his captured crewmates toward the occupied amphitheater. For the moment at least, the protesters had two more hostages.

"Damn."

Sulu hated leaving his friends behind. The *Copernicus* had its own phaser banks, with enough firepower to possibly stun the entire mob into submission, but Sulu held his fire. As Captain Kirk had stressed before, their mission was not to wage war on the protesters. Sulu had no choice but to let the mob have Chekov and Banks for the present. He had his orders.

But that didn't mean he had to like it.

The *Copernicus* took off over Oyolo, circling above the area below at a high altitude. He took cover among the clouds, cruising through the enveloping mists while navigating primarily by sensors. It was actually a beautiful night to be flying through the atmosphere. He could have enjoyed the flight, if not for the dire circumstances and the knowledge that his shipmates were at risk.

Now for the hard part, he thought. *Waiting.*

A chime alerted him that the *Copernicus* was being hailed. Sulu wondered what had taken them so long. He pressed a control to respond.

"This is the *Copernicus*," he said, "responding to your signal."

"Oyolu Air Command to Starfleet shuttlecraft," a voice replied. *"Your presence in our sovereign airspace is not authorized. You are ordered to land at the nearest military airbase. The coordinates are being transmitted to you on this signal."*

"Uh-huh," Sulu muttered quietly to himself. "Not going to happen."

Even if the Oyolu authorities could be trusted, which was dicey at best, he couldn't afford to be tied up dealing with bureaucratic hassles, not when the captain and the others were depending on him to extract them when the time came.

"What's that, Air Command?" he said, feigning communication difficulties. "I can't read you." He scrambled the frequencies to interfere with the transmission. "I'm experiencing technical issues."

Bursts of static fragmented the incoming transmission.

"*Zzzt—unauthorized—zzzzt—repeat—zzzzt—surrender—*"

"I'm sorry," Sulu said. "You're breaking up. . . ."

He cut off the hail altogether, preferring his own thoughts to orders it was better to pretend he hadn't heard. He doubted that the Oyolu authorities had bought his "technical issues" story, but at least he had provided Ambassador Riley with a fig leaf to hide behind if and when the diplomats had their say on the matter. At the moment, Sulu was more concerned with just how far the Oyolu would go to defend their airspace—and how the rescue team was faring on the ground. Back on the *Enterprise,* Uhura was monitoring communications on Oyolo. If Captain Kirk and his team were captured along with Chekov and Banks, she was to alert Sulu immediately.

No news is good news, he thought. *I hope.*

Twenty

"Are we there yet?" McCoy asked. "Not that this hasn't been a delightful stroll, but . . ."

A brisk march had taken them from the moldering catacombs to a labyrinthine tangle of dilapidated sewers and utility tunnels beneath the devastated city. A foul stench permeated the unlit tunnels as they made their way through fallen rubble and pools of stagnant water. Slime coated the grimy stone walls. Water dripped from the ceiling. Along the way, they had encountered insects, reptiles, and some "interesting" combinations thereof, but no lurking Oyolu, which was good enough for Kirk. As scenic hikes went, however, he preferred Yosemite.

"Almost," he promised. "I think."

He consulted his tricorder again. It would be easy enough to get lost in this subterranean maze, especially since they'd occasionally had to detour around collapsed tunnels and gaping pits, but the tricorder's navigational programs had kept them on track. Filmy cobwebs clung to his field uniform as he approached a moldy brick wall at the dead end of a side tunnel. His boots splashed through a greasy, scum-slick puddle. In theory, their objective was on the opposite side of the wall.

"This should be it," the captain announced. He used the tricorder to scan beyond the wall. He was not as adept as translating the readings as Spock would have been, but he didn't pick up any humanoid life-forms directly ahead. "Doesn't seem like there's anybody on the other side."

"Thank heaven for small favors," McCoy said. "Maybe the fates are actually on our side?"

Knock on wood, Kirk thought. His phaser was set on disrupt so he pulled the trigger. A brilliant blue glow briefly lit up the tunnel as Kirk carved an opening through the brick wall, dissolving its constituent parts into atoms. Concerned with the wall's structural integrity, he made the doorway as narrow as possible while trying to avoid anything that looked too load-bearing; the last thing they needed was the din of a collapsing wall attracting unwanted attention. Kirk held his breath as the glow faded to expose the chamber beyond. He caught a glimpse of a darkened sub-basement cluttered with random crates and storage containers, sparse racks of threadbare costumes, and theatrical props.

Bingo, Kirk thought.

As anticipated, the tunnels abutted the hidden dressing rooms and storage areas beneath the occupied amphitheater. Lenore had mapped the sub-levels back

on the *Enterprise* and Kirk had committed the map to
his own memory as well as the tricorder's. Scouting out
the basement, it appeared that they were about three
levels below the outdoor stage where the hostages were
being held. Kirk listened closely, but he couldn't hear
any voices filtering down from above them. He imagined that the lower levels were probably soundproofed
to some degree in order to prevent any activity down-
stairs from disturbing the performances onstage. He
tugged on the collar of his white turtleneck undershirt;
it was uncomfortably hot and stuffy in the confined
spaces, not to mention musty, which he hoped would
discourage any of the protesters from seeking shelter
down here. He was already sweating through his sturdy
green sweater. Perspiration threatened to make his yellow makeup run.

*Let's hope those horns stay in place, just a little while
longer.*

Kirk switched his phaser to stun. Weapons in hand,
the rescue team crept into the apparently deserted
basement. Their night-vision goggles allowed them to
scope out the area as they advanced cautiously through
a warren of dark storerooms and cramped, narrow hall-
ways. Kirk noted that the assorted costumes and props
were fairly worn and cheaply constructed; he guessed
that anything remotely practical had been looted long
before. Prospero's wizardly cloak hung forgotten upon
a hook; it was hard to believe that only days had passed
since he had been startled to find Lenore on Oyolo.

Now her future, innocence, and sanity were all very much in doubt.

We're depending heavily on intel provided by someone who may or may not still be a ruthless killer.

Kirk pushed the troubling thought out of his mind. He couldn't afford to worry about Lenore's true nature right now. He needed to keep his wits about him and concentrate on the task at hand: liberating the hostages without initiating a bloodbath. A "grove" of lightweight prop palm trees, left over from *The Tempest,* packed the next compartment. A full-sized replica of a sailing ship's wheel was propped up against one wall. Kirk winded his way through the theatrical clutter in search of the stairs to the next level.

They found company instead.

An amorous Oyolu couple had sought privacy below the theater. Pressed up against a wall by her preoccupied male companion, the woman gasped out loud as Kirk and the strike force inadvertently walked in on them. It was debatable who was the most startled.

"Wait!" she shouted, shoving her lover away. "Behind you!"

Furious at the interruption, the male wheeled about and charged at the intruders. In the dim lighting, it was possible that he had been deceived by their Oyolu disguises and not yet grasped their true nature. Nevertheless, Kirk realized instantly that he needed to nip this awkward encounter in the bud before either the man or the woman could raise an alarm.

"Sorry," he said. "Wrong place, wrong time."

Phaser beams stunned first the man, then the woman, who dropped to the dusty floor of the sub-basement. Kirk felt a surge of relief.

That could have been a lot—

A turquoise beam shot from the shadows, dropping Del Gaizo, who hit the floor hard. Kirk spun around to see a *third* Oyolu standing at the bottom of a ladder up ahead. His eyes were wide with mixed shock and anger and a small disruptor was gripped in his hand. Had he come looking for the missing couple or had he been hoping to join the festivities? Kirk didn't know or care. Only one thing mattered now.

"Take cover!" Kirk ordered, ducking behind the sturdy ship's wheel. "But don't let him get away!"

Realizing he was outnumbered, the Oyolu turned back toward the ladder, but a blast from Kirk's phaser disintegrated the lower rungs, cutting off his escape. Desperate, the man dived into the grove of artificial trees, seeking cover as well. He fired out from behind one of the tree trunks. A turquoise beam shot above Kirk's head.

Damn! Kirk thought. They didn't have time for an extended firefight, but he didn't want to seriously injure the trapped Oyolu by blasting straight through the prop trees with a phaser beam at full power. Thinking fast, Kirk decided to rely on gravity instead.

Darting out from behind the wheel, while McCoy and the others provided a degree of cover, he slammed his shoulder into the nearest prop tree, causing it to topple over into the others. The ersatz palms fell like dominoes, burying the unfortunate Oyolu and knocking him to the floor. In time, no doubt, the man could have shoved the lightweight props aside, but Kirk and the others didn't give him a chance. Multiple stun-beams converged on the trapped Oyolu, rendering him senseless.

Kirk wiped his brow, sweating from the exertion.

"Del Gaizo?" he asked.

McCoy was already checking on the fallen crew-man. "Just stunned," the doctor reported. "But I assume we can't just let him sleep it off?"

"Negative," Kirk said. Lugging the unconscious security officer around on a covert mission was not an option any more than leaving him behind was. "Do what you have to to rouse him."

McCoy nodded. "I'm going to have to risk a heavy dose of stimulant." He loaded a hypospray. "Just a smidgen of cordrazine should get him back on his feet, although he's going to have a doozy of a head-ache later on."

Beats becoming another hostage, Kirk thought. He looked on as McCoy applied the hypospray to Del Gaizo's neck. The man's eyes snapped open and he sat upright with a jolt. "Hey! What the—?"

"Easy, Lieutenant," McCoy said. "You're going to be okay."

For now. Kirk grimly contemplated the trio of

stunned Oyolu. That had been too close. They couldn't risk another chance encounter. *We need to pick up the pace if we're going to maintain the element of surprise.*

Relying on Lenore's map, they ascended a spiral staircase to the staging area directly below the stage, which was thankfully unoccupied. Kirk located the wall-mounted control panel governing the stage effects. The touch-sensitive controls appeared fairly user-friendly, complete with pictorial icons indicating the function of various controls: lighting, sound, and so on.

Just like Lenore described, Kirk thought. *Perhaps we can trust her . . . this far at least.*

He used the tricorder to scan for the viridium patches worn by Chekov and Banks. According to the readout, the courageous officers were directly above them, possibly with the rest of the hostages. Sensor readings, along with echoing footsteps, also indicated the presence of several other humanoids one level up. Those were presumably the armed protesters holding the hostages captive. With any luck, they weren't expecting what Kirk had in mind.

"Over here, Bones," Kirk whispered as he turned the control panel over to McCoy. "You up to playing stage manager?"

"I'm a doctor, not a . . . oh, why do I bother?" McCoy got into position. "You can count on me, Jim."

Kirk figured that if McCoy could perform complicated surgical procedures on a wide variety of sentient species, he could operate the computerized control panel, especially after Lenore had briefed them on how it worked. Kirk signaled the alert security officers to get into position.

"Take your marks, people. It's showtime."

"You wanted to see the hostages?" W'Osoro asked, sneering at Chekov. "Join them!"

Dragged roughly onto the stage by their captors, Chekov and Banks were thrown in with the other prisoners, who reacted with surprise to the new arrivals. Armed guards patrolled the elevated bleachers circling the stage, which was also occupied by a large number of protesters who were not at all happy that A'Barra's alleged assassin remained beyond their grasp. Verbal attacks had yet to turn physical, but it struck Chekov as only a matter of time.

"What's this all about?" Doctor Tamris asked, leaping to her feet. Recognizing her from their surveillance of the hostages, Chekov was glad to see that she appeared more disheveled than abused. She stared in confusion at the new prisoners. Her antennae twitched. "What's happening?"

"Lies and chicanery!" W'Osoro snarled. "It seems Starfleet would rather play games than bargain fairly for your safety." He glowered at Chekov and Banks. "Is that not so, Starfleet?"

Chekov shrugged. "It seemed like a good idea at the time."

Despite his casual retort, the security chief realized

that their situation was perilous in the extreme. He and Banks were surrounded by an angry mob who had just been cheated of its prize and the people in the mob looked as though they wanted to take out their frustration on the nearest convenient target, which, in this case, would be the two defenseless Starfleet officers. The possibility of violence hung in the air like a swarm of voracious Denevan parasites. It wouldn't take much, Chekov guessed, to bring the wrath of the crowd down on top of them.

Maybe I am unlucky, he thought.

"This is no laughing matter, Starfleet." W'Osoro's hand rested on the grip of his holstered disruptor. "Understand me, these unfortunates," he said, gesturing at the other hostages, "are owed some mercy for their generous aid to my people. Their only crime, as far as we know, is unknowingly harboring a viper in their midst. But you and your captain are deliberately shielding A'Barra's killer . . . and may have even conspired to have him assassinated aboard your ship!"

"That's not true!" Chekov protested. "We are doing our best to find out who is responsible for the deaths of Minister A'Barra and General Tem."

"Tem?" W'Osoro spat at Chekov's feet. "What do we care who executed the Scourge of Azoza, aside from wanting to commend them on a job well done? A'Barra's death is all that concerns us. How is it that he came to be murdered upon your vessel? Did the Pavakians put you up to it?"

"Commander Chekov is telling you the truth," Banks blurted. "I wish we could give you the answers you want, but we're still trying to solve the mystery ourselves."

"There is no mystery! The whole system knows who killed A'Barra, just as she and her father killed so many others. Lenore Karidian, the notorious assassin you brazenly pretended to be." He wheeled about angrily to confront Banks. "And who are you, imposter, since you are obviously not as valuable to Captain Kirk as his precious Karidian?"

"Lieutenant Debra Banks of the *U.S.S. Enterprise*," she answered. "I wish I could say that I was pleased to make your acquaintance, but that would be a violation of my Starfleet honor code."

Chekov admired her spirit, if not her tact or instinct for self-preservation. Her flippant response went over about as well as could be expected, which was to say not at all. W'Osoro drew his weapon from its holster and jammed its muzzle up beneath her chin.

"You mock me? Mock our desire for justice?" He was practically shaking with rage. "Perhaps your captain will take our demands more seriously if we send you back to him minus your head."

"Wait!" Chekov shouted, eager to reclaim W'Osoro's attention. "I am the commanding officer here. I take full responsibility for the deception . . . and our failure so far to bring A'Barra's murderer to justice."

"Very well then, Starfleet commander." W'Osoro turned his weapon on Chekov instead. His patience exhausted, he seemed on the verge of exploding like an overloading disruptor. "Perhaps it is you we should make an example of."

"W'Osoro, hold!" A female Oyolu burst from the crowd. Her horns were smaller and less elaborate than the males'. They sprouted like thorns from her brow, giving her a devilish appearance. "Think before you act. This is not what we agreed. We want Karidian, not more senseless killing!"

Chekov was relieved to hear a voice of reason among the protesters. The unnamed woman sounded genuinely concerned that W'Osoro's temper might lead him to do something rash.

You and me both, Chekov thought.

"Stay out of this, Enune!" W'Osoro snapped at her. "We gave them a chance to settle this without bloodshed, but they chose trickery instead. Perhaps, like the Pavakians, Starfleet responds only to demonstrations of force!"

"But is that what A'Barra would have wanted? Executing hostages in his name?" She took hold of W'Osoro's gun arm, attempting to restrain him. "Calm yourself. We need to think about this."

He yanked his arm free of her grip. "The time for calm has passed. Justice for A'Barra can be delayed and denied no longer. We must show the galaxy that our demands cannot be taken lightly, nor can we be treated as fools. If Starfleet blood must be spilled to avenge the Defender, so be it!"

"No!" Enune got between W'Osoro and the hostage. "You're not thinking straight. I can't let you do this!"

"Out of my way, Enune!" He waved his weapon in her direction. "This is for A'Barra!"

"Are you sure about that? Or is this about your own ego and bitterness?"

Chekov considered joining the debate, but he decided it might be better to keep his mouth shut and hope that the cooler head prevailed. He signaled Banks to keep quiet as well. More Oyolu joined the argument, shouting loudly over one another as they debated what to do with their new prisoners. Enune's more measured approach seemed to be in the minority, but Chekov was glad to discover that the crowd was not entirely unanimous in its desires for his immediate demise— and that the chain of command among the protesters was somewhat less than ironclad. Everyone seemed to have an opinion.

"Kill them both," someone argued. "And a hostage every hour until Kirk gives in!"

"Are you mad?" another Oyolu argued. "Then the *Enterprise* will launch a full-scale attack . . . and we'll never get the Karidian woman!"

"Coward! *Someone* has to pay for A'Barra's murder. Why not these two?"

The consensus seemed to be turning against them. Chekov wondered where Kirk and the rescue team were. If the strike force was waiting for a distraction, they couldn't ask for a better one.

Now would be good, Captain.

The tempest struck without warning. Artificial thunder and lightning shook the stage, catching both captors and captives by surprise. Shifting lights created the illusion of storm-tossed seas, adding to the chaos. Startled gasps and exclamations interrupted the heated debate, competing with the roar of crashing waves. Disoriented, the guards in the bleachers looked about in confusion, unsure what had triggered the storm. Only Chekov and Banks knew what the illusory storm heralded. A grin broke out across Chekov's face.

The cavalry was here.

"Duck!" he shouted to Banks. "Keep your head down!"

All at once, Kirk and crew shot up from below, propelled onto the stage by trapdoors previously used to launch airy spirits into view. Taking advantage of the confusion, the strike force fired stun-beams at the startled Oyolu, who were still trying to grasp what exactly was happening. The four-person team made every shot count, taking out the nearest threats immediately. Stunned bodies crashed to the floor of the stage, the thudding impact drowned out by the amplified roar of the tempest. The snipers in the bleachers hesitated, reluctant to fire into the chaotic scene, where blinding thunderbolts and rippling lightning effects made targeting the intruders a challenge.

Kirk lobbed a spare phaser to Chekov, who eagerly

plucked it out of the air. "Hope we didn't keep you waiting, Commander."

"No, Captain!" Chekov opened fire on the Oyolu, even as Banks claimed a weapon as well. "Excellent timing, sir!"

Twenty-One

Momentum was on their side. Kirk wanted to keep it that way.

Turbulence, both real and simulated, consumed the stage. Energy beams, flashing alongside the mock lightning, took any number of Oyolu hostiles out of the picture. Phaser firing, Kirk was pleased to see Chekov and Banks joining the fracas, adding to the strike force's numbers. Locating the hostages, Kirk made his way across the stage toward Tamris and her fellow prisoners.

But W'Osoro got there first. Drawing a disruptor from his belt, he came up behind Tamris and placed the muzzle of the weapon against the back of her head. "Stay back!" he shouted at Kirk. "Drop your weapons or I will vaporize her skull!"

His attention was fixed on Kirk, which proved a mistake. All but ignored by her captor, Tamris raised her arms as though to surrender, but then spun around and knocked W'Osoro's gun arm aside with one arm while delivering a substantial chop to his throat with the other. The weapon went off, but the lethal beam shot harmlessly into the air, even as Tamris deftly hooked her leg behind his knee and, executing a flawless takedown, swept him off his feet. W'Osoro toppled backward, smacking his head against the stage, and the Andorian made sure he stayed down with a series of rapid-fire strikes to his head. He moaned weakly, barely conscious, as she claimed his disruptor.

Kirk was impressed and surprised by the way the Andorian handled herself. "Not your first free-for-all, Doctor?"

"I used to be a mercenary," she explained, "before I saw the error of my ways."

Watching her open fire on the Oyolu, Kirk could believe it. *Looks like Lenore's not the only relief worker atoning for her past.*

Not that he was complaining; they could use all the help they could get. Inspired by Tamris's example, the Horta surged forward like a living wall of red-hot lava. Alarmed Oyolu fired wildly at Jorgaht, but the beams barely scratched his dense silicon-based hide. Steam rose as he left a trail of charred flooring behind him. Acid sizzled in his wake.

"A wicked dew drop on you all!" a gravelly voice issued from Horta's universal translator, threatening his former captors in the words of Caliban. "'A south-west blow on ye and blister you all o'er!'"

Nearby Oyolu fled in panic from the oncoming alien. Although ordinarily a peaceful people, a Horta could incinerate flesh and bone as easily as it bored through solid rock. Kirk had no idea if Jorgaht was bluffing or not, but he couldn't blame the terrified Oyolu for choosing the better part of valor when faced with an angry Horta protecting his friends and colleagues.

Hell hath no fury, Kirk thought, *like a devil in the dark.*

A trapdoor opened in the floor, revealing a stairway leading down beneath the stage. Kirk recognized it as the same passage Prospero and Miranda had used to make their entrances and exits a few nights ago. Mc-Coy's head popped up in the entrance to the "cave" below.

"Over here!" Bones called out. "Get a move on, will you. We haven't got all night!"

"You heard the doctor!" Kirk ordered. "Everybody down below, pronto!"

Taking the initiative, Chekov hustled Tamris and her fellow hostages down the stairs, while Kirk, Banks, and the rest of the strike force provided cover for their retreat. Rallying, the remaining Oyolu began to fire back, but Kirk ducked behind Jorgaht, using the Horta's lumpy impervious form as a shield. Sizzling energy beams crisscrossed the stage, sometimes bouncing off Jorgaht, even as the theatrical tempest raged all around them. Frantic guards fired from the bleachers, only to be dropped by expert shots from Banks and the other trained security officers. Kirk was impressed by Banks's marksmanship.

"Nice shooting, Lieutenant," Kirk congratulated her.

"Thanks, sir." She stunned another sniper with a well-placed phaser beam. "These folks are more angry than expert. Makes 'em easy pickings!"

Kirk waited until the last of the humanoid hostages had vanished down the stairs, before signaling Banks and the others to follow. Crouching low, they scrambled for the entrance, with Jorgaht right behind them. Eschewing the stairs, the Horta burned straight through the stage to drop like a meteorite onto the floor one level below. The impact rattled the rafters.

"That everyone?" McCoy shouted from the control panel.

"Yes," Tamris replied, keeping tracking of her people. "Thank you so much, Captain!"

"Don't thank me yet."

Kirk nodded at McCoy, who closed the trapdoor shut behind them. A blast from Kirk's phaser disintegrated the stairs for good measure, just to discourage pursuit. He doubted that such measures would delay the Oyolu for long. According to Lenore, there were any number of ways on and off the stage. Speed was of the essence if they wanted to make a clean getaway.

"This way," he said. "Follow me."

Encountering no resistance—yet—they hurried down through the theater's sub-basements and into the fetid tunnels beyond. None of the hostages objected to the stomach-turning stench; after several hours in captivity, they didn't smell too fresh themselves. For a few moments, Kirk allowed himself to hope that they might be able to retrace their steps all the way back to the abandoned cemetery, but then he started to round a corner and a sizzling red energy beam shot past his head, blasting the tip off one of his prosthetic horns. He ducked back behind the corner.

"Watch out!" he warned. "We have company."

Furious voices and footsteps could be heard rushing toward them through the tunnels ahead, even as Kirk heard more Oyolu charging after them from behind. Somebody had obviously figured out what the rescue team was up to and had called in reinforcements. From the sound of things, the fugitives were only moments away from being up to their ears in furious Oyolu, and the way ahead was no longer a viable escape route.

"They're after us coming and going," McCoy muttered. "Any bright ideas on how we're going to get out of this?"

"Yes, actually." Kirk beckoned to Jorgaht, who scuttled up beside him. An acidic odor emanated from the Horta. "We need another way out of here. Think you can oblige us?"

The Horta's laugh sounded like an avalanche. "Can a human move through air?"

Kirk backed away, giving Jorgaht space, as the Horta rotated at a right angle and burrowed straight into a solid stone wall, carving a new tunnel to the surface. Kirk gave the steaming edges of the tunnel a few moments to cool before herding everyone else into the newly formed passage. He plucked his communicator from his belt.

"Kirk to *Copernicus*. We have the hostages. We're going to need that extraction."

"*Copy that*," Sulu responded. "*On my way.*"

Once again, they were relying on the viridium patches in their uniforms, which Sulu could use to zero in on their location. The patches, which were based on a highly classified new Starfleet technology, emitted a long-range signal that was all but undetectable unless you knew what you were looking for. Not even the Klingons or Romulans were onto the trick yet, so Kirk doubted that the Oyolu were.

Jorgaht burned through masonry and bedrock faster than an industrial borer, heading upward at a forty-five-degree angle. Kirk and the others had to scramble to keep up with him. Periodic phaser bursts caused the tunnel to cave in behind them, cutting off their pursuers. Kirk heard them blasting away at the fallen debris in a furious effort to keep after the fugitives. They showed no sign of giving up anytime soon.

They get points for persistence, Kirk thought. *Lucky us.*

Within minutes, Jorgaht broke through to the surface. Emerging from the tunnel after the others, Kirk found himself in what appeared to be a ruined plaza surrounded by the charred husks of broken and burnt-out skyscrapers. A cracked and empty fountain contained only a muddy puddle of rainwater. Weeds sprouted between the paving tiles. A toppled stone statue was missing its head. Feral mammals snarled and glared at the intruders from adjacent alleyways, keeping their distance for the moment. No lights shone within the wreckage or upon the plaza. A hot summer breeze blew powdered stone and ash past Kirk's boots. More evidence of the vicious conflict that had trashed so much of the planet.

"Good God," McCoy said, moved by the devastation. "People used to live here."

"And they may again," Kirk reminded him, "provided the peace talks continue." He searched the sky impatiently, looking for the *Copernicus*. The desolate plaza was hardly the most attractive of landing sites, but beggars couldn't be choosers. *Come on, Sulu. Where are you?*

"Captain?" Tamris held on to her captured phaser rifle. "What now?"

"Wait for it," Kirk said, as confidently as he could.

To his relief, the shuttlecraft soon came swooping into sight. Deftly steering a course between the totaled buildings, the *Copernicus* touched down on the plaza. Its aft hatchway dropped open, forming a ramp, and the hostages rushed aboard. The shuttle had limited seating, but its lifting capacity was such that Kirk wasn't worried about overloading it. They were going to be crammed in like sardines, but it was doable.

But what about Jorgaht? The Horta could presumably contain his corrosive secretions, making it safe to rub shoulders with him, but he was still going to take up a lot of valuable room. Kirk briefly considered strapping Jorgaht to the roof of the shuttle; Hortas had been known to survive the vacuum of space for considerable periods.

"Don't worry about me," Jorgaht said, as though reading Kirk's mind. "I can burrow so deep those rioters will never find me."

Kirk appreciated the offer. "But you could get trapped here for who knows how long."

"I'm in no hurry and there's plenty of good minerals to eat down below. I'll show myself again when the political situation has calmed down a bit—and you can negotiate my departure with the legitimate authorities, instead of an anarchic mob." He chuckled via the translator. "I like to think there are still *some* sensible people to deal with on this planet."

He has a point, Kirk thought. Jorgaht was in no immediate danger and the protesters were hardly the official government of Oyolo. Riley could probably arrange for Jorgaht to be recovered later, under somewhat less desperate circumstances, assuming they could prevent a full-scale war from breaking out in the meantime.

"All right." Kirk peeled the viridium patch from his uniform and affixed it to the Horta's communicator. "This will allow us to track you if necessary. Take care . . . and thank you!"

" 'What stronger breastplate than a heart untainted! Thrice is he armed who hath his quarrel just!' " the

Horta emoted. "Now go, before those ruffians catch up with you."

Kirk couldn't argue with that. They were pushing their luck the longer they stayed on the planet. He hurried aboard the *Copernicus,* claiming the shotgun seat next to Sulu. He glanced back over his shoulder at the rescuers and rescued packed into the passenger cabin. They all looked very uncomfortable, but nobody was complaining.

"Everybody aboard and accounted for?" he called out.

"Aye, Captain," Chekov responded. "And I believe we are all eager to depart."

"And then some," Banks added, "sir."

That was all Kirk needed to hear. "Get us out of here, Mister Sulu."

"Aye, sir." Sulu called back to the passengers, "Hold on tight."

He engaged the thrusters and the *Copernicus* lifted off into the sky. Peering down through the forward port, Kirk saw Jorgaht disappear back into the planet's depths. He would be safe if he stayed far underground, deep beneath the planet's crust. Kirk vowed silently to see to it that the valiant Horta made it off Oyolo eventually.

We couldn't have escaped without him.

Not that they were out of the woods yet. Gravity and acceleration shoved Kirk back into his seat as the shuttlecraft climbed steeply toward the upper atmosphere. Grunts of discomfort escaped the cabin as the crammed passengers were thrown against one another. Kirk winced on their behalf, but he figured it could be worse. At least they weren't being held hostage anymore.

"You in a hurry, Mister Sulu?" Kirk asked, noting the steepness of their ascent.

"With reason, Captain."

He adjusted the frequency on the shuttle's communications panel. A harsh voice invaded the cockpit:

"Oyolu Air Command to unauthorized Starfleet craft. This is your final warning: Land at once . . . or we will shoot you down!"

"There's been some concern about our presence in their airspace," Sulu explained. "I may have somehow failed to acknowledge their earlier warnings."

"So I gather."

Kirk had to wonder who exactly was issuing the threats. The actual Oyolu government or just an element of the planet's air defense force that was sympathetic to the protesters' cause? Not that it really mattered at this juncture; Kirk was not about to trust the hostages or his people to the tender mercies of the Oyolu, who were still justifiably worked up over A'Barra's assassination—and who probably weren't going to look kindly on tonight's covert invasion of their sovereignty. When it came to smoothing things out with the Oyolu authorities, Kirk preferred to do so from the bridge of the *Enterprise* and not from an Oyolu holding cell.

Annunciator lights flashed crimson on the control panel before him. Threat sensors detected a battery of surface-to-air weapons locking onto the *Copernicus*. It seemed that the Oyolu had not just been idly rattling their sabers.

"Incoming!" he said urgently. "Maximum shields."

The command came naturally to his lips, even as he operated the controls himself, dialing up the deflectors to full strength, and none too soon. The energy beams slammed into *Copernicus*'s shields, buffeting the shuttlecraft so that it rocked violently from side to side. Passengers screamed as they were tossed about the cabin and into one another, cushioned somewhat by just how tightly they were packed. Kirk was glad that Jorgaht had stayed behind; a massive Horta bouncing around the cabin like a loose boulder could have broken bones.

Emergency alarms lit up the control panel. The deflectors had repelled the initial barrage, but at a cost. The shields were already down by approximately thirty percent and *Copernicus* had taken a beating. Auxiliary systems kicked in to compensate for the damage, but Kirk knew there was a limit to how much the embattled shuttlecraft could endure.

"Evasive action, Mister Sulu!"

"Yes, sir. Way ahead of you, sir!"

Copernicus banked sharply to one side, momentarily escaping the phaser assault. Sulu rolled the shuttle over so that its impulse engines and warp nacelles were turned away from ground-based phaser cannons. Loose articles, including a data slate and an empty coffee cup, tumbled from the floor of the cockpit onto the ceiling and Kirk felt his stomach turn upside-down as well. He was suddenly grateful for his mandatory anti-gravity training.

"Enterprise *to* Copernicus!" Uhura's voice came over an emergency channel. *"The Oyolu have mustered air support to bring you down. A flight of warcraft are heading your way."*

"Acknowledged," Kirk responded. "Thanks for the heads-up."

He and Sulu exchanged worried looks. Kirk found himself missing that Klingon bird-of-prey they had commandeered a few years ago. *A cloaking device would come in handy right now.*

"Here they come," Kirk said. The hostile craft appeared on the tactical display screen as a formation of flashing red icons. "I'm reading charged weapons banks and a battery of air-to-air missiles. Estimated contact: fifteen seconds."

Sulu grimaced. "You sure I can't discourage them with our phasers?"

"I'm not sure Ambassador Riley would approve."

"I was afraid you were going to say that." Sulu sighed. "Flight not fight then." He took a deep breath. "Brace yourself, everyone! Next stop: *Enterprise!*"

Sulu red-lined the *Copernicus*, accelerating at nearly full impulse out of Oyolo's atmosphere. The g-forces, testing the limits of the shuttle's inertial dampers, were comparable to those of an old-style NASA rocket blasting off from the Earth, and Kirk hoped again that the passengers were tightly packed enough to cushion one another. Friction with the atmosphere caused the deflectors to glow brightly red outside the hull; even still, Kirk thought he could feel the interior of the shuttle getting uncomfortably warm for a few moments, before the last misty traces of the atmosphere gave way to the blackness of space. Sulu didn't slow down until they were safely beyond the planet's orbit and heading back into the demilitarized buffer zone. Kirk hoped that the Oyolu military would not be so rash as to pursue the shuttle beyond their borders.

"That was quite the getaway," Kirk praised Sulu, after he got his breath back. "I'm glad we had you at the helm."

"My pleasure, sir."

Kirk knew that Sulu was up for promotion to captain and would probably get his own ship soon. There was even talk of him taking command of the *Excelsior* in the near future.

I'm going to be sorry to lose him.

Doctor Tamris forced her way through the crowded passenger cabin to the rear of the cockpit. Her blue skin looked faintly green, but she managed a smile anyway. Kirk could only imagine how relieved she was to have her people out of danger. Finding quarters for all the rescued relief workers was going to be a bit of a challenge, but he was sure the *Enterprise* could accommodate them.

"*Now* can I thank you?" she asked.

Kirk smiled back at her. "You're welcome."

At some point he would have to inform Tamris that Lenore was indeed a suspect in the murder investigation, but that could wait until the former hostages were safely aboard the ship. Kirk's smile faded as he recalled that, although the hostage crisis had been resolved, the larger issue of the assassinations remained, not to mention the matter of that missing warhead. He had a lot waiting for him back on the *Enterprise.*

Meanwhile, he overheard McCoy checking on Chekov and Banks back in the passenger cabin. "The two of you both in one piece? Those hooligans didn't rough you up too badly, did they?"

"We are quite well, Doctor," Chekov said. "Which is something of a pleasant surprise."

"Don't I know it," McCoy said. "That reminds me, Chekov. The test results came back and I found out what was causing your sneezing fits. Turns out that . . ."

Kirk listened with interest.

Twenty-Two

"So, it seems we could be worse off, Mister Spock," Scotty said. "We could be one of those poor souls on Oyolo."

The hostage crisis on the other planet dominated the news reports on Pavak, where local pundits and authorities were already threatening vague repercussions should Kirk give in to the demands of the Oyolu "terrorists" and deliver Lenore Karidian to their enemy. Needless to say, the seizure of the refugee workers was also being cited by the more bellicose end of the Pavakian political spectrum as proof that the Oyolu were violent barbarians who could never be trusted. Never mind, Spock mused, that he and Scott were essentially being held hostage as well, albeit under less harsh and hazardous conditions. That the unruly crowd outside the fort continued to grow made him wonder just how different their situation truly was from that of the unfortunate captives on Oyolo.

"We may well find ourselves in similar straits soon," Spock said, "if this crisis continues to escalate."

"Aye, it looks that way all right." Scott glumly observed images of the occupied refugee camp. Reports were that at least fifteen volunteers had been taken hostage. "What do ye think the captain will do?"

Spock regretted that he was not aboard the *Enterprise* to render assistance, but he trusted Captain Kirk to deal with this crisis in their absence. The *Enterprise* could function without him. Indeed, by all reports, they had fared quite successfully during the brief period that he was deceased . . . aside from losing the first *Enterprise,* of course.

"If I know the captain, he is already planning a rescue mission. Indeed, I would not be surprised to learn that it was already under way."

Scott nodded, seemingly buoyed by the notion. "With Captain Kirk leading the way, no doubt."

"And Doctor McCoy registering his extreme disapproval of whatever may be transpiring," Spock added. "Or so I would theorize with a significant degree of confidence."

Pogg arrived without warning. A stony expression offered little hint of his decision until the door slid shut behind him.

"There is no time to lose," he said tersely. "Put on your jackets and play along." Allowing them only moments to dress for outdoors, he cuffed their wrists with pliable restraints, drew his disruptor, and marched them toward the door, which opened before them. "Keep moving," he said loudly, presumably for the benefit of the guard posted outside in the hall. "Don't give me any trouble."

The guard gave them a puzzled look. "Brigadier-General?"

"We have received new orders," Pogg stated. "The prisoners are to be transported to a more secure site."

"More secure?" the guard said. "I don't understand."

"Are you questioning me, soldier? This decision was made well above your rank. You don't need to understand it. You just need to do as you're told."

"Yes, sir!" The abashed guard saluted crisply. "My apologies, sir!"

Pogg returned the salute. "Remain at your post. The prisoners' effects are to remain undisturbed until they can be collected and examined."

"Yes, sir! You can count on me, sir!"

Spock found himself indebted to Pavakian military discipline as Pogg briskly escorted them from the barracks to the landing field, where the *Galileo* remained just where they had left it. Night had fallen on Pavak and the temperature had plummeted even farther. The cold stung Spock's face and frosted his breath. He decided that he was ready to depart Pavak.

Should that prove possible.

Pogg pulled rank as necessary to speed their escape, but one last guard stood between them and the shuttlecraft. She glared at Spock and Scotty with obvious enmity; clearly, she was among those who blamed Starfleet for General Tem's assassination.

"Stand aside, Private," Pogg ordered. "New orders. I'm transporting the prisoners to a more secure location."

"In their own spacecraft?"

"That is not your call, soldier. You have your orders."

Alas, this particular guard was not as easily cowed as the one back at the barracks. Her eyes narrowed suspiciously and she raised her wrist-communicator toward her lips. "I'm sorry, sir, but I need to verify this before I can let you through." Her other hand held a weapon. "Please lower your weapon, sir."

Pogg's disruptor was still drawn and pointed at his "prisoners." He turned it toward the guard. "After you, Private."

"It appears we have something of a standoff," Scott said. "If ye don't mind, I'll just step to one side, out of the line of fire."

"An excellent idea, Mister Scott." Spock began to step to the opposite side. He held up his bound wrists to indicate that he posed no threat. "Perhaps we can settle this misunderstanding in a peaceful fashion."

"Wait!" The guard's anxious gaze darted from side to side, struggling to keep track of all three men, while keeping her weapon aimed at Pogg. "Everybody, stay put!"

"Don't mind me, lass," Scott replied. "I'm not going anywhere."

Spock took advantage of the guard's distracted state to effortlessly snap his cuffs and advance on her from the side. A nerve pinch swiftly and efficiently dealt with the situation—and spared Pogg the necessity of firing on one of his own soldiers.

Nevertheless, Pogg stared numbly at the stunned form on the tarmac.

"We couldn't let her call in," he murmured. "There are no new orders . . ."

Spock had already deduced as much. He appreciated the other man's distress, but he knew that time was of the essence. "We must hurry, Brigadier-General."

"Yes, of course," Pogg said, roused from his bitter contemplation of the fallen guard. He hastily removed Scott's cuffs as well. "It's only a matter of time before my ruse is discovered."

Scott entered an access code to open the *Galileo*'s starboard hatchway and the men hurried aboard the shuttlecraft. Scott sat down at the helm and fired up the engines with admirable speed, while Pogg took the co-pilot's seat and activated the comm unit.

"This is Brigadier-General Pogg," he ordered. "Lower the defensive force field immediately."

A confused voice responded. *"Sir?"*

Pogg repeated his fabricated new orders and added an embellishment to forestall any objections. "We have reason to believe that Kirk has mounted an operation to remove the Starfleet inspectors from our custody. It is imperative that they be transferred from this facility immediately."

"But . . ."

"Did you hear me, mister? Lower the shields!"

"Yes, sir!"

Scott kept a close eye on a display panel. "Shields down," he confirmed.

"Then I suggest we depart without delay," Spock said.

"You don't need to tell me twice, Mister Spock!"

Scott engaged the thrusters and *Galileo* took off into the cold night sky. Spock strapped himself into a passenger seat just behind the cockpit as the shuttle cleared the shields. Pogg's ruse had gotten them this far, but Spock had not forgotten the phaser cannons in place around the fort. The shuttle was not, as they said, free and clear just yet. Their attempt at flight might end as quickly as it had begun once the unauthorized nature of their departure was determined.

For a moment, it appeared that they might make their escape without further complications, but then a stentorian voice blared from the cockpit.

"*Galileo! You are ordered to return to Fort Dakkur immediately. Failure to comply will carry severe consequences.*"

Scott cursed under his breath. "Sounds like they're onto us, sir. I don't suppose ye have any other tricks up your sleeve?"

"Just one." Pogg swallowed hard before speaking into the comm. "This is Pogg. I have been taken hostage by the prisoners. Hold your fire. I repeat: Hold your fire!"

Spock admired Pogg's creative mendacity, which bore favorable comparison to Captain Kirk's. "Let us hope that they value your safety more than our captivity."

"They might not," Pogg admitted, "but at least this might give them pause . . . long enough for us to keep from being shot down."

"Galileo. *Surrender at once.*"

"No!" Pogg pleaded, buying them precious time. "Hold your fire! I beg you!"

"*I repeat, surrender at once. This is your final warning.*"

Were the Pavakians bluffing? Spock had no desire to find out. "Mister Scott?"

"I hear you!"

A burst of acceleration shoved Spock roughly back into his seat. Scott was hardly the pilot Sulu was, but what was needed now was speed—not precision flying—as well as an instinctive knowledge of just how far the shuttle's engines could be pushed without burning out. Under the circumstances, Spock could not have asked for a better pilot at the helm.

But would that be enough?

"Cross your fingers, buckos," Scott said. "I'm giving it all we've got."

Within moments, *Galileo* exited the planet's atmosphere, heading out into space. Spock experienced a very human sense of relief as Scott went to full impulse and they left Pavak behind.

"Is that it?" Scott asked. "Did we make it?"

"I suspect so," Pogg said, looking no less relieved than the escaped Starfleet officers. "You two were valuable as bargaining chips, but not so much so as to warrant a full-scale chase across the solar system. Plus, I imagine that the saner heads in our government are reluctant to provoke a major confrontation with the Federation and Starfleet . . . or so I gambled."

Spock wondered if that same reluctance had also inhibited the Pavakian military from shooting down the shuttle when they had the chance. It was one thing, after all, to detain a pair of Starfleet weapons inspectors indefinitely; it was another thing altogether to blast them from the skies when they attempted to depart the planet.

"It seems your instincts were correct then," Spock observed. "Which was fortuitous for all our sakes . . . and perhaps two worlds as well."

"Setting course for Sumno," Scott announced. "Estimated time to arrival: four-point-two hours."

Outward Six, bearing Major Takk, and perhaps the missing warhead, had a substantial lead on them, but Spock drew some comfort from the knowledge that Starfleet shuttles were significantly more advanced and capable of greater speeds than their Pavakian counterparts. He could only hope that advantage would increase their odds of recovering the warhead before it could be put to horrific use.

"I must thank you, Brigadier-General," he said, "for going to such lengths to liberate us. I know that could not have been an easy decision for you."

"It was not," Pogg said. "I would have much preferred to turn this matter over to my superiors, had I only known how far up the chain of command the corruption went. But, under the circumstances, I could trust nothing but my own judgment—which I don't mind saying was a very uncomfortable place to be."

Spock sympathized. He had, on rare occasions, disobeyed orders himself, as when he had "borrowed" the *Enterprise* to return Christopher Pike to Talos IV. He understood full well how difficult a conflict between conscience and duty could be. . . .

"I believe you made the only logical decision," he said. "And I commend you for having the courage to see it through."

"Easy for you to say," Pogg grumbled. "You didn't just toss your career out the airlock."

"Unless we can prove ye had good cause," Scott offered. "Saving the peace—and preventing a disaster— might well restore your reputation and standing."

"Then we had best find that missing warhead," Pogg said, "or your captain may have another fugitive seeking asylum aboard his ship." He sighed in weary resignation. "In the meantime, I don't suppose you have any more of that 'Scotch whiskey' of yours?"

The *Galileo* sped toward Sumno.

Twenty-Three

"You asked to see me, Captain?"

Colonel Gast entered the briefing room where Kirk, Chekov, McCoy, and Riley awaited. Security officers, including Lieutenant Banks, were posted outside in the corridor. Hours had passed since the *Copernicus* had returned to the *Enterprise,* bringing the former hostages to safety, but that time had been well spent. Kirk was running on little sleep, but this meeting couldn't wait.

"That's correct," Kirk replied from the head of the table. "Thank you for responding so promptly."

"I have little else to do while the peace talks remain stalled." She gave Kirk a salute. "My congratulations, incidentally, on the success of your rescue mission. Your reputation is obviously well-deserved, Captain."

"I'm glad to have lived up to your expectations," Kirk replied. "In any event, I promised to keep you apprised of our investigation of the murders. As it happens, some provocative new evidence has arisen."

She arched an eyebrow. "Do tell."

"Why don't you sit down first?" Kirk suggested, indicating an empty seat next to Chekov. "You look tired, if you don't mind me saying so."

In fact, the Pavakian delegate was showing signs of wear. Her tawny fur was not as lustrous as when she first arrived on the *Enterprise* but looked rather dry and lifeless instead. Her eyes were bloodshot and somewhat bleary, while even her pristine white uniform was uncharacteristically rumpled, its creases hardly as crisp as before. Her voice was hoarse and raspy. Once again, Kirk got the impression that she was holding herself together through sheer force of will.

"Thank you, Captain." She dropped into the chair with obvious relief. "I confess to feeling a trifle fatigued. The strain of the last few days no doubt."

"No doubt," Kirk said.

In no time at all, Chekov began to sniffle. He pinched his nose, stifling a sneeze, while making use of the medication he had on hand. Another tablet brought him immediate relief.

"Excuse me," he apologized. "Again."

"You should take care of that, Commander," Gast advised. "It appears to be a recurring condition."

"Oh, it's nothing to be concerned with," McCoy said. "Just a simple allergic reaction."

Gast expressed polite interest. "To what, may I ask?"

"Funny you should ask," McCoy said. "It took me a little while to isolate the allergen, especially with everything else going on, but I got a match eventually.

Turns out it was merely dander . . . from Pavakian fur, to be exact."

"Pavakian?" Gast stiffened. "Should I be offended?"

"No offense intended or warranted," McCoy said. "This is no reflection on your personal hygiene, which I'm sure is impeccable. It's just a random biological quirk, and hardly without precedent in medical literature. Some people are simply allergic to cats or rabbits or shellfish . . . or Pavakians. It happens."

"Trust me, it's hardly without diplomatic precedent as well," Riley said, joining the discussion. "Speaking from experience, you *never* want to seat a Therbian next to a Kazarite at a state dinner, not unless you want the Therbian hacking and coughing before the entrée is even served."

"Fascinating," Gast said in a tone that implied anything but. "My apologies for any personal inconvenience, Commander Chekov but"—a distinct note of impatience crept into her voice—"I believe, Captain, you were about to update me on the investigation. . . ."

"The investigation and Mister Chekov's allergy go hand in hand," Kirk stated. "You may recall him having some difficulty in General Tem's stateroom the night of the assassination."

"So?" she asked. "I fail to see the relevance. It's hardly surprising that one would encounter Pavakian dander in the general's quarters."

"True," Kirk conceded. "But Chekov also got the sniffles in Minister A'Barra's stateroom after his

murder." Kirk's voice grew harder and more confronta-
tional. "Why would there be traces of Pavakian dander
in *A'Barra's* quarters?"

Gast bristled. "What are you implying? Is this a
briefing . . . or an inquisition?"

"That remains to be seen," Kirk said. "Now, in itself,
the dander is not conclusive, but it did open up some
intriguing new lines of investigation. New information
has been uncovered, which is provocative to say the
least." He turned to McCoy. "Your findings, Doctor?"

A data slate rested in front of McCoy, but he barely
needed to look at his notes. "I conducted a thorough
postmortem and tox screen on Minister A'Barra's remains, which confirmed that the poison in his system
was indeed zetaproprion."

"The very medication prescribed to Miss Karidian
to curb her homicidal tendencies," Gast said. "Or so I
am informed."

"To assist in maintaining her mental equilibrium,"
McCoy corrected. "But here's the thing: There are different variants of the same medications, tailored to
the specific physiologies of various humanoids. Again,
as with the allergies, this is to be expected. Different species have different tolerances, metabolisms,
chemistries, and whatnot, and don't get me started
on Vulcans and that green, copper-based stuff they
call blood . . ."

Gast drummed her fingers upon the table. "The
point, Doctor."

"Yes," McCoy said, "it seems the zetaproprion that killed A'Barra was a variant specifically tailored for Pavakians. Among other things, it's being used on your planet to treat both soldiers and civilians for post-traumatic stress brought on by the war."

"Is that so?" Gast said warily.

"You fought in the war," Kirk said. "Doing your duty to defend Pavak and its interests. I imagine you had some fairly harrowing experiences."

"Who did not? War is an ugly business at the best of times, and the Oyolu can be savage and unrelenting foes—as you surely saw for yourself."

"I'm sure we only got a small taste of what you must have endured in the war," Kirk said. "Right there in the thick of things for all those years."

"I don't ask for your sympathy."

"I wouldn't expect you to," Kirk said. "But surely it must have been . . . traumatic?"

"Or perhaps we Pavakians are made of sterner stuff than you give us credit for." Her face and expression hardened. "Let us stop fencing. It's obvious where you are going with this, but it seems to me that you are grasping at straws, perhaps in hopes of creating reasonable doubt where Miss Karidian's guilt is concerned? My own wartime experiences are irrelevant to this discussion."

"Perhaps not," Riley said. "I still have some diplomatic contacts in your government, patriotic Pavakians with a sincere interest in seeing the peace talks succeed, and they allowed me to look at your official military record."

Gast leapt to her feet. "You had no right!"

"That's a matter of interpretation," Riley argued. "Your private medical records are confidential certainly, but your military record is more of an open book. It's no secret that you survived an ambush on Oyolo three years ago, while doing undercover demolitions work behind enemy lines. Your entire squad was slaughtered and you were the only survivor." He glanced down at his own notes. "Your record also states that you were injured and underwent treatment at a Pavakian military hospital before resuming duty and being assigned to General Tem's personal staff."

Kirk felt a twinge of sympathy for the soldier, given what she had gone through, but asked the hard question anyway. "You weren't prescribed zetaproprion, were you?"

"My medical history is not on trial here!"

Kirk kept up the pressure. "I don't suppose you would allow us to search your quarters aboard the *Enterprise*?"

"My personal effects are protected by diplomatic protocol, as well you know."

"Making them off-limits for inspection, yes." Kirk recalled that Gast had made a point of inquiring about the handling of her luggage when first beaming aboard. "Not a bad way to smuggle a disruptor aboard."

Gast gave him an icy smile. "You have a devious mind, Captain, and a suspicious one, it seems. But you are wasting our time. Even if, hypothetically, you could establish that I have been treated with zetaproprion at some point, I'm hardly the only individual who might have access to that particular drug." She rattled off the possibilities. "The refugee camps, the black market, an unguarded hospital cupboard. Karidian, or anyone else, could have obtained the drug in any number of ways. Why, I wouldn't be at all surprised if quantities of zetaproprion were included in the medical supplies you've so generously supplied to the relief efforts on both planets."

"That's true enough," McCoy said.

"Let me remind you, gentlemen, that Lenore Karidian had access to the GRC's medical supplies and that she remains the only known assassin aboard this ship."

"That's another thing," Kirk said. "Who leaked Lenore's true identity to the press? It had to be someone familiar with her history . . . or mine. You mentioned before, that night in the corridor, that you were a great admirer and very familiar with my career. Indeed, you mentioned my 'reputation' just a few moments ago when you first arrived."

"You flatter yourself, Captain," she replied. "And perhaps you mistake a bit of diplomatic exaggeration for sincere admiration. With all due apologies to your ego, you are not of *that* great interest to me."

Kirk didn't buy it.

"Even after the *Enterprise* was assigned to the peacekeeping mission? It seems to me that an intelligent and conscientious officer such as yourself would want to thoroughly research the principals involved in the upcoming peace talks. You could have easily stumbled onto Lenore's story while familiarizing yourself with my career; the death of Kodos the Executioner, at the hands of his only daughter, was big news at the time . . . and has been a matter of historical record for two decades."

"You've found me out, Captain," she said sarcastically. "Yes, I did conduct a thorough background check on you prior to the commencement of the talks, and on Ambassador Riley as well." She turned toward Riley. "Tell me, Ambassador. Is it true that you once took over the *Enterprise*'s engine room while in a state of intoxication?"

Riley refused to be baited. "Let's stick to the matter at hand, shall we?"

"Very well." She sat back down at the table. "In any event, Captain, the fact that I researched your illustrious career is hardly damning. As you said, the death of Kodos is public knowledge. Anyone with an interest in galactic history might be familiar with it."

Perhaps, Kirk thought, *but the galaxy is a big place with plenty of history.* He found it unlikely that the average Pavakian or Oyolu would know that much about a historical tragedy affecting another species in another part of the quadrant decades ago. They'd had their own bloody history to occupy them, unlike Gast, who had every reason to acquaint herself with the subject.

"I'm curious," he said. "When exactly did you recognize Lenore? At the reception that night? You couldn't have known that I would run into her on Oyolo, let alone bring her back to the *Enterprise,* so I'm guessing that was just a happy accident as far you were concerned. Was framing her a last-minute addition to your plot?"

"Who says that I recognized her? Or that I was involved in some manner of plot?" Her nostrils flared. Scorn dripped from her voice. "Your ridiculous theory falls apart on even a narrative level. Why would I want to assassinate General Tem?"

"To sabotage the peace process," Kirk suggested. "The general struck me as genuinely committed to making amends with the Oyolu. You, not so much."

She did not deny it. "Even if that were true, surely murdering A'Barra would have sufficed, without any need for killing my own superior officer. Or are you also entertaining the notion that I only murdered A'Barra, perhaps in retaliation for the general's death? That, I admit, is a slightly more plausible scenario."

Chekov jumped on her comment. "So you're confessing to A'Barra's murder at least?"

"Not in the slightest," she said. "This is all just pointless speculation."

"Then how do you explain the presence of Pavakian

dander at the second crime scene, in Minister A'Barra's quarters?" Kirk asked. "There have only been two Pavakians aboard the *Enterprise,* and General Tem was already dead at that point."

"I have no idea," she said. "Perhaps it was the general's ghost, seeking revenge?"

She was being facetious, of course, but the thought had occurred to Kirk that General Tem might have faked his death and gone into hiding aboard the ship. A *Constitution*-class starship had plenty of nooks and crannies and Jefferies tubes where a "dead" man could lurk undetected. Ben Finney had proved that decades ago. It was remotely *possible* that Tem was the actual killer, but Kirk's gut said no. Tem had struck him as being sincerely intent on ending the bloodshed, perhaps to assuage his own guilty conscience. There had been a haunted, brooding quality to the man—not unlike Anton Karidian. Kirk found it hard to believe that Tem would go to such lengths to sabotage the peace talks.

Gast, on the other hand . . .

"And if we collected samples of your dander from your quarters," Kirk asked, "and compared it to samples collected from A'Barra's stateroom, would we find a match?"

Kirk had already consulted with Riley. They had both agreed that diplomatic rights hardly applied to biological ephemera left behind in her guest quarters aboard the *Enterprise.* And given that dander was essentially sloughed skin cells, Kirk had no doubt that McCoy would be able to isolate distinctive genetic markers and proteins.

"I . . . that is . . . ," Gast said hesitantly. For the first time, she seemed without a ready response, as though this possibility had not occurred to her. "I'm not sure."

"And why is that, Colonel?" Kirk pressed.

She paused again before reaching a decision. "Upon reflection, I see how certain misleading irregularities may be having the unfortunate effect of sending your investigation in the wrong direction. Therefore, in the interests of clearing any confusion, let me confess that I did visit A'Barra's quarters on at least one occasion, in order to conduct an 'unofficial' diplomatic overture. Strictly off the record, naturally."

Riley leaned forward. "What sort of overture?"

"A sexual overture, if you must know." She sighed irritably, as though vexed at having to make such a distasteful admission. "As you are doubtless aware, A'Barra was known to have a pronounced weakness for the opposite sex. It was thought that I could employ my personal charms to wring certain concessions from him, or at least make him more . . . receptive . . . to compromise." A smirk lifted her lips. "Certainly, I had no trouble coaxing my way into his chambers that evening, but this was *before* either murder."

Kirk was skeptical. "You'll forgive me if I find this scenario difficult to accept. From what I've seen, you can barely stand to be in the same room as the Oyolu.

It's hard to imagine that you would ever willingly attempt to seduce one."

"Life is hardly that simple, Captain. I never said that the Oyolu were unattractive. Uncivilized, undisciplined, and ungrateful, certainly, but they do possess a certain exotic appeal and barbaric vitality." She leaned back into her seat, conveying a blasé attitude. "The late Minister A'Barra, for all his faults, was undeniably a charismatic and magnetic figure. Seducing him was hardly an ordeal; I've done far worse in the line of duty." She smirked at Kirk. "But I hardly need explain this to you, Captain. As we've established, I'm quite familiar with your exploits . . . and you too have been known to use romance as a weapon when needs be."

Kirk ignored the gibe. "And when did this alleged encounter take place?"

"Our first night aboard the *Enterprise,* prior to the first full day of negotiations . . . and well before either of the assassinations."

"And was General Tem aware of your 'unorthodox' diplomatic efforts?" Riley asked.

"The general was a man of strict morals and integrity. I fear he would not have approved." A rueful note entered her voice. "Regardless, you must surely comprehend why I did not volunteer this information earlier. While I make no apologies for my actions, which were done for the good of Pavak, you can appreciate that I would hardly wish to advertise them, especially when, at the time, they seemed to bear little relevance to the investigation."

"Or perhaps you knew how bad it would look for you," Chekov suggested, "after A'Barra was murdered?"

"That, too, I suppose," she admitted. "In any case, now that I have addressed your concerns, I trust that I can count on your discretion in the days to come. Airing this sordid little episode would do no one's reputation any favors, least of all the late Mister A'Barra's. Let us keep his memory unblemished, if only for the sake of his various wives and mistresses."

Not so fast, Kirk thought. "Your explanation is very neat, but I'm not convinced." He looked her over. "You appear to be unusually stressed and perhaps a little on edge. Why is that?"

Despite her self-assured manner, trembling hands betrayed her nerves. Her mouth sounded dry. Her fingers continued to drum restlessly against the tabletop. The delicate layer of fur coating her features made it hard to tell if she was flushed or pale, but she tugged on her collar as though the room was too warm for her. She blinked repeatedly.

"You have to ask?" she said. "These are trying times. Coping with the general's death, inheriting his responsibilities in these vital negotiations . . . and now to be accused of murder? Can you truly blame me for finding these circumstances more than a little distressing?" She swept a withering gaze over all present. "Seriously, gentlemen, I have provided adequate and highly plausible explanations for any discrepancies that might have troubled you. Perhaps now you can steer your investigation into more fruitful avenues, such as back in the direction of Miss Karidian?"

Kirk frowned. Despite Gast's glib responses, he felt certain she was hiding something. Spock would call it human intuition, and point out its fallibility, but it had served him well before. *I'm missing something here,* he thought. *One last piece of the puzzle.*

"You have an answer for everything, don't you?" he accused her.

"I have more than answers," she reminded him. "I have alibis for both assassinations, or have you forgotten that? I was with you when the disruptor was fired in the general's stateroom, and I was being guarded by your own security forces the night Mister A'Barra was poisoned."

She's got us there, Kirk thought. That she had foolproof alibis for both murders had not escaped his mind, but the rest of the evidence had pointed to her guilt, even if he hadn't yet figured out how she had pulled it off. Shape-shifting? Telekinesis? Mental manipulation? Hyper-acceleration? Neither Pavakians nor Oyolu were known to possess any such outré abilities, but Kirk had explored enough of the galaxy to know that, as Spock was fond of observing, there were always possibilities. He thought back to that night on E Deck, after the reception. Gast had indeed been with him when the phaser alarm went off. There was no way she could have shot Tem in his stateroom unless she could be in two places at once. And that was impossible, unless . . .

Suddenly it hit him.

"Chekov, what time was that anomalous transporter event again?"

Gast sat up straight. "Transporter?"

"Twenty-three sixteen, Captain," Chekov reported. "Precisely forty-nine minutes before the alarm sounded."

Two sets of disturbing memories came back to Kirk, of literally grappling with himself aboard the old *Enterprise*. Even after twenty years, he still had trouble sorting out his clashing recollections of those ghastly hours when he had been in two places at once. He had faced down himself in engineering, attacked himself in sickbay . . .

"The transporter," he realized. "You didn't use it to beam anywhere. You used it to split yourself into two separate beings."

The same thing had happened to Kirk when beaming up from Alfa 177 decades ago. A generation of scientists and engineers had studied the incident since then, working out the theory and mechanics of how exactly a freak transporter accident had divided Kirk into two identical copies, one driven by primitive impulses, the other embodying Kirk's higher faculties and conscience. The Alfa Effect, it had been termed. Kirk had been thoroughly debriefed on the incident over the years; he gathered that there were now several noted treatises and papers on the phenomenon, although he'd never cared to read them.

But apparently Gast had.

"Good God," McCoy exclaimed, appalled at the very notion. "You're saying she did that to herself . . . on purpose?"

"But there are safeguards now," Chekov protested, "to prevent such occurrences."

"Safeguards can be overridden." Kirk stared accusingly at Gast. "You were a starship engineer before the war. A brilliant one, according to Tem. Maybe even talented enough to re-create the Alfa Effect using the emergency transporter."

The original accident had resulted from contamination caused by a rare mineral substance found on Alfa 177, but now that the basic quantum theory behind the phenomenon was understood, it would surely be possible to duplicate the effect through creative use of the transporter controls. Spock or Scotty would probably be able to offer a fuller technical explanation, but Kirk didn't need to completely understand the nuts and bolts to guess what Gast had done.

"This is absurd," Gast said. "I've heard enough."

She rose to leave, only to stumble against the side of the table. A profane curse escaped her lips as she grasped the edge of the table to steady herself. Her breathing was labored. Tufts of fine fur wafted off her face as though the stress was causing her to shed.

Of course, Kirk thought, finally realizing what was afflicting her. "Doctor, I believe the colonel requires immediate medical attention."

"No!" She staggered toward the exit. "Leave me alone."

Chekov moved to block her departure.

"Out of my way. You have no right."

Kirk turned to Riley. "Ambassador, I have reason to believe that this is a life-threatening medical emergency. Surely we don't want to have another delegate expire under our watch?"

"Far from it." Riley nodded to McCoy. "Please take action, Doctor."

McCoy approached Gast, medical tricorder in hand.

"No, stay away," she protested, but seemed to lack the strength to put up a fight. "I refuse to allow any sort of medical examination."

"File a complaint," McCoy said gruffly as he scanned her with his tricorder. Kirk assumed that McCoy had also already figured out what was wrong with Gast; after all, he'd dealt with this condition before. The tricorder hummed briefly as the doctor examined the readings. He nodded grimly, unsurprised by the results. "This woman is dying."

Kirk could guess the diagnosis. "Transporter separation trauma." He winced in recollection. "I remember it well . . . twice actually. Both of me went through it."

Two halves of the same person could not survive without the other. Both Kirks had weakened the longer they were apart, and would have died had they not been reintegrated in time. Gast had been divided for at least three days now. Small wonder she was in bad shape . . . and getting worse.

"It's fatigue, I tell you." She collapsed back into her chair. "Nothing more."

"In a pig's eye." McCoy lowered his tricorder. "These results don't lie, Jim." He regarded Gast with a mixture of disgust and pity. "You're looking at half of Colonel Demme Gast."

"But is she the good half or the bad half?" Chekov asked, eyeing Gast apprehensively.

"Neither," she replied in a tone of weary resignation, as though realizing that there was no point in dissembling any longer. "I believe I adequately adjusted the parameters to minimize any such polarization with regards to our respective personalities . . . although if my other half ended up with the lion's share of our aggression and killer instinct, so much the better."

Kirk knew a confession when he heard it. "So you *are* responsible for the murders."

"Not me, specifically, but the *other* me . . . yes, she is the guilty party."

McCoy remained shocked. "By why in heaven's name would you do such a thing to yourself?"

"It was necessary," she replied. "General Tem had gone soft. My confederates and I could not allow him to endanger Pavak simply because his conscience had grown too heavy. It was tragic, but it had to be done."

Kirk remembered how little had been left of Tem. He wondered if Gast—the other Gast, that is—had chosen to disintegrate Tem so that she would not have to look upon her dead superior's face, preserving only an arm to make it clear that the general had been the victim of a brutal assassination.

"And A'Barra?" he prompted.

"He was far too stubbornly persistent when it came to continuing the peace talks, despite the general's death. I could not allow him the opportunity to clear his name and carry on his devious schemes to weaken Pavak and cheat us out of our legitimate interests on Oyolo." She smiled coldly, despite her infirmity. "And it is not as though the death of a terrorist leader is something to be mourned. Why wouldn't we want to kill A'Barra if the opportunity arose?"

"And that business about your 'diplomatic' overture?" Riley asked. "Was all that a lie?"

"Without a doubt. Oh, I'm certain that my other self easily inveigled her way into A'Barra's quarters, but no part of me would ever stoop to consorting with that terrorist. The only satisfaction he could ever give either of us was his death."

Kirk encouraged her to keep talking. "And Lenore?"

"As you surmised, a fortuitous gift from the gods, which I took full advantage of." She poured herself a glass of water from a pitcher on the table. The drink appeared to restore her somewhat. "Granted, I already had my alibi planned, but she made a convenient suspect in order to further divert suspicion . . . and keep you nicely distracted."

"Distracted?" Kirk didn't like the sound of that. "Distracted from what?"

"Wait and see, Captain. Wait and see."

She settled back into her seat, crossing her arms atop her chest. Kirk got the distinct impression she had said all that she was going to say.

But that still left a few vital questions: Where was the *other* Gast?

And what was she up to now?

Twenty-Four

Located at the outer fringes of the system, Sumno was an icy dwarf planet comparable to Pluto or Lyrma XI. Its thin atmosphere lay frozen on its surface while the planet's sun was only a large bright disk in the distance. According to Brigadier-General Pogg, who had briefed Spock and Scott en route to the planet, Sumno was home to just one small science outpost that was primarily used as an observatory for studying deep space. Due to its remote location and limited strategic value, the base was staffed by only two or three personnel and was believed to have minimal defenses. It was the last place one would expect to find a missing protomatter warhead, which might be precisely why Major Takk had been dispatched here.

The outpost came into view as the *Galileo* descended toward the surface. The icebound facility reminded Spock of similar outposts on Psi 2000 and Boreal IX. Solar panels, intended to capture whatever meager sunlight reached Sumno, covered the roof of the main habitation building: a low rectangular structure clearly built for efficiency rather than aesthetics.

Support buildings included a garage, tool sheds, and a fusion generator complex located adjacent to the habitat. An impressive array of sensor dishes was set up to capture signals from deep space. Takk's supply ship, *Outward Six,* rested on an icy landing pad carved into the planet's frozen surface.

As the shuttlecraft circled above the base, surveying the scene, Spock employed *Galileo*'s sensors to scan the parked supply ship. "I detect no evidence of the warhead aboard *Outward Six,*" he reported. "A rudimentary force field protects the habitat, inhibiting my scans. I can neither confirm nor deny that the warhead is within the structure."

Pogg attempted to hail the base. "Attention Sumno Station. This is Brigadier-General Pogg. I wish to speak to Major Rav Takk."

Silence greeted his repeated hails.

"Sounds like they're not going to make this easy for us," Scott said from the helm.

"So it appears," Spock agreed. "I wonder if the station's personnel are allied with Major Takk or if he has overpowered them and taken command of the station?"

"It's also probable," Pogg said, "that news of my 'defection' has already reached even this remote base and they have been ordered to shun me."

"That is highly likely," Spock said. "We cannot rely on your rank to secure us access to the station."

"So what now, Mister Spock?" Scott asked.

Spock considered their options. That the warhead was most likely on Sumno was encouraging in its own way; this far out from either Pavak or Oyolo, it posed little immediate threat to either planet. Nonetheless it was vital that the warhead be secured or destroyed in a timely fashion as its continued existence endangered the peace process if nothing else. Furthermore, the warhead's presence on Sumno remained only a theory. The sooner its location could be definitely verified the better.

"We could try to blast our way in," Pogg suggested, thinking like the military man he was. "Do you think this shuttle's weapons can overcome those shields?"

"Most likely," Spock surmised. "But that may not be necessary." He hoped to avoid beaming into a habitat occupied by an unknown number of armed hostiles. "There may be a more effective solution to our current impasse."

He targeted the outpost's generator complex and fired the phasers. Twin beams of ruby energy converged on the generator, disintegrating it. An incandescent red glow briefly lit up Sumno's frozen landscape before dying away, taking the outpost's primary power source with it.

"Attention station," Spock hailed the habitat directly. "This is Captain Spock of the Federation *Shuttlecraft Galileo.* We have destroyed your generator. You will soon lose heat and life-support. We offer you shelter aboard our craft provided you surrender peacefully."

Sumno's extreme environment worked in their favor. It was unlikely that the habitat could endure a long siege, even allowing for backup systems and portable heaters. He directed Scott to keep *Outward Six* in view in order to prevent the station's inhabitants from seeking refuge or flight via the supply ship.

Scott was less inclined to wait the silent Pavakians out. "We still have plenty of phaser power, Mister Spock. What say we hurry things along a wee bit?"

"You may have a point, Mister Scott."

Two mini-phaser banks were mounted to *Galileo*'s roof, with one more recessed into its underside. Employing the full power of the weapons, Spock targeted the solar panels covering the habitat's roof. Cherenkov energy flashed and crackled as the base's modest shields attempted to defend the habitat, but they were quickly overpowered by the Starfleet shuttle's superior firepower. Phaser beams melted the solar panels into slag before surgically removing portions of the roof as well, exposing the interior of the station to Sumno's frigid and airless environment. Spock estimated that the damaged habitat would rapidly become, well, uninhabitable.

"Nicely done, Mister Spock," Scott said, chortling. "We'll see how they can hold out now!"

Not very long at all, as it turned out. Within minutes, Galileo received a transmission from the station:

"Galileo. *We accept your offer. We are coming out. Please hold your fire.*"

Was that Major Takk speaking? Spock had no way of knowing, but he ordered Scott to land *Galileo* within walking distance of the habitat—and within sight of *Outward Six* as well. They watched warily as four individuals in complete environment suits emerged from the habitat and traversed the frozen terrain toward the shuttlecraft. Spock scanned the approaching Pavakians with the shuttle's sensors.

"They appear to be unarmed, at least as far as energy weapons are concerned."

Pogg and Scott both had their own phasers ready nevertheless, as Spock opened the starboard hatchway to admit the men. A tissue-thin force field kept the shuttle pressurized while allowing the surrendering Pavakians entrance to the spacecraft. Spock stood by, phaser drawn, as Pogg and Scott searched and secured the prisoners, placing them under restraint in the passenger cabin. Helmets were removed to reveal three unknown Pavakians . . . and the sneering countenance of Major Rav Takk.

"You had no right to attack a Pavakian outpost!" He sneered at Spock and Scotty. "Is this what the Federation calls peacekeeping?"

"No," Spock replied. "This is what I would term carrying out our designated duties as weapons inspectors." He lowered his phaser. "Where is the warhead, Major Takk?"

Takk smirked. "What warhead?"

"I believe you know to what I refer," Spock said,

troubled by Takk's cocksure attitude. It was as though the man was relatively unconcerned at having been forced to surrender. "A missing protomatter warhead that you reportedly inspected back on Pavak. Unit Zero-Five-Seven, to be precise."

Takk shrugged. "I have no idea what you're talking about."

"Blast it, soldier!" Pogg said, losing his patience. "That warhead was meant to be destroyed. We had a duty to carry out, whether we agreed with it or not. *You* had a duty. Now tell us where that warhead is!"

"Duty?" Takk regarded Pogg with open contempt. "Am I truly being lectured on duty by a traitor who has defied orders and allied himself with those who would disarm Pavak and embolden our mortal enemies?" He spat at Pogg's feet. "I know who you are, Pogg, and what you have done. Do not presume to speak of duty to me. You have no authority here, moral or otherwise!"

Spock surveyed the faces of the other Pavakian prisoners. Their belligerent expressions made it clear that they were in sympathy with Takk and unlikely to cooperate as well. He suspected that the Sumno station had been deliberately seeded with personnel involved in the conspiracy, which implied a considerable degree of advance planning. He doubted that either Takk or his confederates would willingly volunteer the location of the warhead.

"We could search the entire outpost," Scott suggested. "It won't be easy or pleasant, let alone fast, with the heat and life-support knocked out, but it's doable."

Spock considered that option. Even if the warhead was hidden and physically shielded from their scans, they might be able to locate it eventually—if it was indeed on Sumno. The Pavakians' unworried manner continued to disturb Spock. A distressing possibility struck him as increasingly probable.

"I fear we do not have time for an extensive search under these circumstances. The location of the warhead *must* be determined with all deliberate speed."

"That may be easier said than done," Takk said, "assuming I knew anything about a misplaced warhead, that is."

"We shall see." Spock approached Takk, his manner grave. "There *are* other methods of persuasion at my disposal, but I doubt you would welcome them." He arched an eyebrow. "Perhaps you are familiar with the Vulcan death grip?"

Scott caught on to what Spock was attempting. "No, not that! Not the death grip!"

"I fear, Mister Scott, that we may have no other recourse. Sacrificing the major may convince his comrades to be more forthcoming."

"But to kill a man in such a cold-blooded fashion?" Scott sounded appropriately appalled. "Are you truly prepared to go that far?"

"What?" Takk reacted in alarm. For the first time, his smug assurance fractured. "But you're a Vulcan. You would never do such a thing!"

"I assure you, Major, that Vulcans are perfectly capable of killing, provided there is a logical reason to do so." He placed his hand against Takk's neck, as though to administer a nerve pinch. "Moreover, I am only half-Vulcan."

"Wait! Stop!" Panic cracked Takk's voice. "You want to know where the warhead is? I'll tell you everything. Just keep that damn Vulcan away from me!"

"Talk quickly then," Pogg said, taking charge. "Or I'll have him snap your neck faster than a hangman's noose!"

Spock withdrew to let Pogg further berate the suspect. Scott came up beside him and, relying on Spock's superior hearing, spoke in a tone too low to be heard by Takk and the others.

"Mister Spock," Scott whispered, "I wonder just when people are goin' to discover there is no such thing as the Vulcan death grip?"

"A bluff worth trying, Mister Scott. A tactic I first learned from our captain."

Spock returned to the task at hand.

"So you admit to stealing the warhead?" he asked Takk.

"*Rescuing,*" Takk insisted. "Granted, we had to wait until the *Enterprise* arrived and the disarmament process was under way before we had the opportunity to switch out the warhead and substitute a dummy . . . under the cover of the very operation intended to deprive us of such weapons." Regaining much of his earlier confidence, he taunted Spock and the others. "I should thank you, actually. If not for such a massive undertaking, we would have never had the opportunity to get our hands on that warhead. It's ironic when you think about it. Were it not for your craven 'peace process,' that game-changing weapon would still be sitting impotently in an underground missile silo, going unused by our so-called leaders, who lack the will to put it to its proper use!"

"Which would be?" Spock asked, growing steadily more concerned.

"Wouldn't you like to know?" Takk sneered at their worried faces. "But you needn't bother searching the outpost. The warhead is not here. In fact, it never was."

"The devil you say!" Scott challenged him. "Then why head all the way out here in the first place?"

Spock feared he knew. "To create a false trail . . . in the event that the theft of the warhead was detected. To send us on a wild goose chase, as it were, following bread crumbs deliberately left behind to lead any investigators astray."

Spock thought of the Pavakian contacts who had alerted Pogg to Takk's new assignment piloting *Outward Six* to Sumno. He now wondered if those individuals had truly been assisting Pogg after all, or if they had actually been part of the conspiracy to divert attention to the farthest reaches of the solar system.

"Very good, Vulcan," Takk said, gloating. "Your

people's legendary intellect lives up to its vaunted reputation. A shame, however, that you only just now perceived the truth. Yes, the intent was to keep you chasing in the wrong direction . . . while we waited for the moment to strike!"

"Damn you!" Pogg shook his fist at his fellow soldier. "Where is that warhead?"

"On Pavak, of course. It never left the planet. Mind you, it will be paying a visit to Oyolo soon. Their capital city, to be exact."

"But how?" Scotty asked. "Without the impulse booster? A warhead does you no good without the rest of the missile."

"Who needs a missile?" Takk replied. "The warhead is hidden aboard General Tem's own diplomatic shuttle, currently 'under repair' on Pavak."

Spock understood. "The shuttle itself is the delivery mechanism."

"Exactly!" Takk declared. "Oh, our Pavakian shuttles may not be as fast or sophisticated as your Starfleet shuttlecrafts, but a shuttle crashing into Oyolo at full speed, bearing an armed protomatter warhead, will teach the Oyolu a lesson they will never forget!"

Spock had to agree. A direct strike on Yrary, the planet's capital city, would kill millions and most likely extinguish any possibility of peace for generations to come. Yrary itself, as well as much of the surrounding area, would become a contaminated crater unsafe for any life-form. And the environmental danger posed by any surviving traces of protomatter was almost literally immeasurable.

"But the *Enterprise* is patrolling the buffer zone," Scott recalled. "Surely they can intercept the shuttle before it strikes Oyolo."

Takk snickered.

"I would not be so sure of that."

Twenty-Five

Explosions rocked the *Enterprise.*

The unexpected blasts could be heard and felt in the briefing room, where the vibration toppled the water pitcher and caused Kirk and the others to grab onto the table to keep from falling. "What the devil?" McCoy exclaimed. The rapid-fire string of explosions, which seemed to come from more than one location on the ship, caught all present by surprise.

Except Colonel Gast. "Right on schedule," she said.

Kirk shot her a furious look, but he had no time to confront her right away. He stabbed the intercom controls with his finger. "Kirk to Bridge. Status!"

"I'm getting multiple reports of small explosions throughout the nacelle support pylons and in the impulse engineering section," Uhura responded almost immediately. *"No reported casualties yet, but we've taken damage to the warp and impulse propulsion systems."*

Kirk recalled that Gast had once taken part in demolition missions on Oyolo. He had no doubt who the saboteur was: the *other* Demme Gast, who was still at large aboard the *Enterprise.*

"Copy that. I'm on my way to the bridge. Kirk out." He switched off the comm unit and issued an order to Chekov. "Take Colonel Gast to the brig . . . and find her other half." He jumped to his feet and headed for the exit. "Bones, you may be needed in sickbay. The rest of you, you're with me."

A turbolift brought them quickly to the bridge, which was abuzz with activity. Red alert lights flashed as damage reports flooded consoles and bridge personnel moved quickly to assess and compensate for the damage. The atmosphere was tense, but the crew responded to the crisis in a brisk and disciplined fashion. Riley followed Kirk into the command circle. Occupying the captain's chair, Kirk noted that the starry void on the main viewer was surprisingly serene. No enemy or enemy fire disturbed the buffer zone. They were being attacked from within, not without. No amount of deflector screens could shield them.

"Captain," Uhura said, "I'm being hailed by Mister Spock. He says it's urgent."

Spock's timing left something to be desired, but Kirk trusted his friend's judgment. "Put him through."

Spock's stoic visage appeared on the viewscreen. Despite his friend's Vulcan reserve, Kirk could tell at once that this was serious. "What is it?"

"*The warhead.*" Spock concisely explained what the conspirators had been up to—and the immediate danger to Oyolo. "*We have strong reason to believe the attack is imminent, if it has not already commenced.*"

Riley went pale. "Captain, we can't let this happen. Millions will die . . . and so will any chance of salvaging the peace process!"

That struck Kirk as a terrifyingly accurate assessment of the situation. "Where are you? We need you and Scotty back here!"

"We are en route in the Galileo.*"*

"Good," Kirk said. "Make it fast."

"We will endeavor to do so, Captain. Spock out."

"Captain!" Ensign Dazim called out from Tactical. "A Pavakian shuttlecraft has entered the buffer zone, heading for Oyolo. Sensors indicate that it is unmanned. At its current rate of acceleration, it will crash into the planet in approximately thirty minutes."

Spock's estimate would have included at least three more decimal points, but Kirk got the idea. This was obviously the doomsday shuttle Spock had just warned him about. Complete with an armed protomatter warhead.

"Can we intercept the shuttle in time?" Kirk asked.

"Not at present," Sulu reported from the helm. "Impulse engines are offline."

"What about warp?" Kirk asked. Going to warp inside a solar system was risky and they could easily overshoot their target, but it would be a gamble worth taking if it meant stopping the bomb-laden shuttle from hitting Oyolo. "Don't tell me that's down, too."

"I'm afraid so, sir." Lieutenant Anne Magee was manning the engineering station in Scotty's absence.

Kirk did not know her well, but he knew that Scott trusted her. "The intermix chamber is intact, so there's no danger of a warp core breach, but it's going to take time to locate and repair the damage to the power transfer conduits in both pylons. Whoever rigged those explosions knew right where to place them to knock out our propulsion systems."

Gast was a starship engineer as well as a demolitions expert, Kirk recalled. "Warn the repair crews to watch out for booby traps and time bombs. I wouldn't put it past our saboteur to throw a few more nasty surprises in our path."

It was obviously no coincidence that the bombs had gone off, taking the *Enterprise* out of the equation, just as Gast's confederates on Pavak launched their sneak attack on Oyolo. This entire operation had been carefully planned, right down to sending the weapons inspectors on a wild goose chase and staging the assassinations aboard the *Enterprise,* which had served the dual purposes of disrupting the peace talks while simultaneously distracting Kirk and his crew as the saboteur went about her work. It was a brilliant scheme, Kirk had to admit. Almost Romulan in its deviousness.

"Can we target the shuttle with our weapons?" Kirk asked.

"Negative, Captain," Dazim said. "The vessel is not passing within firing range of our current position."

"Blast it!" Riley exclaimed. "They thought of everything."

Kirk refused to accept that. There had to be *some* way to stop the doomsday shuttle, but how?

And to make matters worse, the other Gast was still unaccounted for.

The explosions were music to her ears.

Gast put down the handheld device she had used to remotely trigger the bombs and listened with satisfaction to the red alert sirens going off. The emergency lifepod she was hiding in rattled from the force of the explosions several decks above her, but she knew that she was safely distant from any real danger, exactly as planned. Oyolo was in peril, not her.

As it should be.

A starship the size of the *Enterprise* offered no shortage of places for a well-trained saboteur to hide, but the cozy lifepod, which was housed among several such one-person crafts on R Deck, had proved ideal for her purposes. Intended as a last-ditch survival measure for a crew member who was unable to reach the saucer before an emergency separation took place, the lifepod came equipped with an eight-day supply of food and water, a change of clothes, a survival suit, a basic toolkit, and even a working toilet. Employed only in disasters, and so unlikely to be inspected or disturbed, it had served as a highly convenient base of operations for her covert campaign of sabotage over the last few days and nights. She'd simply needed to refrain from activating the pod's controls and life-support mechanisms to avoid detection. Granted, the pod had not come with a phaser—those were securely stored in the ship's armory—but you couldn't have everything. And she couldn't fire a phaser without exposing herself anyway, thanks to the ship's automated alarm system.

A nine-inch utility knife, commandeered from the pod's survival kit, would have to suffice.

A smile came to her lips as she finally reaped the fruits of her labors, after days of furtively slinking through Jefferies tubes and emergency stairwells to prepare for this moment. Skills honed on various covert demolition missions on Oyolo had allowed her to slip like a ghost through unguarded access tunnels. That Montgomery Scott, the ship's legendary chief engineer, was away on Pavak had been a boon as well. With the fastidious Scott not keeping watch over Engineering, her clandestine tampering with the ship's propulsion systems had been far less likely to be detected.

Alas, the warp core and impulse reaction chambers had been too carefully monitored to risk getting too close to, so arranging a catastrophe capable of destroying the entire ship, or even Engineering, had not been possible. Fortunately, that hadn't been necessary; she'd simply needed to bring about an emergency shutdown that would keep the *Enterprise* out of commission long enough for the attack on Oyolo to succeed.

So much for Starfleet's so-called peacekeeping mission!

She consulted her personal chronometer. In theory, the warhead was already on its way to Oyolo, aimed straight at what was left of their government. Timing had been crucial to this operation; she'd had to wait until just the right moment, synchronized with the launch of the unmanned shuttlecraft, so that the *Enterprise*'s crew would be unable to fix their engines in time to interfere. She had not been idle while waiting, however; she had taken advantage of the time allowed to commit additional acts of sabotage to the ship's backup systems that would hopefully keep Kirk's people occupied for hours to come.

And then there were the booby traps . . .

Mission almost accomplished, she thought smugly. Now all that remained was living long enough to savor the destruction that was about to rain down on the Oyolu's filthy heads. Her lip curled and her blood sang at the thought of the loathsome savages finally getting what they deserved. Pavak had been far too gentle with them all these years. *We should have bombed them into utter submission decades ago!*

Her only regret was that she couldn't personally kill all of them!

She cautiously emerged from the lifepod after first peering out through a viewport to make sure the way was clear. In the interest of stealth, she had traded her Pavakian uniform for a "borrowed" white engineering suit complete with protective helmet. Her plan was to take advantage of the commotion she had generated to blend in with the other crew members dashing back and forth dealing with the crisis; if all went well, one extra technician in a rad suit and helmet would attract little attention.

The insulated anti-radiation suit weighed heavily on her, however, and her limbs were stiff and cramped from hiding inside the compact lifepod. The overly warm environment of the *Enterprise,* so very sultry compared to Pavak's cool, brisk climate, felt even hotter and more oppressive than ever. A wave of dizziness threatened to unbalance her and she had to pause to steady herself. Labored breaths echoed inside her helmet. Her blood pulsed loudly in her ears.

Stay strong, she ordered herself. *Just a while longer.*

Her escalating weakness came as no surprise. She was paying the price for splitting herself in two, that night after the reception, but judged it worth the cost. The trick had proved a creative way to smuggle an extra operative aboard, while simultaneously diverting suspicion from her double. One Gast had provided an alibi, as prearranged, while the other had carried out the dirty work of disposing of A'Barra and General Tem.

Memories of the assassinations were burned into her brain at least. Killing Tem had been regrettable, but easily enough accomplished; he had never once suspected her. And getting to A'Barra had been readily accomplished as well. The promise of some backdoor diplomacy, along with his lustful nature, had been sufficient to gain her admission to his quarters. A quick application of a hypospray loaded with zetaproprion and he had died gasping upon the floor, far too quickly for her liking.

If only I could have taken my time with him, she thought vehemently. *Made him pay for all the Pavakians maimed and killed by his unconscionable terrorism!*

Anger and adrenaline gave her the strength to stride confidently through the gleaming corridors of the *Enterprise.* Busy crew members, responding to the emergency, rushed past her without a second look. Emergency sirens blared through the halls. The smell of smoke and charred circuitry wafted into her helmet. She relished the harsh aroma. It was the smell of "peace" going up in flames.

Another explosion went off several decks above. Startled crew members froze in their tracks and stared upward in alarm. "What was that?" a shaggy Tellarite ensign bellowed. "*Where* was that?"

The impulse engineering section, Gast guessed. *The auxiliary driver coil assembly, to be exact.*

She smirked behind her helmet. It appeared that an overeager repair crew had not been cautious enough to avoid one of her booby traps. *So be it,* she thought mercilessly. There might have been a time when she would have regretted inflicting injuries on unwary Starfleet personnel, but that was before the Federation had chosen to meddle in Pavakian affairs, while treating the bloodthirsty Oyolu as though they were a legitimate civilization on an equal footing as Pavak.

Equal!

The very thought filled her with righteous fury as she recalled the ambush on Oyolo that had nearly killed her three years ago. She had been part of a six-person covert demolition team dispatched to seek out and destroy a suspected Oyolu training camp and arms depot in the densely forested hills outside Usesu. The mission had been going smoothly until they found themselves under fire by superior numbers of insurgents. Her entire team had been slaughtered and she had been captured and "interrogated" for days before finally making her escape. It was then that she had truly grasped the unspeakable barbarity of the Oyolu—and realized that they could never, ever be trusted. You could not make peace with such creatures. You could only subdue them.

Or exterminate them altogether!

The painful memories fueled the volcanic anger growing inside her with every step. Bile churned in her gut. She caught herself glaring at the self-righteous Starfleet idiots passing her in the corridors. The nine-inch knife was concealed in the left sleeve of her engineering suit; part of her wanted to slash at every infuriating crew member she saw.

Control yourself, she thought. *Focus.*

Where was this murderous fury coming from? Was she simply on edge due to weakness and stress, or was this some peculiar side effect of the transporter trick? During the original incident at Alfa 177, at least one version of Captain Kirk had proved violent and out of control. *Perhaps I did not entirely eliminate the polarization factor after all. . . .*

Distracted, she nearly collided with a nameless ensign who came rushing around a turn. He skidded to a halt only a heartbeat away from slamming into her. "Excuse me," he apologized before darting around her.

She gritted her teeth. It was all she could do to keep from slashing his throat.

Clumsy oaf! I ought to—

The feverish intensity of her reaction startled her. This was more than just strain and exhaustion. There was something else affecting her.

I am not fully myself, she realized, *in more ways than one. We need to reintegrate . . . soon.*

Avoiding crowded turbolifts, she ducked into an emergency stairwell and began racing up the steps toward G Deck—and the primary transporter room. The plan was to rendezvous with her other half after the bombs went off and the warhead was launched, in hopes of reuniting into a single being before it was too late. They had employed the emergency transporters before, but it had been thought that, with the lower decks and Engineering in disarray, the main transporter room in the saucer section was more likely to be unattended. She took comfort from the knife tucked into her sleeve. With luck, she would have to dispatch only a single transporter operator.

But was her counterpart still free to meet up with

her? For the sake of operational security, they'd had no contact with each other since the transporter had divided them. Gast's skin crawled as she wondered what had befallen her double during that time. It was strangely unnerving not to know what your other self was doing, but they had agreed that it would be safer that way, with less chance of them being caught communicating. Gast had no idea what might have become of her other half.

Even stranger, she found herself oddly adverse to the prospect of reintegrating with the other Gast, as though that would somehow result in the "death" of the being she'd been for the last few days. She shook her head to try to clear it of this patently irrational instinct. The scientific literature on the Alfa Effect, including Doctor McCoy's own declassified medical logs from twenty years ago, made it abundantly clear that neither she nor the other Gast could long survive without each other.

As her fading strength surely confirmed.

It was possible, of course, that her counterpart would be unable to make the rendezvous. *No matter,* she thought. There was a plan in place for that eventuality as well. Should her other half not join her in a timely fashion, Gast was to beam her atoms into space, eliminating all trace of her existence in order to preserve the other Gast's alibi for the murders. Granted, this would ultimately doom her counterpart as well, but at least the assassinations would not be traceable back to Pavak or one Colonel Demme Gast. She had no shame concerning the killing of A'Barra or the sneak attack on Oyolo, but she would prefer that her name and record not be stained with the murder of General Tem, even if the esteemed military hero had finally allowed misguided pangs of conscience to undermine his resolve, necessitating his death.

Forgive me, General. May you rest in peace.

Climbing more than ten flights of stairs was exhausting. She was breathing hard and shedding by the time she reached the saucer's main deck. Her heart was pounding in her chest and she wanted to kill anyone who got in her way. She loosened the collar of her helmet to let in a little fresh air. Steering clear of sickbay and the auxiliary control room, which was now under heavy guard, she made her way to the transporter room. Despite her fatigue, she managed to maintain a professional posture so as to avoid attracting undue attention. To her relief, no guards were posted outside the transporter room. Where could anyone go anyway? There were no vessels, planets, moons, or space stations anywhere within transporter range.

The door opened automatically and she slipped inside.

Only a single Starfleet officer was manning the transporter control booth. The redheaded woman looked vaguely familiar—Gast dimly recalled being introduced to her at the reception—but her name escaped Gast, for which she blamed her escalating infirmity. She glanced around the transporter complex, but she spotted no sign of the other Gast; she hoped that her counterpart had been only temporarily detained.

One of us had to get here first, she reflected, *and perhaps it's just as well that it's me.*

Fatigued or not, Gast felt better equipped to deal with the transporter operator. If anything, her killer instinct felt stronger than ever. She clasped her hands behind her back as she deftly slipped her gloves off and extracted the knife from her sleeve. The fact that the controls were contained within an enclosed transparent booth posed a challenge, but not an insurmountable one. She merely needed to lure the unsuspecting operator from the booth.

"Yes?" the human woman greeted her. "Can I help you?"

"We've had reports of a radiation leak in this section," Gast lied. In truth, she had taken care not to damage or disable any systems essential to the proper functioning of the transporters. "If you could step out of the booth, please, so I can take a look."

The redhead annoyingly remained at the controls. "A radiation leak? That's news to me."

"This is an emergency situation," Gast said, struggling to hide her impatience. "I need you to—"

A sneeze interrupted her attempt to draw the operator out of the booth. Twisting to the left, she saw Commander Chekov emerge from the landing party staging area on the opposite side of the chamber. Phaser in hand, he crossed in front of the transporter platform to hold her at gunpoint.

"Kindly remove your helmet," he instructed.

Fury and frustration seethed inside her, but she tried to keep her voice calm. "The radiation—"

"Identify yourself," he insisted.

Gast realized that there was little point in dissembling any longer. Discreetly tucking the knife in the insulated tubing at the back of her rad suit, she grudgingly removed her helmet and tossed it to one side. It banged against the floor as she let the *Enterprise*'s unwelcome security chief get a good look at her vexed Pavakian features. She clenched her jaw to keep from snarling. She wanted to spit in his hairless Terran face.

Chekov nodded, seemingly unsurprised.

"I was expecting you, Colonel Gast," he declared. "Or should I call you the *other* Colonel Gast?" He smiled rather too smugly. "Quite the clever ploy, I admit. Reminds me of a story by the great Russian author Dostoevsky, 'The Double.' Are you familiar with it?"

"I can't say that I am," she replied. "I have little interest in alien literature."

"A shame," Chekov said. "You don't know what you're missing."

Gast realized that all her plans had just been sucked out of the airlock. Her mind raced frantically, attempting to calculate her next move. Her eyes darted back and forth, searching for an escape route. Rage made it hard to think straight. Should she resort to fight or flight or perhaps attempt to take a hostage? She began to edge toward the control booth.

"Uh-uh." The other woman drew a phaser pistol from beneath the console. "Don't even think about it."

Banks, Gast remembered. That was the redhead's name. *Lieutenant Banks.*

"You should know," Chekov said, "that the other Gast will not be joining you. I'm afraid she is currently enjoying the hospitality of our brig." He kept his phaser aimed in her direction. "I anticipated that you and your double would want to reintegrate yourself with all deliberate speed, so it seemed logical to assume that you would promptly find your way here. All emergency and cargo transporters are under watch as well."

"Very thorough, Commander," she said. "I underestimated you."

"You would not be the first. I recommend that you surrender peacefully. It is not too late to put you and your doppelgänger back together."

Again, the prospect of merging with her other self elicited a peculiar mixture of attraction and revulsion. Her skin crawled beneath her fur.

"Perhaps, perhaps not," she said. "Ultimately, it doesn't matter. Even if you've apprehended both of us, you can't stop the warhead from striking Oyolo . . . and reducing their capital to a smoking crater of unstable matter! The Oyolu will pay for their crimes against my people. I wish only to live long enough to see them suffer!"

Chekov's smile faded. "Captain Kirk will not let that happen."

"I doubt he has a choice," she replied, encouraged that Chekov could offer nothing more than an empty expression of confidence in his captain. If Kirk truly had a means to halt the attack, Chekov would have said so. "Retribution is at hand. Oyolo will finally learn the true cost of defying Pavak!"

"But that is madness," Chekov said, visibly appalled. "Millions of innocent lives will be lost."

"They brought this on themselves!" she snarled, finally giving voice to the burning hatred in her heart. Spittle sprayed from her lips. "There is no such thing as an 'innocent' Oyolu . . . and there can be no peace with such vile and untrustworthy creatures!"

"That is quite enough." Chekov shook his head in disgust. "We do not need to hear any more of your ravings. Please place your hands—"

A bomb went off elsewhere in the ship. Possibly in the starboard support pylon. The overhead lights flickered and the floor listed briefly to one side. Thrown off-balance, Chekov stumbled across the quaking chamber. His gun arm drooped.

Now! Gast thought.

Seizing the opportunity, she plucked the knife from behind her back and flung it at Chekov. Alas, the tumult and her own debilitated state threw off her aim and the knife merely sank into his shoulder. He grunted in pain as the phaser flew from his fingers to clatter across the transporter platform behind him. Alarmed, and clutching his injured shoulder, he scrambled onto the platform after it.

She lunged after him, propelled by an all-consuming fury she could no longer contain. There was no point in fleeing—she was a dead woman already—but at least she could take this arrogant Starfleet bastard with her. Bloodlust overcame sickness and exhaustion as she tackled him, knocking him off his feet. Snarling, she pinned him to the platform and drew back her fist to deliver a killing blow to his throat. Trained in hand-to-hand combat, she hardly needed a weapon to crush his windpipe.

Good-bye, Commander. Who underestimated whom?

But before she could strike, her fist dissolved into atoms . . . along with the rest of her.

Stuck inside the control booth, Banks was unable to fire her phaser through the transparent partition dividing her from the platform. Thinking quickly, she did the next best thing and energized both Chekov and Gast before her superior could take any more damage. She let out a sigh of relief as Chekov and his berserk attacker vanished into a rippling curtain of energy. The familiar whine of the transporter effect replaced the jarring sounds of violence.

With no target destination selected, their patterns remained stored in the transporter buffer. Operating the controls, she worked swiftly to isolate and separate their respective patterns into individual files. She would have preferred to have a veteran transporter operator, ideally Mister Scott, perform the procedure, but there was no time to request assistance. The patterns could be held in the buffer for only a few minutes before they began to degrade.

Here goes nothing, she thought.

She reassembled Chekov first. A column of energy coalesced into the wounded officer, who was momentarily disoriented by the sudden change in his circumstances. He looked about in confusion, bleeding onto the platform.

"Where . . . where did she go?"

"Still in the buffer, sir." She eyed his injured shoulder with concern. "Are you all right, sir?"

Wincing, he climbed back onto his feet and reclaimed his phaser. "This little scratch? Nothing to be alarmed about, Lieutenant. Believe me, I've been through worse."

He hopped off the platform and raised his phaser with his uninjured left arm. He aimed the weapon at the empty platform from a safe distance. Blood trickled from his wounded shoulder.

"Shall I rematerialize her, sir?" Banks asked.

"Proceed, Lieutenant. But please try not to make any more copies. Two Gasts are more than enough."

Banks had to agree. "Aye, sir."

She operated the controls, more confidently this time, and the assassin reappeared upon the platform, crouched over an enemy who wasn't there anymore. She blinked in confusion, her upraised fist suspended over the bloodstained floor of the platform.

"What—? Where—?"

Banks watched intently, just in case the hate-crazed Pavakian still had more fight in her, but she only managed a few puzzled breaths before collapsing facedown on the platform. For a second, Banks feared that the shock of the transport had killed Gast, who was supposed to be dying from being split into two people, but, on closer inspection, she saw that the prone assassin was still breathing shallowly. Gast lay sprawled upon the platform, moaning faintly.

"Careful, sir," Banks warned, emerging from the booth to cover Chekov with her own phaser. "She might be playing possum."

Chekov cautiously checked on the unconscious killer. "It appears not." He placed a hand against Gast's throat, feeling her pulse. "She's still alive . . . for the present."

"That's good," Banks said. "I guess."

Chekov stepped away from the prisoner. "Contact sickbay. Tell Doctor McCoy he's going to need room for two Gasts."

"Yes, sir." She nodded at his injured shoulder. "Don't you need to report to sickbay, too?"

Chekov shook his head. "The captain needs me on the bridge."

"But . . ."

"There are first-aid kits in the supply lockers." He indicated the adjacent staging area where the landing parties prepared for their missions. "Get one."

Banks knew better than to argue with him.

Twenty-Six

Lieutenant Mark Duncan wanted to be somewhere else.

The *Enterprise* was on red alert, bombs were going off throughout the ship, and the scuttlebutt was that there was an alien saboteur aboard *and* that the Pavakians had launched a sneak attack on Oyolu, violating the cease-fire. More than anything, Duncan wanted to join his fellow security officers in tracking down the saboteur and dealing with the crisis, but instead he found himself posted outside Lenore Karidian's quarters, keeping watch over the suspect who remained confined to the premises. Duncan knew that the actress, who was allegedly an old flame of the captain's, was possibly the killer of two visiting delegates, but even still it seemed a waste of resources to have him on guard duty here while there was a more immediate emergency going on.

Couldn't we just lock her in for the duration?

A loud crash, coming from inside the guest quarters, snapped him out of his musings. Phaser drawn, he unlocked the door and cautiously entered the foyer, on guard for some sort of trick. Karidian had supposedly

killed at least seven people in her time, so he wasn't
taking anything for granted. She had seemed harmless
enough, but . . .

"Oh, crap!"

The suspect was convulsing atop the bed, her arms
and legs flailing wildly. Her eyes were rolled up so that
only the whites were visible. A bloody froth bubbled
at the corners of her mouth. Broken ceramic shards
littered the floor in front of the bed stand, where her
thrashing had apparently knocked over a vase. A discarded hypospray rested upon the bed, just beyond her
fingertips. Duncan took in the scene and instantly put
the pieces together.

Suicide.

"No, no, no, no." He rushed toward the bed, desperate to keep the prisoner from dying on his watch. More
foam bubbled past her lips. An alarming gurgling came
from her throat. Holstering his weapon, he reached to
clear her airway. "No way! You are not doing this, you
hear me!"

She bit down hard on his fingers. Her right hand
snatched up the hypospray and pressed it against his
carotid artery. He heard the hiss of the device against
his neck . . . and then he didn't hear anything else.

A full dose of the sedative, prescribed by Doctor McCoy
to settle her nerves, was enough to instantly knock out
the guard. He collapsed across Lenore, whose spasms
ended abruptly. She shoved the limp security officer

aside and scrambled out from beneath him. Getting off the bed and onto the floor, she glanced down at her unconscious victim.

I'm sorry, she thought. *I had no choice.*

The play had gone off just as planned. No real surprise there; this had hardly been her first death scene . . . or ambush. She spit a mouthful of blood and soap bubbles onto the floor. The blood had come from biting the inside of her cheek—an old actor's trick— while the soap had come from the lavatory. Attention to detail was key to a convincing performance after all. She took a moment to check the guard's pulse to ensure that he was only unconscious. He was lucky, she reflected. The old Lenore would not have hesitated to kill him in cold blood.

But I'm not that person anymore, she thought. *Am I?*

She stared at her reflection in the mirror over the dresser. She thought she knew whom the distraught woman in the mirror was, but how could she be sure? Not for the first time since coming aboard this new *Enterprise,* she doubted her own sanity and perceptions. Was it possible that she *was* the assassin, that she had lost her grip on reality again, that her father's murderous blood had infected her fevered brain once more? She didn't *believe* so, but perhaps that didn't matter anymore. Her mere presence was threatening the fragile peace between Oyolo and Pavak—and putting Kirk and Doctor Tamris and the others in jeopardy.

I'm sorry, she thought again. *This is all my fault.*

Just her being aboard the *Enterprise,* and accused of the murders, put Kirk in a dreadful position, and she felt horrible for adding to his trials during this crisis, which now seemed to include some manner of disaster or emergency aboard the ship itself. The mysterious explosions rocking the ship were what had finally convinced her to take action. Jim had enough on his hands, such as protecting his ship and trying to end a war, without having to worry about her as well, let alone be distracted by past lies and betrayals and regrets . . .

It was funny. There had been times, back at the hospital on Gilead, when she had hated Kirk and had wanted him dead. She'd blamed him for her undoing and had fantasized about killing him a thousand times, in a thousand grisly ways. And there had been other times when she'd wanted so much to apologize to him for what she'd done, and had wondered what might have been had her crimes and delusions not come between them. And now here she was again, back on his ship, making more trouble for him . . . and the entire peace process.

She couldn't bear it any longer. She had to make this right.

Moving swiftly, she stripped the guard of his uniform and changed into the one-piece burgundy jumpsuit. She was grateful for the more unisex look of modern Starfleet uniforms; this disguise would have been much harder to pull off back in the old days when security officers wore bright red tunics and most female crew members wore skirts. The uniform was not exactly her size, but she was used to making do with whatever theatrical attire was available.

Just another quick costume change, she thought. *For one last performance.*

Inspecting herself in the mirror, she hastily fixed her hair to look suitably Starfleet and tugged the ill-fitting uniform into place. Confiscating the guard's phaser, she stunned him to buy herself more time. He would not be raising an alarm anytime soon. She considered binding and gagging him as well but decided that would be overkill. Besides, she didn't have time to go to such elaborate lengths.

She needed to get off the *Enterprise* before anyone else got hurt.

Leaving the unfortunate Lieutenant Duncan behind, she slipped out of her quarters and into the hallway. Red alert lights flashed incarnadine, yet there appeared to be little activity in this section of the ship, which held mostly crew quarters and guest accommodations. She assumed that any other visitors were staying safe in their quarters during the present crisis, while the *Enterprise*'s intrepid crew was dealing with more urgent matters elsewhere. In this respect, the red alert was working to her advantage.

"You! What are you up to?"

I spoke too soon, she thought. Spinning around, she saw Ifusi charging at her like an enraged bull, his head low as though he meant to gore her with his horns.

"Assassin! Were those explosions your doing?"

Protesting her innocence would be a waste of breath, she knew. Instead she fired the stolen phaser, dropping him in his tracks. He hit the floor with a heavy thud. His stunned form landed at her feet. He, too, was lucky that she wasn't a killer anymore.

She ran down the corridor.

"Captain," Uhura called out. "Doctor Tamris and the other GRC visitors are wondering what's happening. They're alarmed by the explosions."

I'll bet, Kirk thought. Tamris and her people probably feared that they'd gone from the frying pan to the fire, but he didn't have time to reassure them now. "Tell them to remain in their quarters, and keep out of the way, until further notice."

The last thing they needed at the moment was confused people roaming the ship. The other Gast had been apprehended, although the repair crews still had to be on the lookout for the vicious surprises she had hidden through the ship's sabotaged power conduits and other hardware. Every moment brought reports of new complications and difficulties left behind by the saboteur, who had apparently been quite industrious over the last few days. Spock and Scotty couldn't get back soon enough, even if there was no way they could possibly return before the warhead struck Oyolo. A digital countdown on the main viewer reminded Kirk that time was running out.

Twenty-six minutes to impact.

The portside turbolift opened and Chekov strode onto the bridge accompanied by Lieutenant Banks. Kirk noted a crude bandage wrapped around Chekov's right shoulder. Red stains seeped through the white dressing, yet Chekov moved briskly and with purpose.

"Reporting for duty, Captain," Chekov said. "The prisoner is secure."

Kirk was glad to have him back on the bridge. "The brig?"

"Both Colonel Gasts are in sickbay, under Doctor McCoy's care," Chekov reported. "They do not look well, sir."

Kirk indicated the security chief's wounded shoulder. "And yourself, Commander?"

"Just a scratch, Captain. The second Gast did not surrender quietly."

So it seems, Kirk gathered. "Good work, both of you."

"Thank you, Captain." Chekov relieved Dazim at the Tactical station. "So, what did I miss?"

Shuttlebay operations were managed from a control room overlooking the cavernous landing bay below. Lenore entered confidently as though she belonged there. Her hike through the ship had been a nerve-racking one, with her expecting to be recognized at any moment, but, in the heat of the red alert, nobody had paid any attention to yet another crew member going about her duties. Lenore expertly concealed any butterflies in her stomach as she inhabited the role of a busy enlisted woman with someplace to be.

It's just another stage, she thought. *Another part to play.*

"Yes?" a harried lieutenant asked, looking up as she entered. "What is it?"

She let her stolen phaser answer for her. A sapphire beam swept the control room, stunning its personnel, who slumped unconscious over their instrumentation panels. She squeezed past them to reach the controls for the clamshell doors at the aft end of the landing bay. Large windows offered her a view of the *Copernicus* resting on the bay below, ready to go. As far as she knew, the *Enterprise*'s other shuttle, *Galileo,* was still on Pavak with the weapons inspectors.

Good, she thought. So far fortune was with her. Perhaps that was proof enough that she was doing the right thing. *Or at least the lesser of two evils.*

An emergency stairwell led down from the control room to the floor of the landing bay, where she stunned several more startled crew members before climbing into the cockpit of the shuttlecraft and firing up its helm controls. Her stint in the GRC, which had occasionally required her to assist in making deliveries to disaster sites and outlying refugee camps, had taught her a little about piloting a variety of vehicles. She hoped it would be enough—and that she could get away from the *Enterprise* fast enough to elude its tractor beams. *Who knows,* she thought. *Maybe Jim will be shrewd enough to let me escape.*

It was better this way. She knew that fleeing only made her look guiltier, but that didn't matter anymore. She fully intended to serve as a scapegoat for the sake of peace; better that the Pavakians and Oyolu blame her for the murders than each other. Perhaps in that way she could finally atone for her crimes, as well as those of her infamous father, and spare Jim Kirk any torturous dilemmas.

The only question had been to whom she should turn herself in to, the Pavakians or the Oyolu? After some consideration, she had decided to set course for Oyolo, in hopes of smoothing over any hard feelings from the hostage crisis and rescue mission. The Pavakians would be displeased, but, as long as the Oyolu did not go easy on her, they might settle for the knowledge that General Tem's alleged assassin had not gotten away scot free. "Justice" would be served and the peace process could continue.

Or so she prayed.

As she'd programmed them, the bay's huge clamshell doors opened at her signal. A low-level force field kept the bay pressurized while permitting access to and from the *Enterprise*. Activating the thrusters, she lifted off from the marked runway and piloted *Copernicus* out of the bay faster than was surely advisable. In a heartbeat, the shuttle had cleared the bay and was accelerating through the vacuum of space. Lenore held her breath, fearing that a tractor beam would lock onto *Copernicus* at any moment, while testing the shuttle's speed limits.

"Good-bye, Jim," she whispered over the thrum of the impulse engines. "I never meant to hurt you again."

Lenore steered a course for Oyolo.

Twenty-Seven

"Captain!" Chekov exclaimed. "*Copernicus* has exited the shuttlebay!"

"What?" Kirk had no idea who could have taken the shuttlecraft or why. A horrible thought flashed through his brain: Could there be a *third* Gast running amok? "Lock onto it with a tractor beam. Don't let it get away!"

"I'm trying, sir," Chekov said, "but the tractors are inoperative!"

More sabotage, Kirk realized. *Gast's handiwork no doubt.*

Within seconds, *Copernicus* would be out of range of the tractor beams, Kirk realized, and the *Enterprise* couldn't even chase after it with the ship's propulsion systems down. Frustrated, he pounded his fist against the armrest of his chair. As if the bombs and the doomsday shuttle weren't enough!

"Uhura," he barked. "Hail *Copernicus*. Find out who the devil took that shuttle!"

"Yes, sir!" She fiddled with the controls of her console. A startled look came over her face as she established contact with the runaway shuttle. "It's Lenore Karidian, sir!"

Lenore?

Of all the possibilities out there, that one had never occurred to him. Thunderstruck, he glanced at Riley, who appeared equally taken aback. In all the commotion since Gast's confession, there had been no time to address the fact that Lenore was apparently innocent after all.

So why was she running?

"Put her through," Kirk ordered.

"Aye, Captain."

Lenore's head and shoulders appeared upon the main viewer. Seated at the helm of the *Copernicus,* she wore a red Starfleet uniform and had her hair styled in a manner consistent with regulations. Her expression was taut but determined. Kirk wondered briefly how she'd managed to evade her guard and escape her quarters. He assumed that Chekov was checking into that at this very minute.

"Lenore?" he asked. "What do you think you're doing?"

"I'm sorry, Jim. I know how this looks, but it's best for everyone. I'm going to turn myself in to the authorities on Oyolo . . . and confess to the murders."

"But you're not a suspect anymore. We've identified the real assassin: Colonel Gast. She's in custody now."

He kicked himself for not immediately informing Lenore that she'd been cleared of suspicion, but with the bombs going off and Oyolo in danger, there had simply been more immediate matters demanding his attention. He had thought Lenore was safely stowed away in her quarters.

"Gast?" Lenore was visibly confused. *"But . . . how—?"*

"It's complicated," he said, lacking time to explain. "But you need to turn around and head back to the *Enterprise* immediately. There's a Pavakian warhead heading straight for Oyolo."

He glanced at the digital countdown: Twenty minutes to impact.

"A warhead?" Her face paled as she grasped what that meant. *"Can't you stop it?"*

"We're trying, but our hands are tied." He hastily explained the situation to her. "So, you see, Oyolo is the last place you want to be right now . . . and we need that shuttle back."

With the *Enterprise* stalled, *Copernicus* was their best shot at intercepting the Pavakian shuttlecraft bearing the warhead. Kirk had been on the verge of dispatching it when word came that it had been hijacked. But was there still time to make the attempt?

"Can I help?" Lenore volunteered. *"Tell me what to do."*

Kirk took her offer seriously. She was already en route to Oyolo, which put her in a better position to stop the doomsday shuttle than anyone else. And he knew from bitter experience just how determined and effective she could be when it came to eliminating threats.

"The shuttle's phasers," he asked Chekov, "could they stop the Pavakian craft?"

Chekov shook his head. Sensor data scrolled across his tactical displays.

"Unlikely, sir. Sensors are detecting high-level shields protecting the target. It appears that, among other things, all power from the life-support systems has been diverted to the deflectors. The hull is also protected by heavy ablative plating." He shook his head. "It's an armored truck, sir. I doubt the *Copernicus*'s phasers can make a dent in it."

Figures, Kirk thought. He wondered if the diplomatic shuttle had always been so heavily armored, due to the constant danger of Oyolu terrorism, or if Gast's fellow conspirators had deliberately fortified it in preparation for this attack. Not that it mattered; from what Chekov was saying, the shuttle could not simply be halted by *Copernicus*'s phasers. Plus, Lenore lacked Starfleet training in space combat. There was no guarantee she could score a direct shot.

But Lenore had another idea.

"What if I collided with it?" she suggested. *"And it hit me instead of Oyolo?"*

Kirk didn't like the idea, but looked to Chekov for a tactical assessment.

"It could work," Chekov said. "A collision at impulse speed, with the warp nacelles partially engaged, could trigger the warhead."

Before it reaches Oyolo, Kirk realized. "But that would be suicide, Lenore."

"I know. This is my chance to finally wash the blood

from my hands, and perhaps even redeem the name of Karidian." Emotion cracked her voice. "*It's very clear to me now that I'll never truly be able to escape my past, so I might as well stop trying . . . for everyone's sake. It's probably better this way. . . .*"

"No," Kirk objected. "I refuse to accept that. You can't just throw your life away."

"*But what other choice do we have?*"

Kirk's mind hit on a possible solution. "Listen to me," he said urgently. "I have an idea."

"*Transmitting intercept data,*" Chekov's voice announced. His thick accent reminded Lenore of the one she had assumed for a production of *The Seagull* many long years ago. "*Please acknowledge.*"

"Data received," she replied, loading the information into the shuttle's automatic pilot. "Initiating countdown."

A computerized voice issued from the control panel before her:

"*Ten minutes to interception.*"

A sensor display indicated the Pavakian shuttle directly ahead. Peering through the forward port, Lenore thought she glimpsed the lethal craft crossing the buffer zone like a shooting star. A shudder ran through her as she contemplated the apocalyptic weapon the vessel was carrying toward Oyolo and its people. If she failed, the death toll would make even her father's body count seem trivial by comparison. Millions would perish instead of thousands.

"Eight minutes to interception."

There was no time to lose. Scrambling, she low-ered the shuttle's shields and placed its warp nacelles in warm-up mode before abandoning the cockpit. She hastily donned an emergency space suit from a supply closet. A rigid shell protected the wearer's torso while the arms and legs were constructed of a more flexible material that allowed greater freedom of movement. The cumbersome suit challenged her quick-change skills, but she managed to climb into it while the com-puter counted down. A detachable helmet and match-ing jet pack waited to be donned.

"Four minutes to interception."

Was it even worth racing the clock? For a moment, she gave serious thought to remaining aboard the shut-tle and paying for her many crimes once and for all. It would be easy; she wouldn't even have to lift a finger to bring down the curtain on her sorry drama. She could exit the stage happily, knowing that her sacrifice had saved the lives of millions. It would be a fitting final act, worthy of the immortal Bard. She might even see her father once more . . .

"And by a sleep to say we end the heart-ache and the thousand natural shocks that flesh is heir to, 'tis a consummation devoutly to be wished."

It was tempting; she had always wanted to play Hamlet, as opposed to Ophelia. A tragic end was probably the best she could hope for. And yet she had worked so hard, for so many years, to earn a second chance. There was much good she could conceivably do, if only she survived. Was it possible her story could yet have a happy ending?

If people like Jim Kirk still believe in me, perhaps I should, too.

Shaking off her morbid impulse, she fastened her helmet and activated the suit's life-support system. The jet pack fit over the oxygen tank on her back, the heavy burden making her long for the weightlessness of space. Sturdy boots thumped across the floor of the shuttle as she hurried to the aft hatchway. Signage warned that the hatch was not to be opened while the *Copernicus* was in flight, let alone in space with the shields down, but she overrode the safeguards and activated the emergency release. The hatch dropped open before her.

"*One minute to interception.*"

Explosive decompression, along with the shuttle's forward momentum, sent her hurtling out the back of the cabin into the weightless void. She experienced a moment of sheer vertiginous panic as she found herself falling through space for the first time in her life. There was no up, no down, only a vast sea of emptiness in which she feared she might drown. Frightened eyes peered out through the helmet's wide visor at the merciless immensity of the cosmos. Her breath caught in her throat.

The jet pack, she remembered. *Use the jet pack.*

Her gloved hands found the thruster controls at her sides. Hesitantly at first, she worked them to bring her headlong motion slightly under control. Rotating in space, she spied *Copernicus* streaking away toward the distant doomsday shuttle, crossing unimaginable distances in a heartbeat.

"Lenore! This is Enterprise. *Can you read me?"*

Kirk's voice came over her helmet's comm system. She assumed that the ever-resourceful Lieutenant Uhura had managed to establish the link. The voice was a comforting reminder that she was not alone in this interplanetary abyss. Swallowing hard, she found her own voice.

"I hear you, Jim. I'm here."

"Did you make it? Did you bail from Copernicus?"

"Yes," she assured him, not mentioning her near change of heart. "I did it. I'm off the—"

A blinding flash, like a star birthing or dying, lit up the buffer zone as *Copernicus* collided with the Pavakian shuttle bearing the warhead. The soundless explosion was awesome and terrifying to behold, rendering Lenore mute and aghast. A blazing ball of white-hot light billowed out in all directions, blowing apart both shuttlecrafts. Hundreds of kilometers away, the hellish conflagration still struck her as far too close for comfort. Static crackled in her ears, no doubt caused by the violent release of who knew what electromagnetic energies. A shock wave, propagating through the interplanetary medium, slammed into her, sending her tumbling head over heels away from the infernal spectacle she had helped to kindle. Jagged shards of metal flew like shrapnel through the void, buffeting her.

"Lenore!" Kirk shouted over the static. *"LENORE!"*

Breathless, unable to speak, she hurled across space like an ill omen. *"When beggars die, there are no comets seen,"* she thought. *"The heavens themselves blaze forth the death of princes . . ."*

Was she the harbinger of her own demise?

"Lenore! Answer me!"

Kirk's voice grounded her, as surely as a bracing dose of zetaproprion. She groped for the thruster controls, only to find them unresponsive. Damage lights flashed inside the helmet and an automated female voice spoke in her ear:

"Life-support compromised. Twenty-three minutes of available air remaining."

Had the shockwave or some flying piece of debris damaged the suit? Lenore had no idea; what was obvious was that her life had been reduced to another all-too-brief countdown. With the *Enterprise* becalmed in space, there was little hope of rescue before her time expired.

"Lenore? Are you there?" Kirk asked. *"We're reading distress signals from your suit."*

She was grateful that she didn't have to waste any of her dwindling air explaining her dire predicament. Life was too short—literally—to dwell on the mechanics of the situation. A peculiar peace came over her.

"It's all right, Jim. It appears I won't be getting a

second chance after all, but I'm content. At least I can
depart this mortal coil in peace. All my sins have been
washed away at last. . . ."

"*Don't say that. Don't give up hope. I'm not going to
let you die out there.*"

"It's kind of you to say so, Jim, but we both know
there's nothing you can do. This is my final curtain call.
There will be no more encores."

Was it just her imagination or could she already feel
the cold of space seeping into her weary bones? Was
that the hiss of escaping air in her ears?

An undiscovered country called out to her. . . .

"Hold on, Lenore," Kirk urged her. "We'll find a way to
save you, I promise!"

He signaled Uhura to mute his audio. As much as
he hated to leave Lenore hanging, he wanted to be able
to confer frankly with his crew without her overhearing
any more bad news. He knew all too well just how limited their options and resources were at the moment.

"Keep talking to her, Uhura. Don't left her drift in
silence."

Uhura nodded at her station. "Understood, sir. I'll
try to keep her hopes up."

Kirk appreciated it. He couldn't think of a better,
more compassionate soul to have on the other end of
the line at a time like this. He looked anxiously at Engineering. "Propulsion?"

"Not yet, sir," Magee responded, shaking her head.

"Impulse and warp both still under repair. I honestly can't say when they'll be up and running again, but . . . not soon enough."

Damn, Kirk thought. "It's not fair. She just saved millions of lives on Oyolo. She doesn't deserve to die in space."

"I agree," Riley said, surprising Kirk. "I was wrong about her, about who she is now. Too bad it's too late to do any good."

Kirk refused to accept that. "No. There must be *something* we can do."

"But what?" Sulu asked aloud. "We're dead in the water."

"I'm well aware of that, Mister Sulu," Kirk said, rather more sharply than necessary. "But we need options."

"Captain?" Uhura interrupted. "I did my best, but . . . she's asking for you."

He hesitated only briefly. If there truly was no hope, maybe this was the best he could do for Lenore right now. After all they'd been through, he wasn't about to let her face death in space without even his voice to keep her company.

"Put her through," he instructed. "Lenore? Can you read me?"

"For the time being," she said. Her disembodied voice haunted the bridge.

"Don't worry. We're working on a solution now."

A wry chuckle came over the comms. *"You're an excellent liar, Captain. You always have been. You would've made an excellent leading man. I can see you as Caesar. . . ."*

He worried that the air was already getting thin in her helmet. It occurred to him that she might want to speak less to conserve her oxygen supply, but if talking kept her calm, he wasn't going to deny her some human contact and communication in what might be her final moments. A few extra breaths probably weren't going to make any difference.

"Stay with me. Don't give up." His throat tightened. "We'll think of something."

"I'm luckier than my father, you know. He never got a chance to atone for his crimes. He died in guilt and despair, but whatever dreams may come, mine will be far more restful, I think . . ."

"Don't talk like that. You've suffered enough. You don't need to pay for your past mistakes anymore."

"That's right." Riley raised his voice to be heard over the comlink. "This is Kevin Riley. I misjudged you . . . and I forgive you. Nobody wants you to die."

"That's good to know, but perhaps all the more reason to make a graceful exit. Always leave the audience wanting more, you know? 'If it be now, 'tis not to come. If it be not to come, it will be now. The readiness is all.' " She sighed wistfully. *"I've always wanted to play Hamlet, did you know that? A shame I'll never have the opportunity. . . ."*

"You'll get your chance," Kirk said. "To play other roles. You have your whole life in front of you."

"*I wish I could believe that, but I was born under an ill star and have never had much luck with happy endings. Tragedy was always my forte.*" Her voice quavered. "*Jim, I'm getting very cold, and sleepy. . . .*"

"Hang in there! Don't slip away!"

"*Keep talking to me, please. Don't leave me alone. . . .*"

"I'm not going anywhere . . . and neither are you."

He could hear her drifting away, both literally and figuratively. Her voice began to slur as she sounded more and more out of it.

"*'Now my charms are all o'erthrown, and what strength I have's mine own, which is most faint. . . .'*"

"No! Stay with us!"

We're losing her, he realized, *and there's nothing I can do!*

"Captain!" Chekov called out. "There's another vessel approaching her location at great speed." A grin broke out across his face as he stared at his tactical displays. "It's *Galileo!*"

Twenty-Eight

"Attention, *Enterprise,* Karidian. This is *Galileo.* We have been monitoring your situation and are prepared to render assistance."

Spock manned the helm of the shuttlecraft while Mister Scott monitored the engines' display panels with his customary degree of agitation. The worried engineer wiped droplets of perspiration from his brow as he eyed various indicators with increasing concern.

"I don't like it, Spock. This boat wasn't built to maintain this kind of acceleration!"

"I am aware of that, Mister Scott, but there was little alternative under the circumstances."

Racing time, they had crossed the solar system from Sumno at warp speed, leaving Brigadier-General Pogg to transport Takk and his confederates back to Pavak aboard *Outward Six.* The odds that they would be able to intercept the Pavakian shuttle in time to prevent the attack on Oyolo had been slim, but a slim chance, as Captain Kirk had demonstrated on more than one occasion, was better than none. Spock had judged the endeavor worth the risk, despite the considerable strain placed on *Galileo*'s engines and warp nacelles, which had required the best efforts of both himself and Scott to operate at such levels without burning out. Spock had been particularly impressed by Scott's ability to coax more speed out of the shuttlecraft than was theoretically possible. As a Vulcan, Spock did not believe in miracles, but, in this instance, Scott had more than lived up to his reputation as a worker of same.

"Indeed," Spock added, "I regret that I must increase our rate of acceleration if we are to reach Miss Karidian in time to preserve her life."

Scott gulped. "But the indicators are already pushing into the red zone. We're exceeding every safety level."

"Would you prefer to let her perish because we arrived a few moments too late?"

"No," Scotty said, sighing heavily. "We need to do what we can to save the brave lass. It's the least we can do after she took out that bloody warhead for us."

That the *Copernicus*, piloted by Lenore Karidian, had succeeded in preventing the Pavakian shuttle from delivering its lethal payload to Oyolo had come as a relief to both men. The *Galileo* had arrived in the buffer zone too late to make a difference in that respect, but perhaps they could still be of use where the endangered actress was concerned, provided they made sufficient speed.

Success was by no means guaranteed, however. By Spock's calculations, Lenore had only approximately eight minutes of life left to her. Retrieving her from space under such time constraints was no simple matter. Both men had already donned environmental suits in anticipation of any possible emergencies, but even still the challenge was daunting. Weightlessness was hardly conducive to haste.

Scott appeared to arrive at the same assessment. "I'm not as spry as I used to be," he confessed. "Perhaps I should take the helm while you go fetch the lassie."

"That will not be necessary, Mister Scott. Time does not allow for an extravehicular rescue."

A puzzled expression betrayed Scott's confusion. "Then what are you suggesting?"

"To quote an old Vulcan expression, it appears we must bring the mountain to Muhammad."

"What do you mean by—?" Scott's jaw dropped as he grasped Spock's intent. "No, you must be joking."

"This is hardly an occasion for levity, Mister Scott. Please verify that you are securely strapped into your seat."

"Aye, Mister Spock." He swallowed hard. "I'll be doin' that all right."

Lenore's tumbling form registered on the shuttle's sensors. An onboard computer reported her speed, momentum, direction, and rate of acceleration, but Spock performed the necessary calculations in his own head as well. A woman's life was at stake; there was little margin for error.

He plotted an intercept course for her. Within

precisely 6.041 minutes, he made visual contact with their target. Through *Copernicus*'s front port, he saw her tumbling toward them. Spock scaled the shields down to their lowest operational setting, then he executed a combined loop and barrel roll so that the rear of the shuttle now faced the oncoming woman. His face was fixed in concentration. Despite his calculations, this was going to be a delicate maneuver, requiring split-second timing. He needed to precisely match Lenore's speed and direction if they were to accomplish their goal.

"Here she comes!" Scott said, peering back over his shoulder at the shuttle's aft viewport. "Ready as she goes!"

"Affirmative."

Spock swiftly reviewed his calculations one last time and pressed an icon on the control panel. The aft hatchway sprang open and Lenore hurled bodily into the cabin, her mass and momentum penetrating the minimized force field keeping the shuttle pressurized. She traveled the length of the cabin before the shuttle's artificial gravity sent her skidding across the floor. She slammed into the rear of the cockpit with what Spock estimated was insufficient force to cause serious injury. He had matched the shuttle's acceleration to hers in hopes of minimizing the impact, while, in theory, her insulated evacuation suit and helmet would provide a degree of protection as well.

Nevertheless, he would breathe easier once he knew she was unharmed.

"You did it, Mister Spock!" Scotty said. "You caught her!"

"Obviously." He closed the aft hatchway and reduced the shuttle's speed for the sake of the overstressed engines. Now that they had secured Karidian, they could afford to make their way back to the *Enterprise* at a more prudent pace. "Please check on our guest if you will, Mister Scott."

"Aye. That I will, Mister Spock!"

Scrambling out of his seat, Scott rushed to assist Lenore, who was sprawled in a heap upon the floor. He hastily detached her helmet as Spock watched intently from the helm. Gasping, she sucked in mouthfuls of fresh air. Her face was pale and her lips blue, but she was clearly still alive, although probably in need of immediate treatment for hypoxia. Spock dialed up the heat in the passenger cabin before activating the shuttle's automatic pilot and joining Scott at Lenore's side. Scott draped a thermal blanket over her trembling shoulders as Lenore managed to sit up.

"Are ye all right, lass?"

"I . . . I think so," she said, shivering within her damaged space suit. Her eyes widened as she recognized her rescuers. She glanced back and forth between them. "Mister Scott. Mister Spock . . . it's been a long time."

"Twenty years, four months, and three days," Spock said. "But, to employ a human expression, better late than never."

Twenty-Nine

Security teams escorted both Colonel Gasts into the transporter room. It dawned on Kirk that nearly a week had passed since a single Gast had first beamed aboard the *Enterprise* with the other delegates. Much had changed since then, and not always for the better, particularly where the devious Pavakian was concerned.

Weakened to the point of death, both Gasts required assistance just to walk. They remained identical in appearance, but the variation in their personalities was growing ever more extreme. One of the Gasts, the one who had actually committed the murders and sabotaged the ship, fought savagely despite her weakness, thrashing and twisting in a futile attempt to break free from the guards' grips. Her bloodshot eyes were wild. Saliva sprayed from her lips as she spotted Kirk. Rage contorted her face.

"You!" She tried to lunge at Kirk but was held back by the sturdy guards. "You ruined everything! You're as bad as those Oyolu scum! I should have killed you all, blown this entire ship to pieces . . . !"

By contrast, the other Gast, the one who provided

her double's alibi during the killings, appeared resigned and despondent. She stared bleakly at the floor, not even lifting her head to acknowledge her counterpart's crazed ranting. She let the guards herd her toward the transporter platform.

"It's no use," she murmured. "It's over, finished . . ."

Hours had passed since the warhead had been destroyed and it seemed that the crisis was indeed over. Repair crews, under Mister Scott's diligent supervision, had restored the *Enterprise*'s propulsion system and were in the process of undoing Gast's insidious handiwork. Thankfully, no crew members had been killed by her booby traps, although a number of casualties were now recovering in sickbay, along with Lenore, who was recuperating from her ordeal in space. According to McCoy, she was bound to make a full recovery, given a little time and rest.

It was unclear, however, whether the same could be said of the two Colonel Gasts.

"What do you think, Bones?" Kirk asked McCoy, who was on hand to provide whatever medical assistance might be required. "Is there still time to reintegrate them?"

"I wish I knew, Jim." McCoy regarded the twin Gasts with concern. "They've been separated for at least three days. That's much longer than you were, and you remember how hard that was on your system."

I could hardly forget, Kirk thought. Two sets of unpleasant memories clashed together in his mind, just as his warring selves had fought physically twenty years ago. By the end, he—*they*—had been so weak they could hardly stand.

"No! Let me go!" the rabid Gast shrieked as the guards dragged her onto the platform beside her more quiescent double. Fury gave way to sheer animal panic as her eyes glanced about frantically, searching for a way to escape. She hissed and kicked and shed. Tufts of dry fur went flying from her exposed hands and face. "You can't do this to me! I want to live!"

Kirk remembered that fear as well: a blind, instinctive, irrational terror at the prospect of rejoining with your opposite half. That fear had killed a test animal—a horned canine native to Alfa 177—when they had attempted to reintegrate it. That fear had almost undone Kirk as well. Only his civilized half, his ability to reason and compromise, had saved him.

"Let me go, you Terran bastards! I won't let you do this to me. I'll kill you first!"

Chekov, supervising the operation, kept a close watch on the crazed Pavakian. He appeared to be recovering as well, although Kirk noticed that he was still favoring his left arm. Kirk made a mental note to submit commendations for Chekov and Banks. They had both come through with flying colors, validating Kirk's faith in Chekov and his security staff.

Well done, Pavel.

"Doctor," Chekov addressed McCoy. "Your assistance, please, in securing the prisoner's cooperation?"

"All right," McCoy said, cautiously approaching the feral Gast. "Just keep a tight grip on her. She looks like she might bite."

"Bite? I'll tear your throat out, you incompetent quack! I'll—"

A judicious application of a hypospray tranquilized the more murderous double. Her eyes glazed over, her thrashing limbs went limp, and her head drooped onto her chest. She stood numbly atop a transporter pad, less than a meter from the other Gast. Drool trickled from the corner of her mouth. A low moan replaced her bloodthirsty ranting.

McCoy backed away and stepped off the platform.

"Given her debilitated state, I administered only a minimal dose," he explained. "Let's get on with this before it wears off."

"My thoughts exactly," Kirk said. "Everybody off the platform except the prisoners."

The guards warily released both Gasts, while Chekov and Banks stood by with phasers ready. For a moment, Kirk feared that the dying Pavakians might collapse onto the platform without anyone holding them up, but they managed to totter unsteadily upon their respective pads. It might have been easier if they'd held each other up, but that same instinctive aversion to rejoining still kept them apart. They turned away from each other, unable to even look at their other halves.

Why is it, Kirk thought, *that we so often fear facing ourselves?*

That was a question to ponder another day. What mattered now was trying to restore Gast if it wasn't already too late. Kirk nodded at Spock, who stood ready in the control booth.

"Energize."

Coruscating columns of shimmering light dissolved both Gasts into energy. Spock carefully monitored the displays on his control panel, giving them his full attention. It was Spock, Kirk recalled, who had put Kirk back together decades ago. Kirk hoped that his science officer could pull off the same feat again. Gast, for all her crimes, deserved a fair trial back on Pavak.

"Merging patterns now," Scott reported.

Twin columns moved together, converging over a vacant pad. The transporter whined as a solitary figure coalesced atop the pad, growing more substantial by the second. The light faded and a single Demme Gast appeared on the platform.

We did it, Kirk thought. *It worked.*

But the materialized figure collapsed. McCoy rushed to examine the motionless form. He checked her pulse and breathing, then hastily administered a powerful stimulant. When that failed to rouse her, he labored for several minutes to resuscitate her before reluctantly giving up the fight. He examined her with a scanner to confirm the truth.

"She's dead, Jim." He shook his head sadly. "It was too late, I guess. They'd been separated too long."

"Maybe," Kirk said thoughtfully. "Or perhaps she

simply couldn't live with her failure and saw no point in going on." He had needed to overcome his own fears to rejoin successfully with his other half. He doubted that either Gast had been in any state to muster that kind of desire to be whole once more. "Perhaps she just could not let go of her pain . . . and hate."

"Hardly the most scientific diagnosis, Captain," Spock said, emerging from the control booth, "but perhaps not inaccurate." He gazed down at the lifeless remains. "In the end, she couldn't escape herself . . . or what she had become."

"Few of us can," Kirk said. "But sometimes it's worth the effort."

Lenore had proved that.

"The shuttle is waiting to take you all back to Oyolo," Kirk said. "I think I can promise you a smoother ride this time."

Doctor Tamris and Lenore had gathered on the bridge to make their farewells before returning to their relief work on Oyolo. Ifusi and Riley were also present to see them off, along with Kirk's senior officers, excepting Mister Scott, who was busy conducting a top-to-bottom inspection of all the *Enterprise*'s systems, just in case. That the late Colonel Gast had managed to bollix his precious hardware in his absence had not sat well with Scott; Kirk knew the engineer was going to leave no stone unturned until he was certain beyond all doubt that the *Enterprise* was absolutely shipshape once more.

"Thank you, Captain," Tamris said. "We're all very grateful for your hospitality, not to mention your daring intervention earlier, but it's time we get back to our work. We're still badly needed planetside."

Kirk was impressed by her bravery and dedication, as well as her remarkable ability to forgive the very people who had taken her and her people captive. No one could have blamed them if they had chosen to never set foot on Oyolo again, let alone head back to the very same refugee camp.

"I have to ask," he said. "Are you quite sure it's safe to return? My strike force didn't exactly make many friends among the Oyolu during the rescue mission. There might still be some hard feelings."

"I appreciate your concern, Captain," she replied. "But we've received assurances from the Oyolu authorities that they can guarantee our security, and now that A'Barra's true killer has met her end, passions are said to have cooled significantly. I've been in touch with Jorgaht, who has emerged from the depths, and he assures me that the coast is clear." She shrugged philosophically. "As much as it ever is in this uncertain universe."

"Fair enough," Kirk said, glad to know that the valiant Horta had not been forced to hide deep beneath the planet's crust for long. "Your courage, as well as your willingness to overlook what occurred before, bodes well for the future . . . and perhaps for peace in general."

"We shall see," Ifusi said skeptically. He approached

Lenore, who appeared none the worse for her harrowing close call in space. "In any event, I must thank you again for your heroism in saving my world. All of Oyolo is indebted to you. Millions still live, despite the Pavakians' treachery."

Riley did not let that last remark pass without comment. "The Pavakian government has denounced the assassinations and the attempted attack on Oyolo in the strongest possible terms. Colonel Gast and her confederates represented a rogue element that did not have the backing of the legitimate authorities. The new envoy, Brigadier-General Pogg, is being dispatched to continue the peace talks, and I'm assured that Major Takk and his fellow co-conspirators will stand trial for their crimes. Furthermore, a thorough investigation into the full extent of the plot is already under way. Pavak has promised to root out every last trace of this conspiracy . . . in the interests of peace."

Ifusi snorted. He crossed his arms across his chest. "After all that's occurred, I have little faith in Pavakian promises. Nor am I convinced that Gast and her fellow villains were truly acting alone."

"But if you let their actions poison the peace process," Lenore observed, "they will have succeeded after all, and both worlds will suffer for it." She placed her hand on Ifusi's arm. "Perhaps you can thank me—and honor A'Barra's memory—by bringing an open mind to the peace talks and ensuring that A'Barra did not die in vain. Too many lives have been lost. Trust me when

I say that it's time to move on . . . and leave the sins of the past behind."

Ifusi mulled over her words. "There may be some wisdom to what you say. I will think on it."

That's a promising start, Kirk thought. More wisdom from *The Tempest* came to mind. " 'Yet with my nobler reason 'gainst my fury do I take part,' " he recited. " 'The rarer action is in virtue than in vengeance.' "

"A laudable sentiment," Riley agreed. "One might almost think Shakespeare was an Irishman." He graced Lenore with a forgiving smile. "Time to let bygones be bygones."

"I couldn't agree more, Ambassador," Kirk said.

He was proud of Riley. The onetime lieutenant had matured into a man of impressive character and ability. Pogg, whom both Spock and Scotty spoke highly of, was expected shortly, and Kirk had every confidence that Riley would eventually help the two parties lay a solid groundwork for peace.

"Thank you, Ambassador," Lenore said, visibly moved by Riley's gesture. "You can't know how much that means to me." She moved along the bridge, making her farewells. "And thank you, too, Mister Spock, for saving me when all seemed lost."

Spock accepted her gratitude with his customary dignity. "I am pleased that Mister Scott and I were able to remedy the situation. And, if I may say so, your personal evolution is quite commendable and a testament to life's endless capacity for growth and progress.

It would have been a waste for such a worthwhile process not to continue."

"Why, Mister Spock, that was practically poetic." She scrutinized his stoic features. "You're different than you were when we first met, twenty years ago. Warmer, I think, and less forbidding. Perhaps even a trifle more human."

Spock arched an eyebrow.

"I will attempt to take that remark in the spirit in which it was intended." He raised his hand in a traditional Vulcan salute. "Live long and prosper, Lenore Karidian . . . or would you prefer Lyla Kassidy?"

"Karidian," she said. "I'm tired of hiding from my past. It's time to accept myself for who I am, the good and the bad."

Kirk nodded. "To thine own self be true."

"Precisely." She sighed and glanced at the entrances to the nearby turbolifts. "Now I suppose I should get a move on. I don't wish to keep Doctor Tamris and the others waiting."

"Take as much time as you need," Tamris said. "We won't leave without you." She stepped into the starboard turbolift. "Good-bye, Captain, officers, ambassadors. And, once more, all our thanks."

The door whisked shut and the lift carried her away. Kirk admired the Andorian's consideration and tact. He suspected that she had departed in order to give Kirk and Lenore a chance to make their goodbyes in private.

"Shall I escort you to the shuttlebay, Miss Karidian?" he volunteered.

"Yes, please," she answered warmly. "I'd like that."

Leaving Spock in command of the bridge, they took the port turbolift. The door closed behind them and they found themselves alone. Kirk let the lift sit for the moment, in no hurry to provide it with a destination.

"So you intend to continue your relief efforts?" he asked. "On Oyolo and elsewhere?"

"Yes, but not out of guilt anymore, but simply to make a difference. It's hard work sometimes, and dangerous, but it can be enormously satisfying and good for the soul, too." She gazed at him knowingly. "Not unlike being a starship captain, I imagine."

"You imagine right," he said, "although even a captain gets some time off occasionally."

"Is that so?" A sly smile came over her lips, reminding Kirk of the alluring young woman he had first met at that cocktail party on Planet Q. "You know, despite all the bombings and battles, there remain a few beautifully unspoiled spots on Oyolo, including, so I'm told, some tropical islands and beaches in the southern hemisphere that were largely untouched by the war. They're supposed to be quite lovely . . . and private."

"An intriguing combination," he replied. "Well, Spock tells me that the disarmament efforts on Pavak are likely to take another week or so, and Ambassador Riley still has to bring both sides back to the bargaining table, so the *Enterprise* is going to stick around in the buffer zone for a while, if only for everyone's peace of mind." He eased closer to her, grinning. "I may have some time on my hands. Perhaps we could explore some of those islands . . . together?"

There could be nothing permanent between them, he knew. They both had their own voyages and duties carrying them in different directions. But perhaps they could finally put the past behind them and enjoy the present while they could.

"I might be persuaded," she said coyly. "What's that thing Spock says again?"

Kirk knew what she meant. "There are always possibilities."

And so there were.

"Let us not burden our remembrances with a heaviness that's gone."

—*The Tempest*, Act V

Acknowledgments

At the end of the classic Original Series episode "The Conscience of the King," McCoy assures Kirk that Lenore Karidian will get the best psychological care the Federation can provide. Rewatching the episode a year or so ago, I found myself wondering whatever happened to her . . . and what might happen if she and Kirk crossed paths again. That was the very specific genesis of this book, and I'm very grateful to all the people who helped me turn that idle thought into the novel you're reading now.

My editors, Ed Schlesinger and Margaret Clark, offered support and advice at every stage of the project, and they waited patiently for the manuscript while I wrestled with snowstorms, deadlines, and a certain giant radioactive lizard. And my agent, Russ Galen, once again took care of the business end of things, allowing me to concentrate on complicating Kirk's life. Thanks also to my friend and fellow *Star Trek* author, Tony Daniel, who helpfully coined the term "zetaproprion" when I needed a name for an experimental drug that somehow didn't get named in "Whom Gods

Destroy." And to author Christopher Bennett, who let me pick his brain regarding the movie era.

While writing this book, I relied heavily on Memory Alpha, Memory Beta, and my extensive library of Star Trek reference books and magazines, but I want to give a special shout-out to *Mister Scott's Guide to the Enterprise,* which was more or less my bible when it came to describing the *Enterprise*-A and the movie era in general. Also due thanks are writer Barry Trivers, who wrote the powerful episode that inspired this book, and actress Barbara Anderson, who first brought Lenore Karidian to life.

On a personal front, many thanks to my siblings in the Pacific Northwest for taking care of our aging parents while I pounded away on a keyboard thousands of miles away. I know just how much time and care you devote to Mom and Dad. I'm sorry I can't help out in person.

And thanks, as always, to Karen Palinko and Lyla and Sophie for giving me a reason to step away from the computer once in a while.

About the Author

Greg Cox is the author of numerous *Star Trek* novels and short stories, including *No Time Like the Past, The Weight of Worlds, The Rings of Time, To Reign in Hell, The Eugenics Wars (Volumes One and Two), The Q Continuum, Assignment: Eternity,* and *The Black Shore.* He has also written the official novelizations of such films as *Godzilla, Man of Steel, The Dark Knight Rises, Ghost Rider, Daredevil, Death Defying Acts,* and the first three *Underworld* movies, as well as books and stories based on such popular series as *Alias, Buffy the Vampire Slayer, CSI: Crime Scene Investigation, Farscape, The 4400, Leverage, Riese: Kingdom Falling, Roswell, Terminator, Warehouse 13,* and *Xena: Warrior Princess.*

He has received two Scribe Awards from the International Association of Media Tie-In Writers. He lives in Oxford, Pennsylvania.

Visit him at: gregcox-author.com.